IN ANOTHER SUN

IN ANOTHER SUN

WILLIAM AUTEN

TORTOISE BOOKS
CHICAGO, IL

Published in the United States by Tortoise Books.
www.tortoisebooks.com

ISBN-13: 978-1-948954-10-5
ISBN-10: 1-948954-10-9

Cover design by William Auten.
Tortoise Books Logo Copyright ©2019 by Tortoise Books. Original artwork by
Rachele O'Hare.

One day we must go;

one night we will descend into the region of mystery.

Only here we come to know ourselves;

only in passing are we on earth.

Cantares Mexicanos

The old things have passed away; behold, new things have come.

2 Corinthians 5:17

In a single sound and in a single action, the present returned to her. She had been elsewhere, floating inside the many gray films of her head, but the rings' familiar metal-on-metal *Shink!* sound jolted her into a light when the demon yanked the curtain open. The single sound and the single action reverberated inside her—the present with its unavoidable wattage and acoustics; time pushing and pulling her; all this time suddenly and once again hers. She knew why she was here—part of it frightened her; part of it was too demanding for her to avoid—and she let it guide her rather than her guiding it, as though for the first time in a long time in her life she had a reason that was simple and direct, and she didn't want to articulate why.

"Sorry," Vanessa whispered after bumping into a family at the front of her group. The navy blue of the father's Dallas Cowboys jacket blended with the room's darkness while the single silver star twinkled under the stage lights. The two boys started punching each other in their shoulders, moved down to their stomachs, and tapped their groins a few times before their father reached behind Vanessa, jerked the taller, older boy, and delivered a hard stare with a gravelly "Knock it off." The teens quickly snapped their attention back to the demon narrating the next scene—a hospital, which Vanessa had anticipated after the demon pulled back the curtain. The boys had behaved better in the previous two rooms focusing on adolescent issues that, Vanessa chuckled to herself, had remained the same since her days in high school. The stout woman clutching a three-ring binder and wearing a headset and black t-shirt and jeans glared at Vanessa after she apologized. Vanessa wondered if she was a member of Tim's church and was in charge of tonight's preview—maybe his boss.

Repositioning herself in the group, Vanessa had returned to the place that she had once called home, and she reminded herself that she was here to see Tim—only Tim—and not to fall too deeply into the past, not to be swayed or pulled in any other direction, especially one that she could not let herself follow fully anymore. She hoped that her own presence would not jinx Tim's performance, that their reunion, all these years later, would not stumble with a new beginning.

An ominous electronic thrum pumped throughout the hospital room. Vanessa had noticed its presence in the previous scene—a bedroom—shortly after the teenage girl finished writing in her journal and downed prescription drugs that the demon encouraged her to take as his arthritic-like black hands capped the pen and set it on the nightstand next to her note. The young, bespectacled actress wept while wrapping herself in sheets and a blanket. Vanessa's group stood at a distance from the bed. Staring at the girl from within the darkness and in that silence was all that Vanessa could do.

The audio track's dissonance wavered among the medical equipment: an IV stand, a gurney, and a large lamp that flooded the miniature hospital floor with a pale green light. The demon paced back and forth, stomping his boots, swishing his robe, intent on making his presence known. A nurse rolled a tray of instruments toward a doctor, who spun on his stool and faced a sheet tented over the knees of a twenty-something woman on the gurney. The demon halted in front of the group and cast his eyes upon them; his spike of a chin bounced up and down

2

while he talked. Vanessa felt that he returned his eyes to her every time he paused in his monologue. The set-up to the scene was so intense that she wanted to laugh, which would have been an antithesis to the intensity, but she sucked in her lips to keep from laughing because of the obvious delay between the pre-recorded voice crackling above her and the demon's irregular hand and head jerks, like poorly timed dubbing for a foreign movie.

The doctor lifted the sheet. His gloved hands reached for pliers sitting on the tray next to him. Vanessa watched the doctor lean into the tented sheet more and more, often diving in all the way to his head. After requesting a tool from the nurse, his arms sawed back and forth, pulled and pushed. The demon circled his dark, jagged body around the gurney as more sounds scraped, twisted, and bounced throughout the room. A heart monitor and respirator increased their rhythms. The demon shuffled closer between the doctor and the patient. Vanessa reminded herself to enjoy how Tim had crafted the robe to resemble bat wings when the demon stood backlit and raised and lowered its arms, but she snapped back to the scene and cringed when she heard the young woman on the gurney ask a question.

The doctor answered through his surgical mask after the demon, passing over the gurney, shifted toward the doctor and, black robe outstretched again, black glove touching the doctor's smock, spoke into his ear. The demon pulled away before the recording ended. Vanessa wanted to snicker but didn't, and she felt that somewhere Tim made a note about this poor timing; thinking of his meticulous attention to detail and perfection, as well as this notebook, probably volumes of notebooks by now, made her smile. The doctor nodded. The woman on the gurney, looking up into the light, shifted her body with the doctor's pull and push, her hands gripping the pillow. The demon lifted his red eyes onto Vanessa and the audience.

The doctor spun around, wiped off the curette, and rolled himself toward the woman. His hands sliding into the sheet, the doctor's wrists rotated back and forth and pulled them out bloodied. He set the curette on the silver tray next to him and, spinning on his stool, held up the pliers in front of the demon and the small audience. Vanessa wanted to cover her face. Nauseous, she focused on the set's details, the sounds, and the amount of work Tim had put into the costumes and special effects for this and the other rooms.

Stamping his foot to flip the lid of a metal trashcan with a bio-waste symbol on it, the doctor paused and looked into the audience directly at the woman wearing the headset, who slightly nodded. The doctor shifted in his seat, and as he started to speak again, the pliers dropped to the floor. A sharp cracking sound quickly followed. The doctor leaned over to pick up the pliers. "Sorry," he said, his voice shaken free of its baritone. "Shoot, sorry."

Vanessa closed her eyes and rubbed the base of her neck.

"Mike, you can't do that during a performance. You just have to go with it," yelled the woman wearing the headset, whipping it off. She dragged a highlighter over a page in her binder. "OK, listen, forget it. Let's take a break. Tim?"

When she heard Tim's name, Vanessa inhaled sharply. A stocky man with a black beard wearing thick-rimmed glasses and a gray hoodie stepped into the operating room's lights. He carried more weight in his gut than the picture on his website, taken from the neck up, had revealed. But Vanessa knew him right away, and the space between her heart and head unfolded.

As he jogged across the floor, his pants covered in paint and plaster, Tim turned his ball cap backward. Looking away and then up, Vanessa saw the gap between the operating room's fake walls and the ceiling tiles above them. She guessed that Tim had used the angles and spaces to his, and the production's, advantage, especially with speakers perched in the corners and the hanging lights filling the gaps between old and new facades, both creating an air of theatrics.

"Come on, man. I don't have time for this," Tim moaned, moving from shadows to lights and back again, his exasperation fading under the sounds of his heavy work boots and a toolbox scraping across the floor. "You have to be careful. You're twisting too hard. Twist your arms, not anything else," he lectured the doctor, who looked confused. The respirator and heart monitor clicked off; some track lights blazed on over Vanessa and the small group and exposed more of the room's wires, props, and staging. The nurse pulled down her mask and took a sip from her Coke bottle. The demon slouched down on a chair and asked for a fan. "It's over there," Tim ordered, pointing to a teenage boy who, after finding and plugging its long extension cord into an outlet, shuffled in front of the group and held it in front of the demon, who adjusted his bulbous blackened cowl.

Vanessa watched Tim uncap a small tube of adhesive and gather the broken props and the pliers after kicking open the toolbox and sliding next to the doctor, who stood up from the stool, pulled off his surgical mask, and snapped off his latex gloves. "I need some air," he groaned and then motioned to the demon who waved the doctor off and pointed his crooked black fingers to his charred chest; he was not giving up the fan anytime soon. From out of the shadows at the back of the room, a young woman appeared, startling Vanessa. Her black t-shirt with white letters—Hope House XV, 1 Corinthians 15:19—contrasted with the green-blue walls and cream-colored tiles of the operating room. She briskly walked over to the far edge of the hospital stage, rounded up additional props and items, and offered photocopies of the script, which the embarrassed doctor brushed aside before dismissing himself through a fire exit. Tossing her head back toward the open door and scratching her head with the highlighter, the purple-haired director sighed.

The doctor flopped onto the stairs; seconds later he pulled a wrinkled script from his smock's back pocket. Vanessa stepped away from the halted scene to rest on a chair by several plastic bins and rolls of fabric. The rest of the crowd dissipated inside the room, leaving behind the smell of heavy perfume and cologne and anxiety.

One of the women in the group welcomed the break, stating that things were getting a little too intense. The family who had stood next to Vanessa broke apart. The dad and mom drifted to a table in the corner of the room. The younger boy split off with boys his age; the older one hugged a girl whose smile exposed a mouthful of braces. They sat shoulder to shoulder against a wall as their phones cast a pale blue over their faces while they swiped, clicked, and laughed without ever looking at each other. The director moved about with the cast and crew. Behind the operating room's counter, the nurse shared a script with the woman on the gurney.

Overhearing their upcoming lines, Vanessa leaned back in the chair while Tim dusted off the demon's robe, which took her mind off the rehearsal.

The demon turned the fan onto his black robe, dramatically billowing it, but also blowing more dust onto it. The pubescent voice inside trying to sound evil didn't sound evil. "I want that thing you were talking about," he squeaked after he lifted his mask.

Redirecting the fan from the mangled face to the robe and cleaning it again, Tim grimaced. "Not this round. We have less than a week now."

Vanessa looked at the door where the doctor had exited—the one leading into the parking lot and the moonlight. The more she overheard and watched the cast and crew practice, the more she felt that she should stand up, walk down the stairs, avoiding the doctor and his puddles of stage fright and theatrical mistakes, slip into her car, and drive away without Tim seeing her. She could text or email him much later and tell him that something had come up, she never made it to the rehearsal, it was thoughtful of him to invite her, and they could try to meet again, preferably in a different setting. Tim stood back, contemplated his adjustments to the demon's mask, and brushed the robe one more time until it shone. Vanessa could not move.

"Let's go to the next scene." The director slipped on her headset and surveyed her binder. "Start the soundtrack again. Tim, the lights over there need some more contrast."

The demon re-laced his boots, stood up, lowered his mask, adjusted his fangs, and held a door open for the reassembled crowd to pass through one by one into the next room.

Before she slid past the outstretched black robe, Vanessa said, "I'm going to stay behind. I know Tim." As she stood directly in front of the demon, the illusion of his towering height and his gangrene-like flesh layered over bulging eyes and a hollowed-out nose broke down to boots with large heels and rubber and paint. "Thank you, though," she continued, flicking the horns jutting from his jaw. "Really impressive.

Tim's amazing at what he does." She headed for a small workshop area, lit by a desk lamp, near the hospital scene where Tim hunched at a table with his toolbox and gear.

"Hey, come on! No touching!" whined the demon, which caused him to miss his cue as his pre-recorded voice looped inside the adjacent room filled with strobe lightning and the sounds of rain and an organ.

Standing behind Tim and watching him work, Vanessa fidgeted with the small new corkscrews of her short hair before tapping his shoulder.

"Vanessa! You came," he said, spinning around and gleaming as he set down some light filters. He took off his thick gloves and hugged her. "It's so good to see you. How are you?"

"Pretty good," she answered, holding onto him until they peeled back and stared at each other. Her body leaning near his, she wiped her eyes.

"You look great. Still a head-turner." He let go of her hands to motion to a shirtless man down the hall. "Hey, Jase," he yelled, "I fixed the motor. It should turn a little smoother now."

The man high-fived Tim and jogged back.

"This really is something," Vanessa said. "What you said on the phone…I'm blown away. You've really turned it up."

"Thank you. Yeah…makeup, lighting, the sets. We're almost at full-costume. It's a lot right now. I don't even know what day it is most of the time."

"I know what that's like." She squeezed her eyes shut. "I didn't think they'd let me in. But as soon as I said, 'Tim Baxter invited me,' they did."

8

Tim laughed, checking something off his clipboard when a young woman brought him bottles of spirit gum. "Did you tell the bouncer at the front door we have history? The cover's free if you sell your soul."

Vanessa grinned. "Who played our demon guide?"

"Josh, who has to get his timing down. He gets easily distracted."

"I noticed that."

"He is sixteen. You remember when I was sixteen, right?"

"I do."

"He says it's the mask, but he really wants this voice box. Not happening." Tim shook his head. "The kid's got potential. We're super-fortunate to have him this year. We keep improving year after year."

"With you in charge, I believe it."

He pointed his thick thumbs at his flannel shirt. "Hours and hours of it. Carpal tunnel, headaches, fumes."

Nodding, Vanessa massaged the back of her neck and pulled her hair. "It's so great, Tim. Your little company. You must be exhausted."

"It's just the three of us. Me, Bryce, and Kev, who's a senior this year. He's helped me since he was in junior high. I don't think I'll be holding on to Bryce much longer. His band's getting hot." Tim jerked his head at the doorway opposite the surgery room. "They're probably still in there, if you want to see the rest. We can catch up later when you're done."

"Thank you, but no."

Tim started sorting brushes. "Well, these have seen better days."

"I should let you go."

"You're back in town for good, right?"

"I am."

"Coffee Saturday? I have to make some purchase orders in the morning, but how about after that?"

"Sure."

"Are you all moved in? I could help you unload." He mimed having defined biceps instead of flabby arms.

She laughed with him and at his goofy smile that she never forgot. "I'm very spartan now. Yes, let's do Saturday. Text me."

Tim touched her hand as she started to leave. "Sure you don't want to stick around? Practice usually lasts until about nine. I haven't eaten dinner yet. We could..."

"It's been a long night. I'll see you soon."

"Good night, Vanessa. Thanks again for coming. I'm so glad you're back."

After she hugged and waved goodbye to Tim, she headed through the fire exit where the pale doctor had excused himself; she stopped on the bottom step of the stairs and turned around, her shoes squeaking on the metal, the autumn air prickling her, memories spiraling around her, echoing. Tim's silhouette moved like a marionette without wires, without anything or anyone having to pull him to the right place and at the right time, this smooth shadow gliding between her and, in the background, the bright lights erasing all of the present features she had seen and all of the past features she had brought with her and could not release. She could not keep herself from returning to the middle, reentering, dropping in between the things out there on the horizon yet to reach her and the things that had loosened on their way down from the sky and the stars, realigning on their own, clicking into place. That so little needed to be said between Tim and her frightened and relieved her; that time had changed what they looked like but had not changed what they had shared between them, and yet so much waited on the edges for her to open to him. To see him would cost more than only time, she knew—and it had—and yet she also knew that not to see him would also cost more than only time.

Canta y no llores. She heard that old song's refrain in her head, a favorite of her mother and father. Sing and don't cry. The chorus stayed with her as she reached her car. For several seconds she forgot where her keys were. She felt along her body and quickly became anxious. She found them buried in the inside pocket, but she didn't remember putting them there. "Stupid," she said aloud to the night air, flinging open the car door, starting the engine, and wiping her face. As she sat in the slowly warming car, the moonlight shone on the gravel parking lot and, on the other side of the fence, the dark two-lane road that brought her here and would take her back. Camino nocturna, she mused, massaging the base of her neck and glancing in the rearview mirror at her cropped hair. She now had nowhere else to go but forward; she had received what she had wanted to receive and, yet, still had more to receive. She had to keep going forward, tumbling with the pieces of her that had been broken apart, off, falling since she returned, the pieces falling quieter the further they fell away from her and into the blank space of time taking her in.

The church cradled an inner fire. It could do nothing else but cradle an inner fire, to act as a conduit for an inner fire. The stucco exterior was once blinding white, the only white at the end of a street choked by debris, smokestacks, rust, and oil stains. But gray was now its color, crumbling with black and brown marks, as though a fire, falling from the sky, had burned it, and after this fallen fire had burned the outside of the church, it scrambled along the ground and, finding its destined home, continued burning on the inside, held in heads, hearts, and hands. The unkempt grass and weeds on the small strip of land behind it remained dry, no matter how much rain passed through during the spring and summer. The church's neighbors were dirt and junkyard lots, a trailer park, a row of rundown houses that the city and police ignored, and shops and businesses affiliated with cutting, grinding, sanding, blowtorching, dirt, sweat, and grease. Six-foot fences topped with razor wire protected each building.

The church's roof, A-shaped, the black shingles curling up at their edges, stood no taller than the cabinetmaker and lumber mill on the left and the machine fabrication company across the street. Were it not for the rooftop cross, the size of perpendicular aluminum baseball bats, glowing purplish-blue at night, or for the sign Bienvenidos a Iglesia Vida Nueva hand-painted in blue and yellow and drilled into the ashen stucco beside two windows fuzzy with mold and the scuffed and rotted doors, the fire waiting inside would not have been so obvious.

In the early days, when Vanessa was young and before he owned the church—when the fire was more like tinder—Calderon hoisted a cheap blue tent on cheap metal poles in the rectangular backyard behind the church. He drove stakes into the grass, between rocks that dissolved into dirt near the metal fence and the bramble threading through it. Rain jabbed the tarp as it dropped, like a plastic bag punctured over and over. Calderon stood with Bible and yellow-legal-pad sermon in hand, the tent's color and shade sinking his eye sockets deeper into his skull, dark-blue blood spreading under his eyelids, and he liked to entreat the small group of families, no more than seven individuals who first joined him back then: "Someday the church behind us will be ours. It will become our house of worship. When I came here to this country, I was led here. I used to work right around the corner, down the block, at a shop that chopped cars in the front and helped people but was sinful in the back and hurt people. But I knew I would be saved, that a great fire would come for me and sweep me elsewhere." He always stopped to wipe sweat and humidity from his brow, sniffling as he did, his voice plateauing before taking off again. "And it did. I am here because of this fire I have to share with you...and that you need to share." Adjusting his tie, he stared over them and into a space framed by their heads and the base of the blue tent, a space filled with the church's back doors sealed by two-by-fours, broken windows, and paint peeling from wood and stucco. "Sed y hambre." His body winced as his voice boomed to those who listened to him. Calderon stared into this space, and his eyes locked on the church, as though he was the only one who could see into it, as though he had found the center where the fire would move once the church fell under his name.

By the time Vanessa's family had been brought to Calderon, the church was his. The fire was no longer spoken of in the future tense, as it had been under the blue tent. The fire found its way inside, illuminating the church's musty wood-paneled walls, the dirty floor tile, and the rusted folding chairs. The fire provided a large wooden cross sitting in a gold stand at the front of the sanctuary, flanked by a plastic table with two faded and wrinkled reproductions of the paintings *Christ at Gethsemane* and *Christ Our Pilot*. Vanessa and her parents learned there was no escaping the fire.

The location and the time of Calderon's sermons changed but not the theme. "Every day," he said to the rows in front of him packed with families and individuals, "I would pass this old church, boarded up, abandoned...but not empty. I saw it time and time again on my way to work, eating lunch out there...right out there, on those very front steps facing this church...on my way home after work, and standing in that tent in the field behind this. I passed this old church. I had to come to it, not it to me." He smiled then, holding his finger in the air before brushing the pink scar running from the top of his left cheekbone, just below his eye, to his jaw, a scar that widened or shrank like a river following curves and bumps. "I knew...I knew, hermanos y hermanas, that one day the Lord would deliver me, and us, to it, that we would find the means to purchase it. And we did. From dirt out back...that little tent...our little tabernacle in the woods...to this."

Calderon's name was fire, and the fire could not be removed from his voice or his sermons. The fire appeared inside when Calderon broke open scriptures, crackling slowly with his breathy repetitions of verses; or it burst intensely at the end of his sentences or in the middle of them, over a key word or idea he needed the congregation to see clearly and to remember. Fire that saved; fire that judged; fire that cleansed; fire in the past; fire in the present; fire in the future; fire to burn; and fire to heal. Fire cleared paths. Fire destroyed paths in order to brighten another one to be travelled. "El Camino Torcido o el Camino Recto," his voice bellowed as his frail arms balanced two roads in the air.

He emphasized that someone was either close to the fire or someone was in the fire; there was no middle ground. Fire was the medium through which everything passed; it exposed and recalled everything. Without fire, Calderon said, nothing else was worth pursuing or using as fuel or light. Every day and every moment of the day had a fire. Monday through Saturday the fire came at night; on Sundays it burned in the morning, just before noon when it intensified the most, after church and during coffee and small talk, the men drinking coffee on one side at the back of church, the women chatting on the other side, children playing outside in the dry weeds and crabgrass and under the blue tent.

The fire had a permanent home, but Calderon asked for the fire to be taken out, shared with the rest of the world. The fire started with him, but he pushed it past him, past his small wooden pulpit, and into the crowd captivated by him. The crowd and the families did not ignore the fire; they could not run from it because they had nowhere else to go. It was everywhere they were: in their minds, at their meals, in their beds, in their dreams, on the way to work or school, the fire's course consuming, spreading, just as Calderon himself had experienced, just as Calderon said would happen to them.

Calderon followed up with the fires, all of them, every day, pulling an imaginary string from his mind to his heart and then pulling the same imaginary string in front of the congregation, unifying all hearts and minds with that singular, imaginary string. "How has that sermon changed your life?" he asked, his thumb resting on his index finger, pinching and pulling the invisible string. "How has that verse made you see things differently? Mis hermanos y hermanas, what are you doing different today than yesterday?"

Many times, the congregation responded to the fire with confirmations or silence, but even the silence meant the fire had reached them, had exposed where they faltered and could fall apart, or had highlighted a new, stronger foundation they needed to be on. Without the congregation, without Calderon's voice and direction, and without Calderon, the fire would die out. The fire longed for skin and eyes and ears to fall onto.

The fire was transformational and had no name, but it was personal; it was communicable. Sin. Forgiveness. Hope. Past. Present. Future. Heaven. Hell. "El Diablo dice," his voice slithered with his left hand in the shape of horns. Body and time wrapped together in the fire. The fire let everyone in and excluded no one. The fire knew no denomination. It was there for anyone. It was there for the old who had been with Calderon since day one, an origin rekindled again and again. It was there for those who had been brought here with promises of a new horizon, a new ground that the fire cleared, the fire reaching for the place in the sky from where it had fallen.

In the past, Vanessa had heard about the fire and its place inside and outside the church, its heat in the heads and hearts and hands of those near it, its path sparked by Calderon's bellow far behind her or in front of her, its words meandering through her own heart and head but never landing there. Calderon's voice broke her own silence the first time she heard it, and his voice, with its power, would seize her every now and then. "¡Buenos días, mis hermanos y hermanas! Praise be to God." Warmth smothered Vanessa, and she looked at the ceiling of the church, believing the voice started above her in the rotting, spotted beams before rumbling down on her like thunder. She spun in the pew and saw a short man with a round belly standing just inside the front door of the sanctuary, holding his right hand in the air, the first two fingers together, the way she had seen Christ's displayed in images around the church. Vanessa saw how Calderon focused on the space between the ground and the table at the front. But the fire had not found its way into her yet. Sitting in the dusty wood pew between her father and mother, she always held a pen or a colored pencil and had on her lap a tattered notebook for drawing. The sounds of the sermons floated around her, flickering by her ears like insects.

When she was eight years old, she stopped drawing just long enough to feel the fire closer to her. The guitarist at the front had finished playing and nodded to the back of the church, taking his guitar with him as he moved to an empty rusted chair in the front row. After smiling at some of the other children she had been playing with, Vanessa spun toward the front of the church, her chin resting on the pew's cool ledge. Between the rows of old pews and metal chairs, Calderon hobbled down the aisle, his right leg slowly realigning itself every few steps, the fire keeping his legs churning, jerking into place. Watching him, the congregation craned their necks. Vanessa did not bother to look. Calderon wore his usual attire: a white short-sleeved dress shirt, a brown tie, and black slacks. His slicked-back hair shimmered the closer he walked toward the front of the church, a father with an invisible bride. Against his abdomen he carried a Bible. Once he reached the end of the aisle, he stopped but kept his back to the rows. Vanessa glanced sideways out the window at the shadow of wings fluttering by. Her father looked down at her and, from out of his shirt pocket, Roberto slid the small notebook and pen to her. Flora quietly opened her purse and handed over a small box of colored pencils she had bought for her daughter at Dollar General. Vanessa smiled at them both, faced the front again, and became very quiet as she flipped open to where she had left off from the last sermon, cocking her head at the page's landscape where trees and, she imagined, her parents and possibly a river needed to be.

Calderon took one large deep breath, exhaled it, and then turned with his eyes closed. Vanessa glanced up and wondered if he was sick. But then, eyes remaining closed, he smiled broadly as though he stood under an unseen sun shining down on him, this unseen sun deepening the trough of his scar. Calderon breathed deeply again, held it, and quickly exhaled. As he opened his eyes and arms, his voice quickened, the fire bubbling inside, his voice entering a deeper register. "¡Buenos días!" he said with a grin.

"Buenos días," said the crowd.

Vanessa smiled and mumbled with them. She returned to her drawing.

"Did you notice anything different up here this morning when you came in, talking with your fellow brothers and sisters?"

Some in the crowd shook their heads; most were silent.

"Maybe the coffee hasn't kicked in yet," he joked.

The crowd smiled; some chuckled. Vanessa looked up and then looked down at the lines crisscrossing across her paper. Flowers. A sun. She looked outside at the fluttering shadow and began to add more lines, sketching what she saw.

Scratching the side of his sweaty nose, Calderon limped over to the table and sipped from his glass of water. He scooted a narrow wood lectern from behind it to the front of the sanctuary. The cross attached to the lectern's face shone. "Brother Miguel made this for me."

The crowd craned their necks again, and those sitting close to Miguel patted his arms or shoulders, nodding with him. Roberto and Flora turned too. Vanessa added blue to the sky, save for the patches of white clouds.

"Isn't it lovely?" Calderon's voice buzzed. "Very sturdy. Very sturdy." His hands tapped the top of the lectern. "Ah, brothers and sisters, it means we are growing and committed to each other. I remember when I had nothing like this...right out there, behind us...that blue tent...nothing at all but my feet, which I still have to use."

The congregation chuckled with him.

"But this...this means we are more than just a church." He stood behind the lectern, placing the Bible in front of him, his palms gripping the lectern's edges. "Familia," he emphasized, his voice echoing in the sanctuary and over the red flower Vanessa added to the green field. "I can never say that enough. And yet we are also more than a family...a body...un solo cuerpo en Cristo." His voice extended the sound of s in Cristo. His eyes searched the room, bypassing Miguel and his family, and rested on Roberto, Flora, and Vanessa, who imagined sitting amongst the flowers under the sky she had drawn. Nodding to them, Calderon continued, "Let us pray before so that we are pure to receive the Holy Spirit and God's Word."

For the sermon, his baritone voice recharged depth and power, especially for a man of small stature, and his words and the tone used to bring those words simmered in Vanessa, who looked up from her notebook when she heard it. She watched Calderon pace in front of the congregation, flabby arms, elbows cocked, palms in the air, smiling, sweating, strands of thick black hair falling down to his eyes as they searched the room, his paunch billowing in and out, pumping more oxygen into the fire, the voice continuing on, its volume building on itself like smolder. He spoke of God saving the lives of men and women, "those in the church and those waiting to enter our church...guiding them here...becoming part of our family and, by extension," his voice crescendoed, "the body of Christ." He inhaled. "There is but one plan for your life...just one," he went on, holding the Bible in the air and wiping his brow with the sleeve of his shirt. "To be saved through Jesus who, according to Luke Nineteen-Ten, 'came to seek and to save what was lost.' We can't escape that. It draws us in like a moth to a flame. The plan for saving lives was given to Jesus." Calderon held his breath. His eyes rolled toward the ceiling. "There is no other plan."

After nearly an hour of striding back and forth across the front of the church, exhausted, Calderon removed his tie and unbuttoned the top of his shirt. His brow and collarbone glistened with sweat. "One more thing before we break and enjoy lunch, my brothers and sisters, and before Hector plays more beautiful music for us." He opened his Bible and gently lifted out from the pages one square of red fabric, no larger than a sock. Heads in the rows shifted to see it. Vanessa added a second set of fluttering wings and, after she did, looked up, the fabric catching her eyes. Calderon delicately held up the red square. "Do you remember these? Sister Sylvia and Sister Flora made these squares weeks ago."

The crowd nodded. Vanessa stopped scribbling when the red square in Calderon's hands danced in front of her. Calderon looked around the room, his eyes resting on Flora's soft face and purple top in the spring light. He glanced down at Vanessa, who, upon hearing her mother's name, closed the notebook and kept her eyes up.

"And if you remember," he continued, "which I know you do, I said to you that anyone can find this if they look for it. It's everywhere and anywhere like a guiding light. It's as common as dirt." Calderon pointed his hand, which held the Bible, down toward the ground. "I said, 'This is the blood of Christ that burns for you.' This is the blood of Christ, my brothers and sisters. His single drop," Calderon raised his hand holding the single patch, "gave us more than we could ever imagine. It multiplies, it grows, it forgives…and it is ours. And it can cover us." He shook the square. "And I said to you a month ago that each drop of blood you hold we will bring together. I quoted to you First John One-Seven: 'The blood of Jesus Christ, his Son, cleans us from all sin.'" Calderon raised his arm. "I said those many Sundays ago, 'Go on, reach under you, you'll find yours, my brothers and sisters.' And you did. Remember? You found your own square under you." Calderon's volume increased as he smiled and closed his eyes.

Vanessa watched the congregation nod, and she remembered her mother letting her pull out the red square from under the pew many Sundays ago and then handing it to her parents before returning to a drawing.

"And then I asked each of you," Calderon continued, "to write your name and your children's names and your family's names…all those with you…with us now…on each square. Remember? Your name in blood…in Christ's blood. We passed around those markers in the collection plates? And then we all placed those squares of blood in the collection plates. You remember that?"

The crowd nodded.

Calderon placed his Bible on the new lectern and walked to the end of the plastic table. He then motioned to the audience. Two men stood up, one at the front of the row and the other who trotted forward from the back. Calderon grimaced with a smile as he waited on the man at the back of the church. From under the table at the front of the sanctuary, the two men grabbed a large red blanket, unfolded it, and shuffled away in opposite directions from each other, stretching the blanket until more and more red cloth unfolded. "You see?" Calderon asked, pointing to the full blanket. "Each square is here. Each square with your names here stitched together."

Vanessa stared at the large red block in front of her, the thick white stitching connecting fifty squares, black names written within. She searched for her and her parents' names, but all the names were so small, little islands in the middle of a red ocean. She smiled, looked at her mother and father, reopened her notebook, and returned to imagining where the next flower should bloom in the field of scribbled green.

"Isn't it beautiful?" Calderon asked, gliding his hand over its surface. "Flora did an amazing job."

Hearing her mother's name singled out at church, among the congregation, her mother's name singled out not by her father or by her but from within the fire, the source of the fire standing so close to them, Vanessa quickly twisted in her seat and stared at her mom when Flora cried out from the crowd, "Sylvia helped too," and nodded to Calderon. Vanessa had never seen her mother do something like that. Her mother retreated back to the pew, her voice fading, her face blushing. Roberto hugged Flora, and both of them softly leaned into Vanessa, who had forgotten about finishing the yellow flowers she had placed alongside the blue river that cut through the green field.

"Cuidate. Que dios te bendiga." He pronounced the closing benediction, blessing them all, passing God's blessing onto them, asking them to take care, and finishing with a sermon-ending prayer.

"¡Aleluya!" sang the crowd.

After the service, Vanessa waited with her parents in the line leading out of the back door of the sanctuary and into the yard. Standing in the doorway, Calderon spoke to, hugged, and kissed everyone passing through. She wanted to wander off with her friends or explore the small garden by the side of the church where she had seen the winged shadows flutter while she sat inside the sanctuary, but her parents sandwiched her between them. When they reached Calderon, his bad leg perched on the concrete steps leading into the backyard, the pastor wiped sweat from his forehead with a handkerchief. "Flora," he called out, smiling.

Her father positioned himself in front of her mother.

Calderon shook Roberto's hand and said, "Ah, Brother Roberto, I wanted to thank you for filling in the other day at the sod plant. I know it involves the back more so than construction jobs. Hard, demanding work."

"I was happy to do so," Roberto responded before extending his hand.

Calderon leaned in. Wedged between the two men, Vanessa heard the pastor whisper, "But I don't believe I've received tithe on that job yet." Calderon leaned back into the doorframe and smiled at her father and then smiled at her.

"I'll double check."

"Gracias, Brother Roberto. Muchas gracias."

Vanessa felt her father's body tighten as he inhaled and heard him force out, "See you Monday night as usual."

By the time Calderon had nodded and replied, "Yes. May God continue blessing us with your family's presence," Roberto had walked into the yard to help other men set up tables, carry chairs from inside the church, and move dishes of food.

Stepping down a stair, Flora rested her hands on Vanessa's shoulders and said to Calderon, "Thank you for the recognition. It was very kind of you." She looked down at Vanessa, smiled, and smoothed her daughter's shirt.

"You did all the work," Calderon cheered.

"Sylvia, too."

"Oh, I know, yes...yes. It's beautiful and potent...a true symbol of who we are."

Flora nodded, and as she started walking away from the steps, excusing herself from blocking the way of others, Calderon touched her forearm. "Just a minute... I'd like to talk to you about a business opportunity." He spoke briefly to church members behind Flora, shook their hands, and eventually pulled Flora off to the side where white flowers bloomed near a window.

"Let me get Roberto," Vanessa heard her mother say.

"No...no...not now. Tell him after I've talked with you. Listen...it's a business opportunity. I have obtained some money and would like the church to have a panadería. It'd be nice to have a stream of income...for us...and for you. Don't you think?"

Vanessa watched her mother shrug her shoulders.

"More importantly, it'd be great if a responsible, mature woman from my church ran it."

"I do all things equally with my husband."

"That's fine, but I want to give it to you, Flora. I think you're ideal for it."

"Let me talk to Roberto," she said, starting to walk away from him, pulling Vanessa by her hand.

"I need an answer by the end of today, Flora. Paperwork, phone calls, the city."

Sweeping her long black hair back, Flora looked down at Vanessa and then up at Calderon. "I am still cleaning and working at the laundromat. And Roberto's construction job is…"

"No, I know," Calderon cut her off, closing his eyes. "I'll have someone replace you. One of the new women. I like to reward my family members with something new and challenging after they've been here a while. You've earned this."

"That's very gracious of you," she replied. "We are ever thankful that you help us."

Calderon nodded and traced the scar on his face. "You're all doing so well here. I'm so blessed to have you. And that's why I think this business venture is perfect for you." He stuffed his hands in his pockets. "It can be all yours, Flora. You'd be in charge. You have that in you. I've seen it."

Her mother flattened her skirt and stared down at Vanessa for a few seconds. Flora looked up, sighed, and turned to Calderon. "OK…let's talk more but with Roberto."

"That's fine. I'm glad you'll do this."

"I haven't agreed just yet."

"And you haven't said no, either. Besides, how can you say no?" Calderon smiled at Vanessa and then hobbled to the line forming in front of a Crock-Pot. The line of people pulled back and let him go to the front.

"What was that all about?" Roberto asked, licking clean a spoon as he walked over to Vanessa and Flora.

"Mamá's running a bakery," Vanessa said, staring at the insects flittering around the small garden with the white flowers underneath the windowsill.

"Yes, we're running a bakery," Flora said.

"What?" Roberto turned his head toward Calderon, who balanced shaking hands and loading his plate with food. "Pachucho," he grumbled, staring at the pastor.

"Roberto." Flora's voice mixed a gentle coo with a small scold.

Roberto looked at his wife and then at Vanessa. His slim shoulders rose and fell with the breath he surrendered. "What does he want?"

"He wants us to run the church's new bakery." Flora kissed her daughter on top of her head. "M'ija, how would you like to help Mamá be a baker?"

"Cookies?" Vanessa asked as she ran off toward the nearby garden, her hands opening and closing like a shell in front of her face. She stopped when she caught something.

"Cookies. Lots and lots of cookies. Sugar and frosting," her mother responded. "Asaderos..."

"Animal and flower cookies?"

"Sure," her mother chuckled. "Whatever you want." Flora shrugged her shoulders at her father. She kissed him on the cheek and made her way to a group of women who had started singing as a guitarist strummed a few chords.

Roberto looked at Vanessa. She opened her hands to him. Inside was a silver and black moth that, when she and her father leaned over it, pushed out its underwings and revealed a bright orange pattern like a sunset spreading apart dark clouds. Her father nodded and then kissed her hands as they watched it fly away. "We are too poor to be beautiful butterflies," he said.

3

"Let's see..." The latte twitched in Vanessa's hands. Her eyes roamed the coffee shop and then returned to Tim's face. "I forgot what I was going to so say. Oh, so, after I graduated, I went to grad school at UC Denver, but that was *not* for me. Did I tell you this on the phone when we talked?"

"You mentioned grad school and Denver." Tim scooted his chair closer to the table.

"Yeah, so I left and went to work at MetaBrand."

"The PR firm, you said."

"That's right."

"I want to talk to you about that, actually. Sounds fancy...the Big Time."

"The oh-so-exciting world of public relations," she scoffed. "The firefighters, they called us. Putting out the fires management and projects created."

"Like what?"

"You name it. We were hired for everything and anything under the sun. Tech, though, was becoming our specialty, especially after 9/11. Privacy and data mining were our cash cows."

"We're being watched. *1984*," Tim joked, bobbing his thick eyebrows up and down.

"I was very good at my job," she continued after laughing with him. "I loved it. I rose up the ranks. I made executive staff. Perks, bonuses, company credit card, stock options. I met Dan there, did the whole American-middle-class thing. Big house in the 'burbs, boat, SUVs."

"You did it."

"What do you mean?" she asked him.

"You became that all-American story we all want to be." He stirred the straw in his soda. "Pull yourself by your bootstraps. Make something of yourself. I remember you telling me years ago you wanted a life that would show how much your parents sacrificed for you."

"Yeah…" She sipped from her drink while looking away from him.

"How long were you in Denver?"

"Ten years. Ten years that felt way, way too long."

"That is a long time."

"Things changed for me. You know…life."

Tim cleared his throat, shifted in his seat, and grimaced. "I know a thing or two about that."

As his mere presence pulled her closer, Vanessa glanced at him and noticed the low sunset-tinted horizon setting earlier each day and pushing through the glass windows and front door, barely half of it above the roofs of the shopping plaza; several of the stores' windows filled with Halloween decorations; and the trees and their leaves translucent with the beginnings of oranges, yellows, and reds scattered amongst the greens. "Dan and I grew apart…in more ways than one. The other side of the cliché of the American dream is true too. You lose sight of what's important, of what's in front of you. You get sucked into it. I quit."

"MetaBrand?"

"Yeah. Kinda." Her attention drifted toward a nearby wall with a black-and-white print of an old bridge over a river. Snow on the river's edge rose from the water and covered the feet of the massive stone bridge. Two people strolled across the middle where a procession of carved knights, their shields, and their swords arched over them and the pathway. The couple—current lovers or former lovers—held hands; they were by themselves; and the light from an unseen source in the photo unified everything.

"What does 'kinda' mean?" he asked.

"It all fell apart for me by last year. No one was going anywhere. No one. Stalemate. They were going to get me to leave one way or another."

"Did business slow down?"

"No. I couldn't give them any more, and Dan and I couldn't give any more to each other. We were done. The whole thing was connected like fabric, you know? Pull one string, and the whole thing unravels." She exhaled. Sitting across from her, Tim waited for her to let more out into the light, but she clung tighter to herself. "There have been some major changes in my life in the last year and a half."

"No, I figured as much," he said. "I could tell when we talked on the phone this summer. You called me out of the blue. Not that I'm complaining, but I figured you were either nostalgic or...well, you said you were moving back. I thought something else had happened. Maybe your dad had gotten sick or something."

"It didn't have anything to do with my dad."

"I can relate. These past couple of years have been a change for me too, and I'm not..." Tim stopped mid-sentence and scratched the stubble on his throat. "Listen," he picked back up, "we don't have to talk about that or any of this. Let's save it for another time."

"Yes, let's save it for another time," Vanessa replied. "Because I want to do so much more, many different things now that I have all this time on my hands. Well, as long as my dad gives me days off."

"Are you back at the bakery?" Tim burst out laughing. "Because if you are..."

"I know, I know. It's high school all over again."

"Same spot?"

"No, he moved it closer to Fontaine Square. Still the best empanadas in town. Recetas de mi mamá, my mom's recipes, thank you very much. And get this..." Her hands drumrolled on the table. "My papá moved."

"Where did he move?"

"Near Cherry Street."

"Not upstairs from the bakery anymore?"

"Nope," Vanessa said, gleeful at his response. "He got a nice little old home. Perfect for him and his growing collection of music. When he bought that CD player, look out! I fear for the day he finally figures out iTunes."

"I'll have to come by and order so many sweets," Tim chuckled.

"And coffee," she added.

"Oh, of course, the coffee. I mean, *still* the best coffee in town...big coffee drinker that I am." He smiled broadly at her.

"*Still* am, right?" she teased.

"Duh." He lifted his Italian soda into the air until the large cloud of whipped cream broke apart in the raspberry-red sky. "You said you had a condo?"

32

"Yeah, it's nice. I told myself, OK, I'll move back home but not *home*. Thankfully, after all the Denver nonsense, I didn't have to."

"I think I could move in with my parents if I had to."

"I always liked your parents."

"Yeah, I lucked out. They were good parents...still are. Vanessa?"

"Hmm?" she said after breaking her stare at the photo of the bridge.

"Your condo?"

"Oh... It's a very bare, basic condo. You'll have to see it."

"I'd like that. What do you want to do with your time, assuming Mr. Ochoa gives you time off?"

"Travel. I really want to travel. And when I did, it was never for personal...always business. But now with some time on my hands..."

"Where do you want to go?"

"California. Always wanted to go there."

"Hollywood? Disneyland?"

"No, but those would be fun," she chuckled. "No, up north. We...Dan and I...MetaBrand...were up there many years ago for a meeting. It's gorgeous and wild up there. Life would be not what I've been used to. Dan was such a homebody. Business all the time, every time. I'm no spring chicken anymore. El tiempo vuela. Time flies." She sighed and drank her coffee. "Enough about me. What about you?"

Tim scratched his beard. "After graduating high school, I took some courses at the vo-tech school. Welding, plastics, fabrication. Basic intro stuff. My dad was a little horrified that I was serious about this and not college or something else. But I couldn't bring myself to do anything but what I love. So, I broke away from school all together. Bored. I was really bored unless I was doing this. I wanted my own stuff, my own interests, but I wanted to do more with it. I thought about California, too…Hollywood. Never made it out there."

"I remember you talking about that," she said. "You've done this for so long."

"I think my dad finally saw that I was good enough at it that I could make a living. He turned around. I don't want to make it sound like he was a jerk about it all, but you know…Dr. and Mrs. Baxter. Plus, I think the idea of getting my feet wet with the church with all this helped him too…and me. I could try out these skills and not suffer too much if things went south or if I had to get a 'real job.' But I just kept on teaching myself and many years ago went to a conference for that kind of stuff. Paid for that myself."

"Good for you."

"I got back, scraped some money together, got some machines and some materials, formed my LLC. The church helped me get started. They were my first client and patron."

"Night's Watch."

"Yep."

"Great name for a company."

"Thank you. So, yeah, I've been doing masks and costumes and makeup ever since."

"Mainly for churches?"

"The bulk of my business is from faith-based places. Movie and television companies, churches. I don't want to say no to clients. I want to do all kinds of work. I would like more…different outlets."

"So, I have a confession." She leaned closer to Tim. "I did a little cyber stalking and found out that your haunted house has made some *serious* national news."

"Yeah, it's really taken off." He blushed as they looked at each other; his cheeks matched the liquid in his glass.

"I remember you showing me those sketches for... Oh, what was that play you talked so much about? Our junior year, I think."

"*The House on Maple Street.*"

"That! Yes! You had sketched up what *all* the characters and sets should look like. And your dad let you build stuff...really big stuff."

"The façade for the town hall and the interior living room and the flesh-eating alien insect."

"Yes, in that huge storage shed in your back yard."

"Reluctantly, but yeah, ol' Steve Baxter did," Tim chuckled. "That thing was a full body suit made out of cheap latex and plastic trash can pieces that I carved up. I found these metal rods in a dumpster near a home that was being renovated in my neighborhood. And the paint...this bright caution-yellow and obnoxious neon green."

"I remember that!" she laughed.

"I drove to all the hardware stores I could. It was the summer of doing that and landscaping with Alan Weaver, my buddy. I was so miserable in that shed. I'd come home from mowing all day, and then I'd get inside that shed. It was so hot and humid."

"Oklahoma summers. Now *those* I haven't missed. Was that the same summer we all went to Adventure Island every day?"

"It was. We'd go to youth group and then book it over there as soon as we were let out. Out late." Tim leaned back and crisscrossed his scuffed work boots. "Ah, the old hangouts. I was so good at Skee-Ball back then. Don't get me started on laser tag."

"You took out a whole birthday party of seven-year-old girls," she snorted.

"Hey, those little girls were *brutal* to me. 'Please mister, don't shoot us.'" Tim held up his hands. "Then, BAM! They came out of nowhere blasting me. Good times back then."

"Yeah…" Her voice faded as a line of customers moved in front of the black-and-white photo where the setting and the hour of that moment inside the picture frame—the stone, the knights, the snow, the water, the moonlight—remained unchanged on the bridge hanging in twilight like a string of pearls. "Those scenes at the haunted house the other night… They had an effect." Vanessa looked at Tim's face; he had not turned away from her. "What about the demon's voice?"

"I took Josh and recorded him. He was ecstatic that day. I picked him up after school and brought him to my studio, had my computer all set up. I think he deliberately messed up so he could stay there. It took longer than I planned. He was all over the place. No, I mean, seriously," Tim chuckled, "all over the place. The kid was by the plastics, the paints, the masks. He was like a puppy getting into stuff. I wanted to buy this modulator that would be built into the mask, but time and money. More money than time, to be honest. We had to have that pre-recording. I hate it, though, because it really cheapens the experience. I want the actor and the character to be one."

"Time and money," Vanessa echoed. "Have you ever seen that show about special effects people? It's a reality show or a competition."

"*FaceOff!* Yes, I have."

"You should get on that."

"Oh man, I love that show. I do want to be on it."

"What's stopping you?"

"I don't know."

"Tim, you have all this talent. You should look into it."

"I do want more than where I am."

"More than church gigs?"

"Yes, but I mean beyond the church and the production companies I've worked for. I want more, but it's *outside* that. I can only ask for so much to be provided."

"Why not reach out to other companies and studios?"

"Funny you should mention that." He became very quiet and looked down at the table. "I want that to happen. But I think they'll have to find me and help me out, not me reaching out to them. I need some PR."

"Oh, do you?"

His eyes suddenly swelled with tears.

"What is it?" she asked.

"Demons." His hands brushed the air and then pushed his glasses up his nose.

"You mean like the ones you make?"

"Sort of. I made one, that's for sure."

"One for a movie or...?"

"I'm just happy to see you," his voice trembled.

"Me too, Tim. Me too."

He cleared his throat. "This place is good. I usually go to this café down by my shop. Buzz. Great name."

"That is a great name. Where's your shop?"

"Off Emery and Thompson. Near that equipment rental place and the ice-skating rink."

"I remember that."

"We spent a lot of Sunday evenings there after youth group."

"Is it big?"

"About two-thousand square feet. There's some land at the back and an old parking lot. The church owns it and bought some sheds. I keep a lot of things in there."

"I'd really like to see it."

"I'd love to show it to you." After several seconds of silence, Tim's bottom lip quivered. "It got broken into two years ago."

"Oh, that's terrible. I'm so sorry, Tim." Vanessa reached out her hand.

He touched her fingers but then pulled back to wipe his eyes. "It's OK. All my cabinets and storage bins were pushed over. Everything was dumped out. The worst was that one of my airbrushes was turned on and used to paint an upside-down cross and a pentagram on the walls. Really horrible to see."

"I am so sorry. Was anyone hurt?"

"No."

"At least you're OK. No one was hurt. I know it's yours, but it's just stuff."

"Yeah, but those symbols. It was really embarrassing, especially when Pastor Rick and the cleaning company came over. The cleaning company is owned by one of the church members, and Rick's wife runs her own accounting business and helps me with my budget. She knew about it. He obviously knew about it. Everyone at the church knew about it."

"I'm sure they all understood."

"It's just…"

"What?"

"Nothing."

"Tell me."

After taking a long drink and pumping his knees up and down, he said, "I did it. I'm the one who trashed my own studio with the pentagrams and the upside-down crosses." His large torso crumpled forward as though he had lost his breath from a punch to the gut. A woman ordering a muffin stared at him before turning back to the counter.

"Shh, it's OK." Vanessa rubbed his back until he was calmer. "Why did you do it?"

"I knew it would get a lot of press coverage. And it did…*a lot*. I got all kinds of support from churches all over the country. From small churches to the huge mega-churches. Pastor Rick has a big network. It did what I thought it would do. Attention and more work, but not from the places I hoped. My Halloween business that year rose forty-five percent. My sales have been insane these last two years. I don't get to keep much of what I make. But all these production companies contacted me…granted, all Christian. Steady work, but I had hoped for something else, you know? Like I said, something outside. Anyway, I was interviewed by news stations, got a ton of Web exposure, and it just slipped out. It took off like wildfire. I said I did special effects for Christian organizations and I own my own FX business, which is true. I am a Christian, and I love creating special effects, but it has been tied to me ever since. I never said I was harassed. I never said I was threatened. I never said that I, as a Christian, was harassed or threatened. I never said

Christians live in a dangerous world. I never used the word *persecuted*. I didn't do any of that. I messed up. I know I did. I got selfish and greedy and deceitful. And the sad thing is that I don't have the courage right now to come clean." He let out a big sigh. "The media made it sound like all I did was religious work. I was guilty enough to go along with it. The images of the store, the pentagram and upside-down cross, were just...a catalyst. I was selfish and stupid, and now I have to live with it."

"What colors did you use?"

"What?"

"The pentagram and the cross...what colors?"

"Are you being serious right now?

"I am. Yeah."

Tim chuckled a little. "Red...*blood* red."

"What other red could it be, right?"

"Exactly. And black."

"Together?" she asked.

"Of course." Tim smirked at her. "The black added a drop shadow to everything. It's the gloss black I use in many of the scenes for the haunted house and my fabs. It's like fresh oil. A matte black would not have the same effect. And that red...well, I mean, come on. It's my own special formula." He leaned in. "You should have seen it. It looked like blood dripping down the walls. I was that good. Everyone thought that the perps had killed something in the room and used its blood to make the cross and the pentagram. The cops were looking for a carcass." He wiped his face with a napkin. "Do you see what I did?"

Vanessa nodded. "I understand, Tim. I do. I really do."

"I do want real money. Unless it's one of those mega-churches or a production company, I have to do major discounts for the small guys, often for free." Tim leaned back in his chair; the irises of his eyes switched between green and brown. He tugged on his chin before saying, "It's always been about the work, but I want some things I can call my own."

"No one else knows this?"

"No."

"And the police?"

"They thought it was hoodlums."

"What did you tell them?"

"I came to my shop that morning and found it that way. Let's change the subject."

"Sure."

"I guess you'll be here a while?" he asked.

"I don't want to be here, but I had nowhere else to go. I needed to be with my dad. I had to start over."

"He's a good egg, but I don't think he ever liked me."

"He liked you in his own kind of way. Tough exterior but a big softie inside. He didn't like most of the guys in my life. You made the cut…just barely." She smirked at him. "But my mom liked you. She felt something good about you the first time you came into the bakery."

"Your mom was a good egg, too. It's weird how everything gets handled."

"What do you mean?"

"You specialized in PR, lost your job, got divorced, came back home to help your dad."

"What does PR have to do with this?"

"I could use some good PR."

"Tim…"

"Just saying."

"Those are just circumstances. They're not...levers and pulleys."

Tim smiled at her. "I got to tell you my story. You can tell me yours."

"I did," she snapped and, realizing that she snapped at him, smoothed her sweater over her shirt and jeans. "I hated grad school, worked at a depressing white-collar job for ten years, watched my marriage dissolve, watched my life slip so far out in front of me, and now I'm helping out at the bakery again like I did when I was a teenager and in the town I swore I'd never return to."

"That's not all there is to it. I can tell there's more."

"What do you want to know?" She crossed her arms.

Tim glanced at his phone. "Let's get together again. We can talk more about all this. It's late, and I have some touching-up to do before practice tomorrow afternoon."

"OK, I'm meeting my dad for dinner anyway. It was good to do this." Vanessa slid her chair out, stood up, and felt as though she dangled in the air, caught between the present, the future, and the poetry of the past.

Tim opened his arms and hugged her. "Yes," he spoke in her ear. "Let's do this again. Being so close again, it'd be stupid not to keep this up. Tell your dad I said hi."

As she wrapped her arms around his shoulder blades, she closed her eyes and smelled cologne on his neck. After he left, he sat for several minutes in his car. The brake lights glowed, the exhaust pipe rumbled, and a car waiting on him honked and sped off when he didn't vacate the parking space. Vanessa looked once more at the photo. The front door chimed. Vanessa spun around and realized that someone she didn't know had opened it.

※

The bareness of her condo shocked her less and less the more she left and reentered it. Stepping into that space of white walls, white ceiling, and light-stained hardwood floors and cabinets was like stepping into a field underneath a blinding sky. The only darkness was the fireplace's black square, surrounded by a limestone mantelpiece and filled with fake logs that retained the same charred marks no matter how many times the previous tenants had used them. The only colors came from the futon that she bought the day after moving in; the silver block of her old laptop; some clothes barely filling the master bedroom closet; the books that she had arranged from cool- to warm-colored covers on the fireplace's mantel; and the pool and landscaping outside her second-floor balcony's door.

The condo was large enough for someone with many large things, but Vanessa was no longer that person. She could have lived in a cheaper place, but that meant living in an area of town she left many years ago. Money wasn't an issue. She had the divorce settlement and the hefty resolution from MetaBrand, sums that she had only heard about when people won the lottery. With all the zeros printed on the checks and floating in her bank account, she had more money than she had ever seen and more money than she had ever needed. The books and the car were the last things that reminded her of her previous life, of Dan, and of the places she had been and where she wanted to go.

Part of her wanted to admit that maybe Tim was right: things in life move into place at their own timing like gears twisting into their correct spots at the correct seconds, internal workings lining up without strain. Fumbling with her keys and flipping on the lights in the entryway, Vanessa sighed at that possibility and at the words *fate*, *purpose*, and *meaning* swirling in her head, those words trying to snatch her up and place her in a clean, observable line from there to there. She rinsed a glass in the dish drainer, topped it off with ice and water, and standing at the kitchen sink, massaged the back of her neck. She cut off any more thoughts about such a possibility and those words, dumped two ibuprofens into her hand, and shuffled to the balcony.

Her back against the vinyl siding, she plopped down to the concrete floor and stretched her legs through the balcony's small iron fence. She thought of the past summer, when she moved into the condo, moving, she thought, between an elongated band of private, emotional heat, one end weighed by the past while the other end, in front of her, spiraled out, loose, undefined. During those first weeks back, she found calm by sitting on the balcony and watching birds or squirrels skitter on the trees. The trees were green then, sharply green, the sun lighting the tips of their leaves into arrowheads piercing a crisp, cloudless sky. But as she opened the door tonight, the cool autumn air spilled in, the nights longer, the days shortening, the trees starting to turn into the colors of fire. The high she had felt being with Tim again waned until she felt a need to find a dark corner and place all hopes and worries inside it until spring returned.

Her head throbbed on the top right; a tingling pain grew into a small pressure floating between the fluid of her brain and her skull like a ghost knocking more and more on a calcified door. She calmed down by telling herself that the headache was because of the caffeine from the latte with Tim or because of the white wine at dinner with Dad. When she stood up, she wobbled and latched onto the balcony's doorknob. Blood rushed to her brain and flooded out any memories or thoughts she had of the day, of the time she had spent with her father, of Tim, of what Tim had revealed to her and what she had yet to reveal to him. Numbness prickling over her body, dizzy, other senses spiked, she could smell the coffee shop from hours ago and its roasted air on her sleeves, the smell of dinner's grilled salmon on her sweater, her father laughing with her over memories. She saw Tim toast his red soda with extra whipped cream to her, and she saw her father toast his tumbler of whiskey to her. They all spoke of Flora. They all spoke of the past, more so than of the present or the future. She cried as the day overshadowed her: reconnecting with Tim; having another dinner date with her dad at their favorite restaurant; sitting on the balcony and watching the trees and the sky and listening to the night slowly lengthen; knowing the duties awaiting her at the bakery tomorrow morning; and realizing on her drive home tonight that the diner and the motel on the other side of the road had not changed since she last drove on that road over a decade ago. The day had overshadowed her fractured life and the hopes of putting it all back together again.

She breathed slowly and deeply and walked from the balcony into the living room and then, scared by the silence inside the condo, back onto the balcony. The first night she slept in the condo, she woke up convinced that she had lost her hearing, that her health had declined again and in another way. The walls of her condo were very thick; no noise penetrated them, but outside cars drove by on the streets beyond the complex with their steady hum of engines and tires and the occasional deep bass of a stereo. Vanessa looked at the lights from the street and from the other units wrapping around the pool with their soft blue-silver lights glowing over the water. She toyed with the idea of going to the bakery at this time of night and making herself a large pan of something gooey and chocolatey and woven together by sugar and memory, something that she could eat by herself at the table in the prep room under a single lamp.

A message blinked on her phone. *Thanks again for today, see you soon*, Tim had texted under a picture of him and a full-size skeleton waving at her from his shop. She covered her mouth as she laughed and shook her head. He had also sent a second picture not long after the first one. She clicked it open and covered her mouth again as she zoomed in on the drawing and squinted at the words *Aztec Wheel of Time — 1996* written in his sloppy teenage-boy handwriting. The paper had yellowed, curled and split in the four corners, gray stains in the middle of the paper, but the colored pencils and the ink had remained vibrant, and teenage Tim had drawn the heads of the calendar's animals as perfectly as she remembered them the day her mother first sketched them on the walls of the old bakery. Rabbit, Jaguar, Snake, Dog, Deer, and Eagle all faced the right side of the page. Tim had flipped them along the horizon until they all stared at the symbol for Death with its cream-colored skull embellished with small red circles inside large yellow circles. Behind Death, Tim had drawn House, a tall, narrow building with a red door and a yellow roof. On the other side of House was Flower, its red roots ballooning into yellow petals. And beneath his sketches, Tim had written call numbers from the downtown library, three rows of them, and circled them. In different ink at the bottom of the paper, he had also scribbled lines from an Aztec poem: *You have transformed into a Flower Tree, you have emerged, you bend and scatter; you have appeared before God's face as multi-colored flowers.*

Shutting off her phone and closing her eyes, Vanessa felt a new pulse in her head, one competing against the headache—the headache icy and prickly, the new pulse warm and melting.

The gate to the pool clicked shut, and she watched two shadows scamper off. Water dripped behind them as they left wet footprints. She stared at the water. Her breathing slowed. Taking off her shoes and rolling up her black slacks to the knees, she made her way down to the pool.

Bending a little over the water, she watched her shape break and re-form and break again. She rotated her neck far to the left and right and then up and along the neighboring buildings. Her headache faded but then returned. Lights went out one by one, and the night was darker than it had been when she first stepped onto the balcony. She stood up and removed her jeans, looked around, and peeled off her sweater and shirt. Into the water, wearing only her bra and underwear, she slipped as quietly as she could and dropped into its chill.

She mused that she could sleep there, underwater, just floating, and remembered the times she swam with her friends in high school at the community pool, her body floating in the middle of light and motion, her friends kicking around her. She thought how far she had come, always wanting to be in the water, magnetized by it, but having no clue how to swim. She thought of the first time she went off the diving board. The ladder was so high, but up she went, mainly on a dare from Tanya but also to impress Jacob. Looking over the edge of the board, Vanessa froze, the air much cooler up there, the breeze having picked up after she climbed the ladder. Every little movement bobbled the board and scared her.

"Come on…go!" whined a little girl in pigtails, goggles, and a pink and yellow one-piece. She was much braver and more aggressive than Vanessa would have expected from someone half her size. The little girl huffed and began putting her small hands on top of the board, ready to bypass Vanessa. "One at a time!" whistled a lifeguard. Sighing and huffing more, the little girl backed down. "Then go!" she shrilled. The lifeguard and Vanessa made eye contact before the lifeguard whistled at someone else. Vanessa heard her friends chanting and yelling at her far below the board. They splashed their legs as they clung to the side of the pool in the shallow end. "Do it, V!" yelled Tanya. Vanessa watched Jacob flirt with Veronica Sanchez and her lithe body. Vanessa pulled down her long black t-shirt, sucked in her belly, and rolled her shoulders back, flopping her long, wet, black hair behind her. The lifeguard looked up at her again and was about to blow Vanessa down when she ran off the board and plummeted into the water below.

The splash shocked her, stung her body, and nearly knocked her out. And as Vanessa sank, she panicked. She opened her eyes and saw that she was so far underwater that the surface seemed just as far away above her as it did when she stood over it on the board. She felt trapped inside a glass box, clear blue light glowing all around as she hovered. She pushed herself off the pool's floor and, kicking and gasping for air, bobbed up and down on the surface. "Help!" she tried forcing out. No one paid attention. "Help!" Her brain, scrambling and firing away, struggled to push another plea out, and she believed she shouted for help out loud. Kids laughed and screamed.

As she bobbed, Tanya, Stephanie, and Melinda rose above and fell below the surface. No one, not even the lifeguard who whistled at the little girl, came for her, even as Vanessa violently pulled in water and the summer air, mixing them together. She spit out the water as quickly as it filled her mouth, and then something in her told her to kick and propel herself forward. But she didn't move; she believed she was moving, but she remained in one place, thrashing about.

Suddenly she felt a large splash next to her and two strong arms wrap around her stomach. Another lifeguard had snared her, dragged her to the side of the pool in the deep end, and pressed her against the coarse wall. She coughed up water and spit into the trough with its bubbles and dead bugs floating past her. Before the lifeguard drifted away, he said something, but the water plugging and buzzing in her ears reduced his words to a mumble. Her friends glided toward her. "V, you a'right?" asked Tanya. Her friends patted her on her back and helped her out of the pool. "Damn, V," Jacob said as her hearing returned and the haze lifted from her eyes. She remembered that he laughed at her.

Vanessa thought of this as she leaned back against the edge of the condo's pool and its own coarse wall. She could see her balcony's open door, the warm yellow light inside, and the blankness of her walls as compared to her neighbors' congested walls. A few more condos darkened, and she was alone in the cool water with the blue light taking over. The cars passing by and the chirping crickets lessened. She realized that these were the sounds of night she had missed in the suburbs; that her condo was filled but empty; that these sounds were out there and had been waiting for her; that these were the sounds of her youth as she listened to them penetrate the thin walls of the camper by Vida Nueva, the apartment above the old bakery, or her first apartment in Denver—a weaving of sounds that her recent life had pulled apart; sounds that reminded her of an earlier life, of standing in the night and wondering what was out there, what was beyond the very things given to her, of listening to Calderon and his sermons, of listening to the sounds of a guitar played on her father's records, of her mother's voice.

Vanessa rested the base of her head on the pool's edge, which numbed her neck. The headache had neither increased nor decreased. A haze, spreading from the right side of her head, drifted across her mind, smudging the past and the present, blurring the future, and she felt sick, but not for home or for returning to it, though she had returned home and had begun accepting its irrefutability, and so she slipped into this haze without sleep, this feeling she had felt before, these disjointed parts of her inside this haze, some pieces reassembled from memories, some to be assembled once dropped into place from above.

4

As the last of their coworkers straggled downstairs, Dan stood in front of a coat rack that had, behind its hooks, a mirror framed in brass that billowed like clouds. He folded his blazer across his arm and stared at his reflection, the angled room, and Vanessa behind him and then jutted out his chin so he could adjust the collar of his shirt. He took his right hand and feathered the graying sides of his hair before glancing at himself one more time. Out of the corner of his eye, he watched Vanessa walk over to the coat rack. Her purse hung on the hook under where his blazer had been. "Told you I'd keep it safe all night." He grinned as he faced his reflection. The copper ceiling tiles intensified the warmth of the golden light that broke up the monotony of snow falling outside the windows.

"Yes, you did," she said. "Thank you. You just can't trust anybody these days."

"You can't, especially with all these white-collar professionals." His smirk deepened the wrinkles around his eyes and mouth. "I was trying to get your attention all night."

After sliding her purse's strap over her shoulder, Vanessa touched his elbow. She had made eye contact with him many times over their colleagues clinking and guzzling drinks, enjoying the hors d'oeuvres of the private party nestled upstairs in the restaurant, and congratulating her and Dan on a job well done. Standing before their company, the owners and CEOs recognized Vanessa and Dan after the party had commenced and praised her for "leadership," "quality," and "action." She stood in the crowd watching and listening to all this, feeling eyes on her, feeling the occasional pat on her shoulders from those around her, but after the rousing praise from MetaBrand's owners, Dan left her side, squeezing her wrist before he did, the crowd splitting down the middle as he charged through, to reiterate to everyone what had been expressed, "that without Vanessa we wouldn't be celebrating tonight, that without her we'd be any old startup in Denver still trying to make it big. We've arrived." Never in her two years at the company had she imagined herself in such a spotlight.

"Last call?" Dan asked, finishing one more bacon-wrapped date and nodding toward the stairwell.

"Yes." She placed her wine glass on a tray held by a man dressed in all black and wearing a black apron. His jet-black hair was slicked back and highlighted his dark eyes and brown face. "Thank you so much," she said, her voice slower, tender, her tone directed not at where she was— the present celebration lifting her—but where she had come from—a past that humbled her; her heart filled with the two moments that it lived in. The server smiled and continued gathering empty glasses and plates.

Dan placed his hand on the small of her back as they drifted down to where some of their coworkers had snuck to watch the beginning of March Madness. Vanessa's heels clicked the wood floor while the bottom of her dress slid down each step like a red wave retreating back to sea. Hours ago, she went up those stairs for the first time, having months before seen them glowing from the first floor, and she had wondered, in the many late-night meetings, dinners, and drinks that she and her team had here, where the stairs led and what was up there. Individuals, couples, and groups promenaded past her, glistening in their shoes or dresses, their laughter fading as they ascended around the corner, carried

52

up. Now she descended the stairs herself, from where she had been invited, twisting down in the golden light, glistening in her own dress, having not only been up there, solving a personal curiosity, but also having been suspended in momentary elegance and attention.

"I think we're it," Dan said as they slid into a booth. "Everyone came for the free drinks and food and then left." He chuckled. "And when you and I are the reason for tonight."

"It wasn't just us. The whole company."

Dan pointed his finger at her. "River Walk done under budget and ahead of schedule. Everyone loves it. Everybody's talking about it. New office space here we come, and more importantly, new clients here they come."

"I know a lot was riding on this. I can never tell when they're happy, only when they're not happy. A lot of people came crying out of meetings during this project. I had my share of tears."

"I know. People notice. I tell Dave and Brian mostly everything."

"Mostly?"

"Mostly." He winked at her. "MetaBrand is taking off, and you're outshining everyone in your department. You're the best to run it."

"What about Ellen?"

"You've made yourself known when she can't."

"She's been good to me. She hired me. She's my first real boss at my first real job."

"River Walk in less than four months. That's you, not her."

"She told me she's been here six years."

Dan adjusted his cufflinks. "She's not going to be with us much longer. Just between us, OK?"

Vanessa nodded.

"We were going to do it before Christmas, but you stepped up before things got too ugly. Hey," Dan shouted as he flagged down a server zooming by the booth, "we're ready for some drinks and menus *now*."

"This isn't my table, but I'll be sure to…"

"Well, look, we've been upstairs in the private room. We're with MetaBrand. Give us some waters and menus. We've been here a while."

The petite, youthful server briefly stared at Dan. She balanced several plates and glasses on her tray and quickly looked up when the bar roared when a jump shot tied the game. "I'll let someone know." She smiled and walked away.

"This place should have kept its staff from 1929. That one guy over there has been here since they reopened years ago. Look. His collar barely covers his neck tattoo." Dan nodded toward the man taking an order from a couple sitting at a table. "Dave knows the owners, so we helped them with the rebranding. The Charles." His voice flared as his hands arced across an imaginary marquee illuminating a corner of downtown Denver. "I directed that project when I got here."

"I know." Vanessa pulled her cardigan over her shoulders and leaned forward so her long curls wouldn't snag on the booth. "I guess I can safely assume a pay raise and a bonus during my annual review in addition to my upcoming new title, which I don't know about."

"Look at you being all assertive and throwing out numbers for bonuses and reviews." Dan's face lit up. "Think you can hold onto this wave until next December?"

Vanessa's eyes glistened as she nodded.

"Annual review is nine months from now."

"I know."

"You just had one, too…knocked it out of the park, I heard."

"Yes, I did."

"Well, then… Got some numbers in your head?"

"I do."

"At least five percent?"

"Oh, *please*. I know what you execs drive and where you live, and I know which clients we have in the queue."

Dan continued smiling at her before laughing out loud. "Good. You deserve it. Now and nine months from now."

A different server brought menus and waters. "Any drinks to start off with?"

"The stout for me, and she'll have…"

"White wine, please."

"Very good," the server said before leaving.

"Hey, what kind of ring is that?" Dan pointed to Vanessa's hand. "I remember seeing it from day one, and I've been meaning to ask you."

She flattened her hand and spread her fingers across the wood table. "My dad made it for me. It's from both of my parents, but he made it. A birthday gift. I got it for my Sweet Sixteen."

"Mazel tov," he replied. He reached for her fingers, touching them lightly, and pulled the ring under the tangled burn of vintage filament dangling above the table. "Is that a piece of wood?" He stared at the splinter floating inside a clear dome.

"It is. It's from a tree that my father saw when my parents were younger."

"Must mean something powerful to have it in a ring and wear it."

"It is. My parents came to this country right before I was born. Like, two weeks before I came into this world."

"It has a story."

"It does."

"And?"

"And according to them, this tree had fallen into the river, and my father took a piece from it." She looked at her ring and, as her father had described it to her years ago, saw the tree rustling in the water, the roots firmly in the ground, the break near the bottom where the bark burst like yellow stuffing and the bare limbs dangling over the river scratched translucent lines across the surface, waving back and forth across the current like a polygraph. The river that day was gray and brown and limped under a cold February wind. Her pregnant mother stood on the other side, waiting and shivering, soaked from the waist down, her face as pale as the moonlight; her father waded across, paused midway, and then turned back, stunning her mother and Coyote, who was ahead of them both and waited on a dirt path. Splashing into the river, against the current, her father reached back, broke off a small piece of bark, and slid it into his pocket while holding above him the whole time the two plastic bags they brought with them—all their things that could fit inside. "My father claims," Vanessa continued, smiling while she saw all of this, "that as soon as they crossed, the tree snapped free and floated down the river." Vanessa pulled back her hand and reached for the water glass with her other hand. "He nearly drowned doing it. But he got that one piece in time."

"They crossed the river."

"They did. They came over before 1984. They were granted amnesty."

"You may have mentioned that one time, late at night." Dan removed his tie after the server brought them their drinks; he unbuttoned the top of his dress shirt.

"Was I drooling over a stack of design specs and my laptop?"

"Yes, and I believe it was this very booth."

"Not this one," she said. "A booth over there. I remember because Carolyn kept complaining about the breeze from the front doors. She started wearing that jacket every time we worked here."

Dan laughed. "You never wore a jacket. Where's Carolyn today?"

"Oh, come on, she was on the team. She coordinated a lot for us."

"Are you ready to order?" the server asked.

"The angel-hair primavera for me," Vanessa answered.

"Steak and green beans," Dan said.

"Very good. Your orders will be out shortly."

"They're heavy on the garlic," Vanessa said.

"How do you know that?"

"I've been close to you after you've had them."

He grinned while she blushed. "We should have this part of the restaurant named after us. The River Walk Team Pub. You've really thrown yourself into all this."

"I love it."

"It's like a religion."

"Are you religious?"

"Out of left field," he replied with a laugh. "No, not anymore. Mom's 'spiritual,' my dad not so much. I'm like him. Now, my grandma, she's religious. I loved my grandma. She had all these tall tales, folklore, old wives' tales, that kind of stuff. I remember I had this severe congestion one time when I young...coughing up huge chunks of green mucus. And Babunia said, 'Vo'ka and cig-rettes.'" He spoke with a gravelly, Eastern European voice. "She made me hold a shot of vodka in my mouth while she blew cigarette smoke in my ear. Then I gargled the vodka and spit it out, but not all of it."

"And?"

"It worked. Babunia was pretty proud of herself that day." He raised his pint of beer. "Congratulations again. We wouldn't have done it without you. To you."

"To us." She clinked her glass with his.

"So...I guess you'll have all this time to date again. So many eligible bachelors in the greater Denver area, educated and savvy...maybe some hippie from Boulder. Your dance card'll be full."

"No, I have the Omaha project coming up and, after that, Memphis. I've never made time for it in the past, don't really have time now, but there are always exceptions." She curled her hair behind her ear; her sun-shaped earring glowed in the light.

"Not taking the first thing you see."

"Right."

"That's the way to do it, I think. Wait for the right moment."

"I guess you can finally focus on finding Mrs. Miller."

"True. I've waited long enough." Dan took a deep breath and leaned in closer. "So, how about that date, finally? We kept putting it off until this project was done, and now..."

"Now it is."

"That's right."

"Which date? We joked about so many."

"The time-share with Dave and his wife up in Aspen. We could be up there in time for spring break."

"Spring break? No, I'm not spring break material. I'm twenty-seven and in bed by nine. Besides, my spring breaks in college involved studying and being boring...which was all the time...basically what I do now."

"Did you work?" Dan asked.

"Oh, of course. This Latina didn't ride for free, even at a state school. I worked in the cafeteria. You?"

"I didn't have to work, but I wanted to. My dad didn't grow up rich, but he worked his tail off. My grandfather cleaned a radio station and Babunia was a damn fine seamstress. Dad started selling cars at seventeen. I ried one semester at CUNY, but it wasn't for him. He went back to selling cars and eventually bought the dealership when the owner retired. Then he bought more and more. Pretty soon he had a nice little auto empire. It was nice to be sixteen and your dad's one of the biggest auto dealers on Long Island. Lot of options for a high school boy."

"I bet." Vanessa imagined Dan's father, a little portly man with gray hair and a mustache, wearing a tweed jacket and handing a set of keys to a teenage Dan who sat behind the steering wheel of a car that wasn't like the ones the boys from her high school preferred—the cars that rumbled and crackled, the outsides outlined with loud, metal flair. She imagined a flop-haired Dan inserting a CD into the car stereo that wasn't anything she had heard from the cars idling in the parking lots of her teenage years. She imagined this adolescent Dan cruising around town while his car drew the attention of curious girls and jealous boys. "Chido car, I bet," she said.

"Chido?" he asked.

"Something cool. You know...a chido car."

"I did have some cool cars. One was my favorite. It was used, but it looked new. Pontiac Firebird. Special Edition V8. Black. Tan interior. One of my dad's guys at the shop waxed that thing every Saturday morning. I helped wax it every now and then. Now, *that* I wanted to do. It was the closest thing I could do to get to that car. My dad teased me about selling it even though he knew I had my eye on it. He'd say, 'Five guys came by today asking about that. I think we're getting close.' One day I showed up to help in the office, and it was gone. My heart sank. Minutes after we closed for the day, my dad rolled it out front, handed me the keys, and had this big grin on his face. He said, 'The gas is there, and the brake is, well, you may never use it.' It was a fun car. My dad is a good man." Dan spun his pint on its coaster and stared at the table for several seconds. "Years later," he continued, "one of my undergrad friends and I started a, shall we say, consulting firm out of his dorm. We provided content for students at other universities, not ours. That was decided early on...a rule set in stone. No students from our university. It would raise too many red flags and get us in some serious hot water."

"And by content, you really mean essays."

He fluttered his eyebrows.

"OK. Give me your pitch."

He downed the last of his stout, shifted in the booth, and brushed back his hair. "We had three levels. The Bronze Level was free advice. We didn't tell them much...maybe pass on a list of books after a basic library search. Not too much effort on our part. Super simple. But we'd always remind them that we would be happy to do *more* for them. The Silver Level was more…maybe one theme or a page or two from an essay, taken out of context, so they couldn't just piece something together without us. Not really content-content. Gold, of course, was the whole kit and caboodle. We either resold essays someone had made for us…outsourced, of course…"

"Of course."

"…or we'd hire out someone to write the requested essay."

"Wow. No problem with ethics, huh?"

"It wasn't about ethics," he said as their food arrived. "Like I said, we would only sell to students outside our university. It wasn't our problem if someone got caught plagiarizing. We just sold it. Whatever they wanted to do with it was their business, not ours. It's like blaming a gun manufacturer for deaths. Some of our clients, though, did tell us that they'd sign up for the Gold Level, get these great essays, and just cull them for content, and write their own, feeling too guilty to turn them in. I made this program that tracked who, what, when, where, number of pages, themes, universities, all that. I made it searchable. We made use of phones, fliers, word of mouth."

"And the prices?"

"Well, at first it was just to buy a little more than some frozen pizzas and cheap beer."

Vanessa giggled and looked around the bar; no one paid any attention to them.

"But, you know," he continued, "we learned, grew, and yeah, we made a profit."

"I have a feeling you cashed out early in life."

"Let's just say, by the time we figured out what we were doing, I was ready to invest...really invest, with serious cash and capital before graduating."

"You paid other students to write?"

"They produced. I sold. We all made some cash and went home a little happier."

"That is...*entrepreneurial*," Vanessa said, shaking her head. "I can see this in you."

"I did the barest amount possible in classes. Whatever. The past is the past. It's all about here and now. The present and the future are what matter. Besides, I found out I was really good at making deals and using tech for that. So, I got into computer science by my sophomore year, and..."

"And the rest is history."

"I did, however, enjoy my time at one of Rutgers' finest fraternities."

"I had a feeling about that."

"Is that a deal-breaker?"

"No." Vanessa laughed. "Do you remember the first time we came here?"

"I do. We had just started hashing out who was going to do what on River Walk. We had Carolyn...with her jacket...and Tom and...who else?"

"Kit and Rachael. We had taken up two tables by August, put them together, and set our laptops and folders on them, and all our phones, pens, and pencils."

"Beer and work."

"It was just you and me a lot of the time."

"I'm not complaining."

"I would hope not. I liked it," Vanessa said, glancing at him.

"Me too. HR would've loved to been a fly on the wall."

"Oh, I know."

"Just think, burning out of grad school kept you here in Denver, and MetaBrand was hiring at the right time."

"I wouldn't have left Denver anyway. I like it too much here." She swirled her pasta. "It's this great city that feels isolated. Not too big, not too small. It does its own thing."

"Just like its people."

"Exactly. There's so much to do here."

"So, you like Denver?"

"Very much. I want to see more of the West now that I'm on this side of the country, but Denver's much better now that I'm not in school. I would spend most of my days hiking or being outside. My study habits went down the drain pretty quickly after moving out here."

"I love it here," Dan said, jabbing the final hunk of steak. "You couldn't get me to go back to New York or the East Coast."

"Not even for a deal?"

"Well…" He rolled his eyes. "I visit my parents on the holidays, and my sister lives in Manhattan. Both places have their winters, but here, there's so much growth and opportunity. Good living, good housing, tech startups, being outside. It's a good place to set down roots."

"I miss my dad," Vanessa said, "but it's OK. He needs to run the bakery, and I don't want to ever go back to where I came from. I love it here. I have autonomy and space and a staff now. I never imagined having anything like that to my name. I love my team. I really enjoy what I do, and I'm thankful."

"Good."

"Why?" she asked, blushing.

He folded his napkin and looked at her while she chewed. "Because you're here at the right time. MetaBrand is primed to grow...*aggressively*. All the pieces and key players are in place. You're one of them."

"I want that...and more."

"More?"

"Yeah. Why not go for it all? I want a house and to travel and eat good food...all that."

"You want all that."

"Yes."

"The suburban house in a nice neighborhood."

"Yes, all those clichés," she said, imagining the homes that she had visited when she went to youth group and the ones by the country club where her mother worked before they had the bakery; *Yes, all those clichés* she echoed to herself and saw them again, filled with gold-trimmed mirrors and ivory doorknobs, backyard pools shimmering under the summer sun, and the smell of Christmas cinnamon drifting from the kitchen to the den.

"The white-picket fence..." Dan's voice drifted with hers.

"Yes..."

"And maybe one or two kids running in the backyard..."

"Sure," Vanessa said, closing her eyes, opening them, Dan still there, across from her, his mouth quiet but his words moving, unbroken.

5

Tim flipped the switch to the overhead studio lights, each covered in a metal web, each clanking on one by one. Eyelids flittering, Vanessa glanced around the room and at the shimmering maze of tools, bottles, tubs, workbenches, and the vast amounts of wood, plastic, and metals stored in the shop. Her fingertips glided over the shiny barrels of airbrushes and the shelves of paints organized like rainbows stacked atop rainbows. She looked up and gasped at the row of gray human torsos hanging from hooks. Tim stopped walking and smiled at her as she patted her breastbone and reopened her eyes. The realistic molds dangled in front of her and over the plastic tubs and cans of paint colors—legless, armless, headless, each copy waiting to be lowered down and brought to life with a burst of tinted air, no stronger than a whisper, applied to the surface. *Psst!* Vanessa jumped at the sound of a sharp noise above her.

"It's just the ventilation system," he said, throwing his keys onto his desk next to a stack of white business cards with Night's Watch FX Production in black font. He put one finger in the air, just below tubes stretched like robotic octopus arms from the metal hood bolted to the ceiling. "Wait for it." He smiled at her. "There." His eyebrows bobbed at the sound of a soft hum slowly displacing all the small, invisible things in the air. "Before I got that, I had this huge respirator I'd wear while working. I looked like I belonged to the hazmat squad," he chuckled. "And before that, well, I'd basically get nauseous and dizzy the longer I worked in here. Zero windows. Tried a couple of fans and opened the garage door at the back, and that was like high school."

"This explains so, so much now," Vanessa laughed, wrinkling her nose.

"Yeah, it should."

She strolled over to his desk and the main work area defined by metal and wood shelves, like a cross between an auto-repair shop and a Hollywood back lot. She saw not only a sculpted cowl on a Styrofoam head but also glossy, professional-grade pictures of his work from advertisements, commercials, music videos, the haunted houses, Passion plays, biblical plays, and movies and ranging from the smallest flesh wound to age makeup to full-body pieces—some definitively human, some pulled from the image of a human, some from nature, and some from nightmares. Her gaze swung back and forth. "Look at all this, Tim. These are amazing. You've been busy over the years."

"Yeah, thanks." After his computer powered on, Tim swiveled on his stool and clicked his mouse. "I got an email from *Make-up Artist* the other day. They heard about me."

"And?"

"They think I only do one kind of FX."

"Simple. Show them otherwise." She motioned to his sketches and pieces of foam marked with dotted lines lying around the studio.

"I don't know." He dragged his cursor through his inbox and across the screen. "The church would only allow it if I stuck with my story."

"Tim," she sighed.

"I want to do it. It's just..." He pulled a metal can on his desk toward him, fumbled inside, and tapped a green colored pencil from among an entanglement of pens and pencils. "It's just that I've been branded as this for so long. I've been thinking about things for a while, wondering what to do, and then, this summer, you...last week at the coffee shop. After finding out you're back in town and seeing you and talking with you, I realized I do want more. I really do. I want different things, different...contacts. I want to get out from under the church."

Vanessa's head cocked.

"Not that. Not *leave* the church. I want to break out, have new clients. I want to get from being limited to certain kinds of work. I want to be able to pursue things on my own, creatively and financially. But my story's all off. I'm seen as being one kind of artist. The thing I started...it backfired." Tim tapped the pencil harder on the desk. "Other companies assume I only do one kind of work. I don't want to be a Christian FX artist. I want to be an FX artist who happens to be a Christian." He swept the green flakes broken off from the pencil into a metal wastebasket and then dusted his hands. "Would you help me...retell my story? Or tell it differently."

"PR? Is that why...?"

"No...no," he interrupted firmly. "Don't think that, because that's not it. That's not true at all. I just can't believe that you're a PR person and we're back in each other's lives."

"*Was* a PR person." She tightened her scarf, pulling it like two strings on a package, the black chevron patterns darting in opposite directions over her white shirt. "Just tell the church you want to do these other things."

"It's not that simple. They have expectations. They help with my rent and utilities. Plus, I got those original contacts through them. I feel guilty and greedy at the same time." Tim spun the pencil in his hand before brushing his beard. "There are a lot of opportunities out there to do what I love. Besides, you know *me* and the church."

"I don't know this church, your church, and I don't know *the* church anymore," her voice rose.

"You did once. Weren't those memories good? All those years in youth group?"

"It was just teenage stuff…emotions. Just memories now," she said, leaning away from his desk and glancing at the torsos.

"I know. That's part of it when you're a teenager, and the cliques don't help. But that's human stuff…teenage human stuff, not God stuff, not Christ-like."

As she pressed her back to the wall, Vanessa crossed her arms and looked down.

"And all those times feeling lifted up…feeling bliss?" he asked.

"At the time?" She shook her head. "I would have said the Holy Ghost…absolutely…but now I think the effect was just psychological."

"But the love you felt…"

"Just feelings. It was nice, but just feelings…feelings that I've experienced with a book or a song, too. There was the party, so to speak, of being drunk on those emotions, and then I had the hangover and life to deal with."

"But you felt close to…"

"To you?" she finished for him.

Tim nodded.

"Of course, I did. But I had to get out. It wasn't for me anymore. And I didn't feel that it could answer all my questions."

"Yeah," he said, rocking on the chair and playing with scraps of latex. "You just up and left during our senior year. I know a lot of it had to do with your mom."

"A lot of it did have to do with my mom, but things changed. Things *do* change. I changed. I just saw the youth group as something different...fake."

"Fake?" he shot back.

"At times, yes. Everyone was talking about how amazing Christ was in their lives. I didn't see it. I felt it, I guess, but I didn't see it. It was, like, isn't there more than just words? What about actions?"

Tim dropped his boots from the desk and onto the concrete floor. He shifted in his chair and nodded at her. "You're right. It *is* more than just feelings and words. I've come to realize that too, now that I'm older."

"It became all about being saved. That's all I heard," she went on. "Saving myself, saving my friends, saving...witnessing to everyone around me." She closed her eyes and remembered approaching her friends one day at school during lunch and wanting to talk to them about what she had experienced at youth group and then not having the courage to do it, even though she had written a small speech, filled with Bible verses, and folded it in her pocket. "Everything was watered down to avoiding hell. Everything was about being good and not screwing up. Or so it felt at times."

Tim started to speak but instead looked down. The ventilation system surged again. A soft hum flooded the silence between them. He took a big breath in and exhaled as he leaned his forearms on his legs; his paint-covered hands dangled between his knees. "It's not about being good or bad," he said. "And I say this having to live with my own decision about *this*." He threw his eyes around the shop. "It's about growing and learning, and we're not...we're not 'good' or 'bad' tools. We have *all* these tools available to us. Emotional hunger...sex, greed, fear, pride...love. Pride is the worst because it makes us only focus on ourselves, not our neighbors, not anyone around us, not God. And emotions, they are like those other tools. We can wander about, letting them guide us, or we can use them consciously. But they are one of the raw materials that God gave us to use."

Vanessa looked up at him but kept her arms crossed.

"It's about making choices to build a good thing, move toward a good thing, even knowing that you'll back up as you move forward. It's not about what we intend ourselves to be, but what *God* intended us to be when He made us. He doesn't love us because we are good. God makes us good *because* He made us...because He loves us. But we have to move *to* that, make choices that get us there, and yeah, stumble along the way. But that's part of it."

"That's nice to hear, now, but I honestly think that you can rationalize whatever you want. I was in PR. Believe me, you can." She stared at the paint splatters on the floor by the desk. After several seconds of silence, she sighed. "But there have been things in my life that make me not believe in that kind of thinking anymore. There are things you don't know about." She stood up from his desk area and walked around the open space of the studio. Stopping at the opposite side of the room, she rubbed her fingers over a section of the wall with fresher paint slightly different than the white around it like vanilla ice cream melting on new snow. The section stood out, not so much as a scar running up the length of a leg, from kneecap to hip, but as a long narrow piece of fabric flattened and glued to the wall before being painted over. Its faint ridge created a small shadow that became more defined as the October daylight ebbed.

"That's the spot." Tim adjusted his glasses and leaned in his chair against his desk.

Vanessa's eyes followed her hands up the seam.

"I got a little too much red and black paint there, so I had to sandblast the pentagram off. It was just me in here that week. I gave Bryce a long vacation. I told him I wanted him to have some time for his music because he'd been working so hard for me. Plus, he didn't need to be weighed down because of my decisions. I had to move pretty much everything out back or cover it with plastic to avoid dust. Place looked like a morgue. Which reminds me..." He stood up and zipped up his hoodie. "I have a surprise for you."

"Oh?" she chuckled, glancing at the gray torsos behind him.

"You're standing really close to it. It's up at the front behind the counter. Close your eyes."

Taking her hand, he led her to another part of the studio, near the front windows, she assumed, because her eyelids reddened with the day's light.

"Watch your step." He had her stop walking when he placed his hands on her hips. He rummaged on a metal shelf, set something heavy down on the counter, like a candlestick with a broad base, and unwrapped a plastic bag. "OK, open your eyes."

Two calacas stood in front of Vanessa, their bones and costumes bright in the storefront light. "You made these?" She turned to him. "Of course, you did."

"I started them not long after we met at the haunted house. Painting the costumes took the longest, but it was fun."

71

"Can I touch?"

"Definitely. They're plastic and latex and...dry." He spot-checked the sky-blue flower pinned on the jacket of the male calaca. "Yeah, touch away."

Vanessa crouched in front of the calacas until their hollowed-out black eye sockets looked at her. The male skeleton wore a jacket with vertical white, pink, and orange stripes; the sequence of colors reminded Vanessa of popsicles that she bought from an ice cream truck every summer when she was younger. The male calaca's jacket and bright blue flower and tie popped against his white pants, white shoes, and white gloves. He tipped a straw hat to his lady friend, who looped her skeletal arm through his; her free hand held a bouquet of marigolds. The lady calaca in a puffy Victorian white dress with its brooch and pink belt was ready for a Sunday stroll in a park after church. "Real lace," Vanessa said, touching the thin veil dangling over the skull. She moved her fingers to the broad-brim hat and then over to a small white-and-pink umbrella in the lady's skeletal hand. "I'm glad you made them happy. It's not sad."

"Día de Los Muertos," Tim said.

"Día de Los Muertos," Vanessa repeated and smiled at him as she massaged the back of her neck.

"It's coming up. Two Saturdays from now."

"Yes...yes, it is."

"I remember we talked a lot about it back in the day."

"We did." She cleared her throat. "They're amazing, Tim. Thank you." As she hugged him and stared at the two calacas standing in front of her, she felt lighter, her head and heart very much alive with light pulsing through reopened spaces and time. With their arms entwined and yoked together by the bones they had brought, the two skeletons stood in the middle of these reopened spaces.

"I basically stole the costumes from *Mary Poppins*," Tim laughed, "but there's a reason for that. A theme."

"A theme?"

"I thought we could see a movie in two weeks, right before Halloween."

"What about your haunted house?"

"That's why we'd have to see it on Thursday night. I can't do Fridays and Saturdays."

"Theme," she echoed.

"Theme." He smiled at her.

"Do I get any more clues?"

"Nope."

"Well...OK."

After several more seconds of their embrace, Tim breathed out and said, "You have my secret."

"Which means what?" she asked, pulling back a little to look at him. "I owe you something or I'm supposed to come running back to the church?"

"No...it's just...you have my secret."

"I know I do. But who would I tell, and why? It's between us."

"I know."

"We go way back, Tim."

"I know. We have *history*. I just wanted to say it." He scratched the top of head, pushing the longer black scraps away from his cheekbones. He looked at his phone. "Hungry?" his voice chirped.

"Yes," she answered, her tone rising like his.

He smiled and touched her hand. "Let's get out of here. But before we do, I want to show you something. It's outside." He tossed his head to the loading dock's door.

"Something else?" she asked. "What is it? An ofrenda?"

"Come on," he replied, leading her, hand in hand.

Opening the double garage doors at the back, they went outside the studio and passed through orange and red leaves and a long rectangle of sunlight between the main building and a smaller building. *Psst!* The ventilation system was louder in the outside air, sounding like a metal spike drilled deeper. Tim unlocked and opened the door of the second building, which was a smaller version of his main studio space, filled with storage bins, equipment, and the lingering smells and colors of experiments.

He led her around the corner, behind some paint cans and packing materials. It was colder here. The sound of their footsteps changed from high-toned echoes on the concrete floor to no sound on the wood floor. Gone too was the sound of traffic on the access road to Tim's lot; the ventilation sounds disappeared as well. And the silence was immediate, this room within a room softening all sounds. The ceiling was no higher than eight feet, and the longer sidewalls and the soft white light along the base of the floor enhanced the illusion of the room's depth, gently diffused into layers of pinks, roses, yellows, and oranges thinly washed on the walls and ceiling—a charged translucence. Tim and Vanessa sat on one of the four benches arranged end to end in the middle of the room.

"What is this?" she asked.

"This is the final room."

"To what?"

"The haunted house."

"The one I was in?"

"Yes."

Vanessa looked around the pastel space and felt lost in the feeling of falling deeper into colors and sounds. "It's so very peaceful. Nothing like the other rooms."

"It's supposed to be."

"Why is it here?"

"Pastor Rick doesn't want it used." Tim stuffed his hands in his hoodie's pocket. "He wants to use the haunted house and this time of year to make people think about their choices...the choices we live and die by. He wants the house to raise awareness of people's choice for eternity. He says it's not politically correct, but it's spiritually direct."

"But aren't people just scared when they go through?"

"There's no doubt that fear's a great motivator. But Pastor Rick would say we're not communicating fear, but we are communicating reality and truth. But I know it's too easy to use fear, and that's where Pastor Rick and I stand on opposite sides of the same river. The problem with this, for me, is that it offers too little in the end."

"Why doesn't he want this?"

"The final room they're using is a plain room with members from the outreach group waiting to talk to people who've gone through the house."

"You can't avoid them."

Tim shook his head. "No, they'll be there with Bibles and pamphlets and their own personal stories."

"And you don't like that?"

He glanced at Vanessa and smiled. "I built this, took it over there. It's totally moveable. The room is a golden ratio...the dimensions. I built it this way. Rented a truck, loaded it with Bryce, Kev, and some kids from the youth group. Got it set up, and several members went through and asked, 'Where's Jesus? Where's the chance to witness?' They wanted Jesus, so they got Jesus. I was asked to use something else."

"What?"

"The crucifixion scene that's been used for the past three years. But they said I could enhance it. I guess you could say they said I should enhance it, you know, with all my skills and their vision. I rebuilt the crucifixion scene, the one before the witness room. You were actually four rooms away from experiencing it. You met Jason in the hall."

Vanessa nodded.

"The cross automatically turns once people enter," Tim continued, looking into the colors swirling inside the white room. "And there's thunder and wailing, and two Roman soldiers walk away. They tear apart his cloak and crown him with the thorns. Jesus...Jason...he's bloody...very bloody. I thought it was over the top. They kept asking for more and more blood in the scene. And it ended up being really graphic, to be honest, like, a bad horror movie. But I said, OK, I can do that because it's special FX and you want that, but when it came to the crucifixion, on a different level, I couldn't, really. It was too much. I wanted peace after all the other rooms they experience...something peaceful and quiet and contemplative."

"And empty of Jesus," she said, watching the soft pastel colors tumble in the air.

"Only physically." Tim got a remote control from his hoodie's pocket and clicked a button on it. "I agree with them that it has to be a journey and that the scenes on Earth have to be graphic...to an extent. They're not glorifying violence, but they are exposing serious issues. Change lives at the deepest level."

"But, Tim, all the scenes that I saw that night were violent. And they were issues that can make people feel worse seeing them...seeing themselves in those scenes."

"Not all the scenes. The school shooter...we're trying to reach out to those people who are hurt and confused...offer them love and hope. Besides," his voice flattened, "when it's all said and done, it's a chance for all of us to do what we love to do, each in our own way."

"Yes, definitely for *you*. I can see that, yes."

"I love what I do and that I'm able to do what I love. And yes, we're asking the audience to think about choices and decisions and consequences...a real consequence of decisions. The goal is to get people to realize that their actions are choices, but they always have the opportunity to transform. That's all. It's not about shaming or threatening, at least not for me. It's not about escaping the world but transforming it. Love and hope."

Vanessa rolled her lips in, sighed out her nose, and pressed her lips together.

"We are pushing some boundaries," Tim continued. "And stepping on some toes."

"Except that it's clear which way the crowd is supposed to go."

He rocked his head between his shoulders. "No...no, you're right. We all don't agree on everything, and I don't agree with it all, what we're doing, but it's good. That's what makes us a church. We're all contributing to it. It's my church too," he said, looking down after he did.

"What don't you agree with them on?"

He waited a few seconds before answering her. "I honestly don't know about hell. I don't know if it's a real place or what. I do know...I believe...that it is a spiritual place, one without God and love and hope and feeling completely and utterly destitute. And when I say that, I guess I do believe it is a real place, just not filled with pitchforks and demons."

"Even though..."

"Even though I build pitchforks and demons," he chuckled while closing his eyes.

Folding her hands, Vanessa smiled. Looking around the feathered room, she took a deep breath. "Most of the violence in those scenes happened against women. The date rape at the party where the guy and girl get toasted...he drops a roofie in her glass. The wife getting beat up by the husband. I think the only guy was the school shooter. And that first scene..."

"I know what you're saying."

"Do you? Because that house is pretty judgmental. And all women aren't helpless."

"I know. Judgment is easier than love or understanding." Tim stared at her and paused before speaking again. "I remember when you first showed up at youth group. Even though you knew me, it was like you were alone in the room during the welcome-back-to-school party we had. You were so composed while talking to total strangers. It was pretty impressive for a teenager. You caught my eye then, and it was *more* than just that. There was something else there." He took her hand. "Just like at the bakery. It was like seeing you for the first time all over again. That jolt then, and to be honest, I felt it again when you got hold of me this summer and when we saw each other after all these years. You don't forget connections...what certain people mean. You just don't forget."

Vanessa saw her parents' bakery in its infancy, still being assembled, boxes on the floor and in the corners, her father's tools scattered throughout, often times too close to the serving counter or the food, the walls her mother started decorating, Aztec symbols, the small heads of animals, the Wheel of Time yet to be filled in.

"But then there was so much more the minute I saw you and we started talking. Nothing had changed in all that time we'd been apart. It was the coffee," he laughed.

"It was the coffee," she repeated, chuckling, and covered her face. "You bought all those pastries and sweets. There's no way you and your buddies ate all those."

"Well, I was sixteen. I could eat all that stuff. My high school diet basically consisted of fries and slushies, powdered donuts, and Slim Jims from the gas station. And often the occasional bag of Funyuns." He leaned back and patted his thick belly. "But thirty-four-year-old Tim is in the house now."

"I can relate."

"Look, those scenes…"

"It's OK, Tim, you don't have to…"

"No, I know, I just…"

"You just want to work…be your own boss…be something more than one-dimensional."

"Yes." He looked at her.

"Work not only for churches or only those kinds of places anymore."

"Not exclusively, no."

"Get outside the box."

"I want to add to my roster. Grow, yes, but still maintain who I am and where I started."

Vanessa sighed. "I don't know. I don't know if I can help you. I want to, but I'm so..." She pressed her lips tighter and tighter until they were ghost white, no words trailing behind.

"You don't have to decide now."

"Good, because this room is making me feel emotional."

"What are you feeling?"

"I don't know. I wish I could say." She shifted on the bench. "It's just the lights and the quiet and...is that something like white noise? Or am I hearing things? Are the walls moving?"

"No, it's the lights. It's all part of this." Tim scooted closer to her. "I know there's more. And I know you're not ready yet. But you can tell me when the time's right. You don't have to hide with me. We know each other."

"I know," she replied, leaning into him.

As they sat there, interlocking fingers, shoulders touching, the room's silence deepened. The colors on the four walls slowly spun like lace held in front of a sunset, stretching across the ceiling and the floor, the space within silent and filled with the revolution of curiosity and loneliness, both equal and constant, pivoting, one following the other, one giving in before the other falls away, one waiting on the other to catch up.

6

Every time a car slowed in the middle of the street, especially if the car had tinted windows, and every time a figure, walking on the sidewalk on the other side of the street, stopped, faced the apartment building, scanned the area, and leaned against the telephone pole before moving on, Flora peeked out of the top-floor window and pulled the bedsheet nailed to the frame, closing it as tightly as the late summer wind blowing it back open would allow. Empty liquor bottles, crumbling walls, damaged cars, and shops—some open, some boarded up, some graffitied—lined the street two stories below the bedroom of the apartment where she and Vanessa waited.

One of the figures across the street stopped longer than the others had, lit a cigarette, and cracked his knuckles. When he crossed and headed toward what Flora assumed was the front door of the building leading to the apartment, she panicked and dropped the faded yellow rotary phone into her lap. Her hip and left leg pressing against the wall, her elbow resting on the sill, her heel tapping on the wood floor, she lifted the receiver off the hook but kept her finger down on the switch. The phone rang; the surprise shocked her. The phone buzzed again. Cupping one end and closing her eyes, her finger released the switch as she held the receiver but said nothing.

"Mom!" Vanessa shouted, jumping around the corner. "It's not for you! It's Tanya. She said she'd call."

A teenage girl's voice spoke on the other end, and Flora stared at Vanessa, who, neon bracelets wrapped around her wrist, extended her hand. Flora shook as she handed the phone to her daughter.

"Hey, wassup? Yeah, I know." Vanessa snaked her way back into the cramped living room until the telephone cord tensed like a high-wire between Flora and the doorway.

After a few minutes, Vanessa popped her head back into the bedroom. "Have you seen my stocking cap?" Her black hair looped down to her belt.

"It's eighty-five degrees out. Why do you need your stocking cap? Who's on the phone?"

With her back to her mom, Vanessa laughed into the phone. She quickly pivoted in place and said, "I want to get a nose ring. Will you come with Tanya, Melinda, and me to the mall so you can sign for us? They need someone over eighteen to sign for a minor." She popped her gum. "It's cool and all."

"I will not. Who's Tanya and Melinda? Are they the ones who bullied you at the movies?"

"Hold on." Vanessa muffled the receiver with a sleeve of her flannel shirt. "No, that was Lucinda Perales."

"I know her mother."

"*Don't* say anything to her." Vanessa's eyes bulged.

"She put her dirty boots on top of your head and smashed gum in your hair. Then she poured popcorn down your back."

"Mom, *please* don't. Tanya and Melinda took care of all that."

"Took care of what? What did they do?"

Vanessa slid back into the living room where the light was gray and pale yellow; the old dark trim and doors of the musty apartment absorbed the afternoon's brightness.

Flora's sandals clapped faster on the bottom of her feet. Peeking through the makeshift curtain, she asked, "Who's taking you to the mall?"

"Antonio, Melinda's older brother."

"How old is he?"

"Nineteen."

"No, Vanessa. No. You are not going with him." Flora stopped halfway, at the bedroom door's threshold, and looked over her shoulder at the window. A car drove by. The bedsheet curtain blew open. Sunlight illuminated her face and tired eyes.

"Mom..."

"No, absolutely not. Besides, you can't go out."

"For real?"

"No. Your father is out."

"You mean he's paying off Pastor."

"Don't call him Pastor."

"And?"

"*And*, no. You can't go anywhere now. You know this. You know the rules for right now. You need to stay here. Family first."

Vanessa slunk back into the living room and muttered into the phone. After a few seconds, she walked back into the room and tossed the phone on the mattress. "It's been, like, months since that. We live like prisoners."

"Shh...the neighbors. And don't take that tone with me."

"The neighbors." Vanessa rolled her eyes, flopped on the mattress, and rested her faded black sneakers on one of the unopened boxes constricting the bedroom. "This sucks...really, really sucks." She wrinkled her nose at the smell of natural gas puffing its way every so often from the kitchen's stove shimmied on an old piece of plywood. "This is so lame."

"Stop thinking about yourself." Flora drew a deep breath before speaking. "It'll be over soon. Your father..."

"*Nothing* has happened," Vanessa cut off her mother. "We don't even go to that church anymore. We haven't seen Calderon in, like, forever. I mean, what's he going to do? Roll up in his handicapped car and tell us how bad we are? That you and dad owe him more money?" She gazed at the peeling ceiling. "I hope Dad brought a gun with him."

"¡No quiero esto en mi casa!" Flora quickly scolded her daughter.

"Danny Lopez says Calderon can never be trusted. They went to Vida Nueva for a long time, longer than us, and they lost everything to Calderon."

"I know, Vanessa."

"They had to start all over."

"I know."

"Danny says that when they tried to leave Calderon..."

"Vanessa...stop."

"Just saying."

"Your father knows what he is doing. He's doing the right thing by paying him back...all of what's his. No more of that over our heads."

"Dad's head," Vanessa replied, pulling a string from the hemline of her shorts.

"I beg your pardon, young lady."

"It's Dad's head. It was all his idea, right? I heard him talking to you about it one night."

"When?"

"I don't know. A while ago, I guess. He said he didn't want us being with Calderon any more...that he wanted us to be free."

"Yes, that part is true. Calderon was...asking too much of us."

"The tithe?"

"If you could even call it that."

"Dad says it went up every year we were with him."

"Yes, it did."

"And that Calderon kept most of it himself."

"Yes, he did."

"So how are we any different than him?"

"We are. We're just *different*."

"How?"

"M'ija, it's difficult to explain. Todo combia. We wanted to be free. Being with Calderon had gone on far too long. Fue una pesadilla. Truly a nightmare." Flora's voice faded. She leaned back from the window; her skirt billowed in the breeze. "Do you remember that day we left Vida Nueva?"

"Yeah."

"And you remember when Calderon called me into his trailer?"

"He was, like, a super-creepy padrino by then," Vanessa said as she felt that May day's heat and humidity and saw the after-church lunch in the backyard and her mother with a serving knife in hand, its silver blade layered with cake crumbs, vanilla frosting, and a dark red fruit filling. Vanessa stood near her father and helped arrange chairs and tables under the big tent. Calderon rolled his wheelchair close and said to her mother, "You can't keep putting this off, Flora." His tone was strict, not touched by the fire of the Holy Spirit as Vanessa normally heard in his voice. Calderon moved toward his trailer home at the back of the church, where the grass faded into weeds, dirt, and bramble tangled under the fence. The serving knife clanked as Flora dropped it on the table and wiped her hands on a towel. Vanessa made eye contact with her mother and mouthed, "You in *trou-ble*." Flora rolled her eyes. "Always something now with him," her father mumbled to her, scowling at Calderon. "Bribón." Arms crossed, black ponytail flowing behind her, the greens of her sweater and shoes popping against the dull vinyl siding of the trailer and its two rusty propane tanks, her mother strode up the ramp to the trailer.

Flora lowered her head and smiled. "I sat on the end of this sofa he had in there. It was a cushion covered in crumbs and dust. Stacks of papers and envelopes were so high. On the floor, he had Bibles, papers, pens, and this large printer blocking the window's light. It was dark and smelled in there. He had a trash bag on the kitchen floor, and I could see the shapes of eggshells pressing from inside like little claws. His wheelchair squeaked closer to me until the metal footrests touched me. I jerked away. And oh, his skin...his skin was nothing more than parchment." Flora looked through the hairline cracks running through the windowpanes where she kept watch; she then looked at Vanessa. "'What did you want to talk to me about, Carlos?' 'Carlos?' He didn't like that. 'You only call me that when you think I'm up to something. La poco rata,' he said. We weren't the only ones calling him that," Flora chuckled, flexing her mouth and teeth like a rat's. "He is a little rat. But I liked calling him Carlos. He had stopped being a pastor to me long ago. He had that bola tie and stuffed his fat fingers into it. That made him breathe heavier through his mouth. He said that he noticed that the three of us hadn't been attending church as much as we used to."

Vanessa nodded and stopped playing with the ends of her hair.

"Once your father and I realized what could happen with all this, we didn't want you helping with the nursery or the children. Roberto only helped with the landscaping when he was asked. 'Something else has your attention,' Calderon said. He knew. He said, 'I'd hate for you to fall into the wrong things.' He knew the bakery had become a real gem. Ah, his health had gone downhill so quickly. He thought that we hadn't rid ourselves of the old ways…heritage. He thought I hadn't." Her mother touched her rosary with a small shell attached alongside the crucifix. "He said I was the last holdout of the old guard in his flock. He said that I'm confusing everyone by keeping this. 'Terca,' he said, 'like an old donkey stuck in the mud.'" The apartment's window cast Flora's face in a clear, warm glow. "It's who I am. I can't just throw it away on a whim."

"Dad had no problem."

"He's not attached to it." Flora fingered the hem of her skirt. "Calderon said he was very pleased with the bakery, especially since we helped other families get job skills. He thought I was in charge of the whole show. I told him I don't think of myself in charge. 'I help my husband, who helps me. We both help our daughter, who helps us. We're a family, not a corporation.' He didn't like that. This wouldn't be happening where we came from. I'd be working in a maquiladora. Miserable conditions, violence against women. Certainly not…"

"I know, Mom," Vanessa interrupted.

"Without Calderon, I'd still be cleaning houses in this country," Flora continued. "And your father…"

"I know, Mom."

"I said to Calderon, 'You remind us of this whenever we see you.' He said, 'Unfortunately, after all these years, we've finally reached a fork in the road.' He knew things had begun to appear uneven in the books. He said his people reviewed the books. I told him you had helped with the books. I shouldn't have said that." Flora smiled at Vanessa. "He said that he didn't like to look embarrassed in front of those whom he helps or who helps him. 'So much embarrassment,' he said. I kept telling them that I'd look into the numbers. He said that he had put it off too long. 'I need to correct it.' He was going to raise our rates...the tithe, he called it, but it wasn't a tithe. He was going to raise it from twenty-five percent to fifty. He said that life isn't cheap and the city is raising its rates. He kept saying how much we all need to make sure our family remains intact, that we remain in the good graces of those who help our church continue to grow...keep the fire going. He said his business partners know where we live. He said they wanted to stop by the store and say hi to all of us. They knew which school you went to. He said he didn't want to raise rates. He said that would make him look like a usurer, which is against the Bible. He said there were other options to clear our debt."

"What?" Vanessa asked in a low voice.

"I sprang up from the couch when he got closer with that wheelchair of his." Flora's voice quivered. "He said, 'Not you. You're married.' He said he looked at what your father and I had done to him as a long-term loan that could be paid off. I said to him, 'Oh my God, are you...?'" As Flora's laughter increased, she shook her head. "'You're crazy,' I yelled to him. 'You are *crazy*. ¡Muy loco!' He went on about the store numbers not adding up, month after month, year after year. He called us desperate. 'Little thieves, little liars, little heathens.' He said, 'I have given all this to you.' And in many ways, he's right. Ever since the day we set foot here, he gave us everything we needed. Shelter, food, water, clothes, jobs, a chance for you." She stared at her rosary and seashell and then at her daughter. "He mentioned his other option again. Marrying you."

Vanessa's face grew pale as her eyes widened.

"I laughed. 'You're serious, aren't you?' He said, 'If I raise your rates, Flora, you can't afford it. ¿Entiendes?' Oh, I understood all right. I pushed his wheelchair aside and laughed so hard that I spit on him. He thought I had really spit on him, but I was laughing so much. '¿Qué es esto? What year do you think this is?' I said to him. '*Fifteen* ninety-four? That she's chattel? That we're in some isolated village in the middle of Mexico?' He did not like this. 'What's next, Carlos? Teach her how to maintain the home? Cooking, cleaning, looking after you? Wiping your backside? ¿Las mujeres en el hogar y los hombres en la plaza?' He got so mad."

"The door!" Vanessa interrupted.

Flora's eyes shot toward the window.

"No, the door to Calderon's trailer. I remember you yelling inside."

Flora nodded.

"Did he...?"

"No. Calderon is a creepy padrino, but he doesn't have that in him. Money and greed. He was just very angry at it all. 'I gave you all this! And you steal from me!' I smacked him across the face and yelled for your father. I jostled that handle so hard."

Vanessa remembered her father running toward the trailer when its door flung open. Her mother stood there, her hair disheveled, mascara running down her cheeks, her green sweater fallen off her shoulders like a leaf. "He knows," Flora panted and stumbled off the ramp and into her father's arms. The two of them spun from the trailer and stormed across the dirt and grass. One of her father's hands clung to her mother; his other hand hooked the summer air and swooped down for Vanessa, his face focused on her. Calderon rolled his wheelchair to where the ramp met the front door. Above the trees, the trailer, and the church, scattering blackbirds blocked the sun.

"Calderon changed," her mother continued. "He's very charismatic. Your father never trusted him but went along with it all because we knew we had to get our feet on the ground. We had to stay there until we could leave. That's just how it was. From there to here." Flora motioned toward one run-down wall in the bedroom to one at the opposite end. "We thought it would be a short time until we got work and a home on our own. Not the case. We actually needed him. We hoped that the tornado that came through many years ago would have freed us somehow. But no. Of course, the church was untouched," she snickered. "We had to hold on longer...and be less selfish." She rubbed her collarbone. "When I first met him, I had a feeling about him. Mainly it was his attitude, his approach to spiritual life. It was like a shrill swooping down from all around. You couldn't escape it. It was not like the soft-singing orioles I loved back in Monclova." Flora sighed and looked into a space above Vanessa's untamed hair and the gray light of the rotting ceiling. "We didn't know he'd change this way, but we couldn't leave. We had stability. We had a foundation. Even if we didn't give ourselves completely over to him, we had something in place. It took a while, but we had it. He did give us that." Flora and Vanessa smiled at each other. "But we had to move on. It was all coming together. It was like wearing a mask. Then one night your father and I talked, and we could see a light cutting through the fog. It wasn't an easy decision. In many ways, it wasn't right, but it was a light...*our* light."

"This was your idea too?"

"Yes, together. Your father and I made sure we would survive without Calderon. I was the one who kept noticing we made more than what Calderon thought we would ever make with the bakery. But I was the one who decided to spend my Saturdays at the farmers' market, selling there. Calderon knew about that. He didn't care because he thought that money would go straight to him. He encouraged my business ventures. 'Pequeña empresaria,' he called me. But I didn't think it'd come to this. I thought we could just quietly and peacefully slip away without anything like this. That was the plan."

"Danny says Calderon is like a mafia boss now."

"I know."

"He says Calderon has his own personal coyote bringing him families. They're like slaves, but he does it in the name of Christ."

"I know, Essa."

"That was us, right? I mean, Calderon is creepy like that guy in Texas who had all those people in his church. He had all those wives and kids and guns, and then it burned down with everyone inside. Ms. Reins talked to us about it one day in history class. Coyote brought us to Calderon." Vanessa leaned up from the mattress.

"No, Coyote brought us to this country. We never saw him after that. It was a few years before we got to Calderon. But, yes, they knew each other."

"That's what you always say to me. 'Coyote got us here.'"

"He did, Essa, he did."

"You make it sound like the stork brought you a baby. You make it sound like magic."

Flora smiled and, clasping her hands together, set them in her lap. "Your father is late."

"Did he say when he'd be back?"

"No."

"Then he's not really late," Vanessa chimed.

"Why don't you listen to some music?"

"I let Melinda borrow my Discman."

"Why?"

"Her brother took hers. I gave her mine."

"The same brother who's driving to the mall?"

"No, this is her younger brother, Porky."

"Porky?" Flora tried hiding her smirk.

"It's Gustavo, but he goes by Porky."

"Why?"

"I don't know. He looks like a pig, I guess. He has this mustache."

"Like your father's?"

"No, it's thin. He's weird like the other boys he hangs out with. They all listen to Metallica *and* Michael Jackson *and* Tupac while skateboarding."

"And he's the one who has it?"

"No, Melinda has it...I think."

"You think?"

Vanessa shrugged her shoulders.

"We bought that for you. You can't just hand it out to people you don't know."

"I know Melinda."

"Please be responsible with the things we give you."

Vanessa wanted to snap at her mother, calling her unfair, wondering whose money really bought the Discman and their food and her clothes, anything over the years. She imagined her father handing over a bag of money to Calderon—a simple brown bag that she'd seen her father use for lunch on his way out the door of their old RV to whatever construction or landscaping job Calderon had set up for him. She imagined this exchange happening in the trees behind Vida Nueva, Calderon in his wheelchair grabbing the money like a dog seeking a bone, her father's hands shaking, and the two men going their separate ways. She thought about this and what her father and mother had been through, unknotting here and twisting loose there until they could all float free. She thought about this promise and the knickknacks and clothes that they stuffed in the back of her father's truck and on the seat next to her and how they lay matted on the wood floor or tangled in the sheet and blanket on the dusty and ripped couch in the apartment's living room where she slept. She thought about how she had been waiting for an all-clear signal from her parents when she could resume a normal life before starting school again, going more to movies, going more to the mall, going more to fast-food restaurants, talking more on the phone with her friends— free from anything pulling her back. Vanessa nodded.

"Did you have that awful CD in there?"

"Mazzy Star? Mom, the singer's just like me."

"It's like listening to my uncles drink too much. Once they turned on Cuco Sanchez, they would cry like little babies. Big, tough macho men reduced to tears. Just like your father." Flora winked as the two of them laughed. "What happened to Selena? You used to love her."

"She's...*not* me."

"She sings about happy things...things I can understand. But you're talented and beautiful in your own way." Flora's head flung toward the window. "Is that him?"

"You're really jumpy."

"You don't know how men like Calderon operate."

"Mom, I want to get out. I've done *nothing* except be stuck here all summer. Dad's like my chaperone. Boyz II Men came through town, and I missed them. Danny asked me to go."

"No boys until you're eighteen."

"That's *four years* from now."

"Fine. Thirty."

"You can't tell me what to do when I'm that old."

Flora laughed. "I was that age three years ago, young lady." She rose from the chair at the window, skirt rippling, her body fuller and heavier as a silhouette in front of the window, walked into the narrow bathroom, and splashed water on her pale face. The bathroom's flaking peach paint and the single, flickering light over the sink muted the shine of her mother's long hair. A cop car and its siren blazed by, but Flora did not hear it and did not budge from the running water as she dried her face and hands with paper towels.

Vanessa looked around the bedroom at the unpacked boxes and then toward the window where the breeze twirled the bedsheet. All the fears that exploded in her mind when she first heard the panic and urgency in her parents' voices—a car could sneak up in the middle of the night; a gun could be used; someone could follow Vanessa wherever she went— had never materialized. She rolled over onto her stomach and watched her mom breathe heavily over the sink for a few minutes before reentering the bedroom.

"Your father would say life is hard. This is just the way it is."

"He says that all the time to me."

"Well, I disagree." She sat down next to Vanessa, who rolled onto her back and dangled her head over the edge of the mattress. "Life *isn't* hard. It's not that it's easy. It just that that we don't know about ourselves until we face trouble. Something has to be given up to go on." With her slim fingers, she detangled Vanessa's curls. "Someone else before you had to give. No one comes here to stay."

"You're getting all Aztec again."

Flora smiled. "Quetzalcoatl..."

"I know, I know. He created another world for humans after the previous worlds were destroyed. He used his own blood to give new life. What's next? La Virgen? Light a veladora? ¡Consolarme, mi Madre!" She folded her hands in a prayer position and closed her eyes. The rays of serpentine light backlit the Holy Mother; a crescent moon supported her as she rested on it; stars filled her green shawl.

Placing Vanessa's head in her lap, Flora became serious. "Your abuelita used to say that we need to commemorate each day. Each thing you say and do pulls you from one place and gets you closer to the next. Esto también pasará. This too shall pass."

As her mother caressed her head, Vanessa stared at the shell on Flora's rosary. Her eyes followed its pale cross section, starting in the center, spinning out from the middle, and ending in the air, sunlight, and her mother's breathing. Retracing the white spiral, Vanessa's eyes rotated to the beginning, falling onto the same point.

"Your quinceañera is next year," Flora whispered.

"I don't need one. We can save money and use it for something else for all of us. Go to Mexico and see where you, Dad, and Abuelita lived."

"Your father would never go for it. We are here." Her small hands pulsed over the ground. "You don't *have* to have a quinceañera."

Vanessa's eyes shot up at her mother.

"Quinceañera or sweet sixteen." Flora shrugged. "We'll leave it up to you."

With the two choices placed in front of her, Vanessa imagined the gowns, excitement, and attention when she could be princess for a day. The whole world would stop and be hers. She and her carnalas would dress up and rehearse until the big day; they'd help write, address, and mail recuerdos to her guests. She would have an elaborate, castle-shaped cake frosted and laced in purples and pinks—her mother would make it for her. Her chambelán de honor would come down to either Danny Lopez or Jacob Padilla, who had been flirting more with her in biology class after he broke up with his girlfriend. But those fantasies, fueled by her friends' fantasies, fell away the last few months and revealed a stripped-down ceremony that was more probable and realistic, grounded and not floating high above her, her family and friends laughing and stuffing their faces with homemade and store-bought food at the nearby city park or at the recreation center down the block. No stretch limo, no gown stacked like pastel clouds, no high-heel shoes. Something closer to her, something that had been under her all the time. Sitting next to her mother, looking at her pale face and bloodshot eyes, facing the window and the sounds below it, this feeling returned to Vanessa and melted any remaining fantasies with herself as the source and the middle of it all, riding on its liquefying gold, its presence more potent now in that bedroom than the first time she felt it, wondering what golden light in the world can stay. "I thought for a second you were going to say I could get a car."

Flora laughed. "Neither of those will provide a car. You will have to do that on your own. But no matter what you choose, you should waltz with your father."

Vanessa imagined her father in his best white dress shirt that her mother had picked out for him from a discount store—the shirt with mismatched buttons and a faint coffee stain near the bottom; the shirt her mother added to the basket that day, alongside dishes and silverware from garage sales and the flea market. Vanessa imagined her father in this shirt and his blue jeans swaying with her as she avoided stepping on his boots. "Will you still make a cake no matter what I choose?"

"Of course."

"OK, I'll think about it."

The front door on the first floor flung open. Flora lunged for the telephone. Vanessa leapt off the mattress and dove behind her mom.

"Flora! Flora!" a voice yelled from below.

Vanessa and her mom embraced each other.

The apartment's door rattled and then unlocked.

"There you are," Roberto panted. The light from the window intensified his sweaty face and his dark eyes focused on his family huddled on the mattress as the bedsheet blew over their bodies. Flora began to sob.

Vanessa looked at both of them and felt very small.

Her father broke into a large smile and fell to his knees in front of them. "Ay," he sighed, kissing them both on their foreheads. "Todo está bien...todo. Everything's all right." Catching his breath, he stretched his legs out; the heels of his boots thumped the wood floor. He flopped his arm on the mattress and smiled at them from the crook of his elbow. "He took the money, except the interest." He wiped his forehead. "That is ours. But he won't know it's missing because it's so small compared to what he got. And it's just enough to start again." He pulled a pear from his jeans and shined it on his shirt-sleeve.

"What about that other thing?" Flora asked.

"The money was more important to him."

The shrinking feeling broke apart inside Vanessa and left behind prickling and numbness as blood and time flowed again—the present resuscitated.

Flora relaxed her grip on Vanessa. "So brave, Berto, so brave!" She cupped his face and ran her hands through his hair.

"I told him that we just want out...to be left alone."

"How much was it, Dad?"

Roberto swallowed and looked at Vanessa and then at Flora. He picked a piece of pear from the back of his mouth. "It doesn't matter. We're done with him and that crazy place."

"What happens next?" Flora asked.

"We start again."

Vanessa's shoulders slumped with images of her family throwing boxes and their things into the back of her father's truck again, starting over at a new school, and losing her friends and the places she had come to know. "Are we moving again?" she asked.

"No." Roberto sat on the corner of the mattress. "I talked to Mrs. Acosta. We can stay here until we can pay for it."

"We need jobs," Flora said.

"We'll get them. I'll go to the temp agency. You need to keep baking. You can sell from here, the front door, from the window. Sell them on the corner out front." He looked at Vanessa. "You can help Mrs. Acosta with her units. You can clean, take out the trash, replace light bulbs. You can keep babysitting. You can help your mother bake. And when we get another bakery, you'll help there too."

"Another store?" Flora and Vanessa both asked.

"We'll get another store...one that's ours, *really* ours. And we'll find another church, especially for you," he said to Vanessa. "We want you to go to church and be around kids your own age. A good church...a *better* church."

"I don't know if I want to go. I like hanging out with my friends on Sunday. And now that this is all over, I can..."

"No," Flora interrupted, "you need something like that in your life. It's important."

"It is, Essa," Roberto said. "We'll find one. We'll ask around. We need to get grounded again. Work hard, save money, be good in school." He bit into the pear. "We can sell at the farmers' market."

"There's the state fair," her mom added.

Vanessa grimaced. Trips to the state fair without her parents meant she and her friends rode whatever they wanted, ate whatever they wanted, roamed wherever they wanted. She, Tanya, and Melinda laughed and yelled the entire time on the roller coasters, screamed during one of the sideshows when a girl transformed into a gorilla before their eyes, flirted with boys they met, and avoided Lucinda Perales and her crew with their glossy black lipstick and tattoos underneath their all-black clothes.

"We can sell at your school's football and basketball games," Flora said.

"In the parking lot?" Vanessa scrunched her eyes.

"We have a lot to do. I'll get down to Labor Ready first thing tomorrow morning." Roberto stood up. "I think we should go out tonight for dinner."

Flora stood and smoothed her skirt; Vanessa forced a smile.

"It's a new start. Let's keep it that way for just a little longer," he said, whistling as he walked out of the room.

7

One by one, the letters on the vertical sign brightened and fell like yellow stars down to the ground; vivid red outlines and the buzzing sound of electricity intensified each letter while the green, pink, and blue tips of the sign curled in neon. Vanessa stood under the sign. For several seconds, she tilted her head back, her headache fluctuating with the bursts of letters, and watched the theater's name spell itself out again and again above the glowing marquee—these lights and words charging the night before falling away and starting over.

When Vanessa was in high school, she knew about the Palladium but only because its name meant a dark, dingy porn theater that Jacob Padilla and his friends talked about sneaking into in a forgotten but once vibrant and historic part of the city. When she left for Denver, the theater returned to its glory days of cinematic films and concerts, but she had never seen it until now. Its legend and art deco—white sandstone chevrons, inlay tiles sparkling with the neon lights looping past them, and large light bulbs ballooning up and down the dark, glossy woodwork— did not disappoint her as the towering theater spelled its name again. She thought that those old black-and-white movies that her parents and abuelita talked about would have been shown in a grand place such as this.

Menagerie of Classic Macabre—the marquee's red letters floated on top of a solid sheet of white light. Vanessa read a few fluorescent-colored fliers taped on the windows and main doors:

Hear Bob Holden and His Mighty Wurlitzer!

Every Thur. Fri. & Sat. night

7:30 until the first show at 8

Nodding her head at one of the fliers, her forehead wrinkled at Tim, who shrugged his shoulders and smiled. Although he had kept quiet about his surprise movie, Vanessa had, seeing the marquee and tonight's feature, stitched together some of Tim's clues from the past two weeks as she stepped onto the shiny tile under the marquee and stood next to him at the ticket window. A song from the swing era played through the speakers mounted on the tube-shaped ticket booth. The young woman sitting inside, dressed in a velvety red vest and white shirt, her hair slicked back, spoke to Tim through the brass vent hovering in the middle of the booth's glass.

"Two, please, for the eight o'clock show," he said, paying for both tickets.

"Thank you," she said. "I can pay you back."

"Nope. First one's on me. Next one can be on you."

"Next one?"

"Hmm, maybe you're right." He smirked and handed a ticket to her. "I guess we better see how we do tonight."

The young woman in the booth delivered Tim's credit card to him on a tray that she slid under the glass. Cars, trucks, taxis, and people rolled by on the surface of the ticket booth's glass—their reflections as transparent and ghostly as Vanessa's as she stood in the middle of the revitalized area. Lights, the bustling city streets, the crowds, and the trees shedding their leaves—all these images shone and passed through

Vanessa's reflection as the young woman pivoted on her stool and waited like a fortune teller for the next person to approach.

"Pretty cool, huh?" Tim asked as he cradled two large Cokes and a greasy bag of popcorn while they stood in the warm foyer.

"This place is so great," Vanessa replied, looking at the dark wood stairs and doors, peppermint-candy-striped wallpaper, and ornate sconces. A sand-colored rug with black diamonds decorating the corners cushioned her feet. After walking down the red carpet, she stopped in front of old movie posters and a bronze plaque brightened by two lamps the size of globes. The Palladium – Built 1917 – Opened 1919 – Reopened 2004. As she read the names of the individuals, organizations, and companies that supported preserving the historic building, a small pang ached in her head and heart. Her pulse stuttered. Blood drained from her face. Her headache faded but then returned; dizziness pushed and pulled her. Her mother would have loved this building and everything inside it, and her father would have taken to her to it on one of their dates when they had extra money and time. Vanessa grabbed the velvet rope defining the concession line. The theater reminded her of the observatory in Denver that she and Dan went to many years ago.

"Old and classy," Tim said, munching away as he stood next to her.

"I hope that's me someday," she said. "Or at the very least, I come back stronger and better the second time around."

Laughing with her and looping his arm so she could walk with him into the theater, Tim said, "We should make the most of the *first* time." He winked at her.

The long aisle and the rows of seats filled up one by one. Tim was adamant about sitting near the front, but Vanessa shook her head when they were two rows away from the screen. If they sat that close, the lights and sounds would entangle her. Offering her his arm again, Tim retreated and sent them back up the aisle and into a section of middle seats. He pointed; nodding with him, she let go of his arm but held his hand as she guided them toward the center of the row.

"I can't get over how many people are here," she whispered.

"Yeah, they've really done a nice job with this place. It's a yearly thing now."

"You come every year?"

"I try to. Work this time of year gets in the way. Someday I want to be on the Board here."

"Really?"

"Yeah. It's just a great place. My grandpa used to bring my grandma here every Friday night for a big premiere. They saw so many classics here. *Casablanca*. *From Here to Eternity*. They brought me to *Star Wars* when I was young...the *original* trilogy."

"The original...of course."

Tim devoured a handful of popcorn. "The whole area around here's really taken off, too. All the stores around here stay open late. It's a big family Halloween tradition they've started. Families bring their kids for the little trick-or-treat they have up and down here. This place really gets involved, showing classic monster movies and what we'll see tonight. There's a later show of what we'll see right before the midnight showing of *Rocky Horror*." He opened a box of Milk Duds. "It'll be super-packed by then. I mean, we're talking a line wrapping around the building and down toward the Irish pub on the corner. People will be dressed up in costume...devoted fans. They'll make their money doing this before switching back to indie and foreign flicks after Halloween. And then..."

"And then?"

"They'll have a marathon of *How the Grinch Stole Christmas*."

"Ah, that's so perfect."

"And *A Christmas Story*. Just in time for the holidays. 'You'll shoot your eye out!'"

"Sounds like someone's been a few times."

"I'm a card-carrying regular, but I dressed up only once for that."

"For *A Christmas Story*?"

"No, *Rocky Horror*."

"Oh sure, just once."

Tim raised his right hand. "I swear, just once. But I did sing along." He rubbed his beard. "I don't know what I'd do this time of year if they didn't have this Thursday night showing."

While Tim stared straight ahead at the giant red curtain in front of them, Vanessa snagged several pieces of popcorn and quickly tossed them in her mouth, pretending that she raided his popcorn bag without him seeing, but he knew because he slapped her hand a few times, tilted the bag toward her, offering it, and quickly pulled it away before her hand moved too close. "Still won't tell me what this is?" she asked.

"Nope, but I will say it's one of the most important films ever, and it's played a big role in my life since I was a kid. Plus, it's perfect for Día de Los Muertos."

"OK." She leaned back in the squeaky chair. She was curious to know what awaited her on the other side of the red curtain that towered over the stage like a frozen waterfall. Patrons filled the balconies above them, and as she looked at the balconies, the elaborate embellishments of the theater softened her and helped her forget her headache.

Tim cleared his throat and shifted in his seat. "A couple of years ago, I saw *The Creature from the Black Lagoon* here...in 3-D."

"Glasses?"

"Yep, old-school kind, too. The red and the blue."

"That's great."

"And then last March I saw a Georges Méliès film festival."

"I don't know who that is."

"Big French moviemaker in the Silent Era. Lucas before Lucas. Méliès made *Trip to the Moon* and *Robinson Crusoe*. It was so cool how he filmed it. The tiger on the island has these stripes that glow and move in color, but the rest of the film is in black-and-white. And at the end, he added more and more color. But *Creature* was the best. Old Hollywood monsters are still the standard."

A couple slid past them and sat a few seats down. Vanessa watched them swipe their fingers over their phones. Heads down, they said nothing to each other. She asked Tim, "Did you have a date?"

"For *Creature?*"

"Either...both."

"For *Creature*, yes. But not for last March. I had been seeing this girl I met on one of the dating sites, but she wanted kids and talked about marriage right away."

"On the first date?"

"Yeah. I was, like, stop, please, you're super cute and really smart but stop."

"Too much too soon, huh?"

"Yeah. There's a grad student who's been helping out at church, we've talked a few times, but I'm an old man now." He took his hands out of his hoodie's pockets and tapped his big gut. "Besides, I'm kinda in the middle of something."

As Tim smiled at her, Vanessa wanted to know what he meant. What was he in the middle of? While she and Tim glanced at each other, the sconces on the walls and along the aisles dimmed, the great sparkling chandelier above them faded, and the carved ivory ceiling curving around the chandelier flattened into a cool matte white. A spotlight warmed the center of the stage curtain. A buzzing echoed in the theater, and from out of the stage floor an organ smoothly rose. The couple next to Vanessa kept typing and swiping, their faces lit by the blue screens, until the woman glanced at Vanessa and put away her phone. A shadow walked from stage right and sat in front of the organ. The spotlight shut off and darkened the crowd, the curtain lifted, and the little light over the organ's music stand clicked on, silhouetting Bob Holden at his mighty Wurlitzer.

Tim shifted in his seat and took a long drink from his Coke. He wiped his hands on his pants and leaned back. The sound of the film reel flapped behind Vanessa. The smell of the popcorn rekindled her headache and slightly nauseated her. Tim looked at her, his mouth miming amazement at what they were about to see. She squinted and giggled with him in the dark.

A bright gray light flickered on the screen. The clip shimmied up and down in gray tones and black and white, and before Vanessa realized what was in front of her, Mickey Mouse stood at a crossroads in the middle of a tumultuous storm. The wind had shredded his umbrella, and behind him, a house silhouetted in black, save for its doors and windows brightly lit as eyes and a mouth, moved like a frightened face. The storm bent the house back like seagrass under waves.

Mickey found the door to the house. He shivered inside the creaky parlor and dodged cobwebs and bats. The front door had locked itself shut with chains and a giant padlock after he stepped in. In front of him he watched a crooked staircase seesaw back and forth. A fuzzy spider, as large as Mickey, dropped from the ceiling and scuttled past him. He made it to the upstairs hallway before the lights in the parlor snapped off.

He struck a match, and his shadow avoided the light, its black form growing on one wall and then shrinking and passing under him to be on the other wall. Mickey stepped into a room with an organ. Emerging from off-screen, Death approached Mickey and, pulling back its thick black cloak, revealed its skull to the terrified mouse. *"Play!"* Death moaned, pointing to the organ. His bottom lip quivering, Mickey shrugged and pleaded with his hands. *"Plllaaay!"* Death repeated with a deeper tone, more intense, each syllable's sound drawn out longer than his first command. Mickey sat on the stool, and as he pushed a few keys, Bob played too. Tim looked at Vanessa and raised his eyebrows up and down; the surprise of joy glowing on her face, she laughed with him. Mickey punched a few more keys; Bob did, too; the staccato notes lingered like a steam whistle. And then Death laid its skeletal hands on top of Mickey's, and together they played a waltz piped into the theater by the hands of Bob Holden and his mighty Wurlitzer.

Following a sustained minor chord, skeletons stumbled into the room, and this gang of bones danced and swayed to the music, some of them stopping to play guitar or xylophone on their partners' femurs and ribs. And as the whole room became more animated, as Mickey's and Death's hands worked their way up and down the keyboard, their feet pushing the pedals, as Bob leaned over his own keyboard and pushed his own pedals, pumping in live music, everything that was dead was alive again; everything broken danced.

The clock on the wall and its pitchfork-tipped hands bobbed up and down to the beat. Some skeletons danced the Charleston, some skeletons fell apart and then put themselves back together, but it was the skeletons dancing in a circle in the middle of the movie that kept Vanessa's attention. They spun around and around on the warping wood floor, holding hands, clacking their teeth with delight.

And then it all stopped—the music, the dancing, the organ in the animated room and the organ at the front of the stage. Bob's hands rested in his lap, and in the darkness, he lowered his head. Mickey scampered down the stairs, but the house itself would not let Mickey leave, until finally the front door flew open, and out he went into the stormy night.

Vanessa wiped her eyes and clapped with Tim as the ending credits rolled. Bob bowed to the crowd before sitting back down, pivoting on his stool, and waiting for the next cue.

"So...wanna stay?" Tim asked in a low voice.

"Yes," she whispered back. "Yes, I do. Thank you."

"You're welcome. And...told you."

"You were right...this once," she teased, leaning back in the seat. Her laughter caught the ire of the woman who had been on her phone.

"Every now and then I get it right." Tim reopened the Milk Duds and poured out some for them to share. "They'll show a few more, and then we can get out of here. I thought we could get pizza and some ice cream. Like old times," he whispered to her. "Just down the block."

"Sounds good." She interlocked her pinky finger with his and leaned into her chair as the next movie started—another Disney short from the 1930s with two electrified ghosts yawning and complaining that there's no one left in the world to scare anymore.

8

"I think we're stuck," she said, noticing the growing crowds. People crammed near her removed their coats and scarves, plopped down on seats, made phone calls, and threw up their hands as they shuffled off to the gift shop to buy snacks, magazines, and travel pillows and returned to the rows linked together by the metal bars running under them. Some in the crowd stood around and shook their heads; some vented their frustrations with large sighs; a few, with boarding passes in fists, stormed off from the gates where they had waited for so long.

"What's that?" Dan asked. His attention bounced between Vanessa's words, the flat-screen TV above him, and his phone.

"Our plane."

The Departures screen on Vanessa's right twinkled with Cancelled or Delayed. Across from her, the conversation intensified between an airline's ticket agent and a short but firm man pleading at the desk. He spoke quickly as he laid his arm across the width of the desk; his family huddled behind him. Vanessa heard an Indian accent overwhelm the man's English as he punctuated how the ineptitude of the agent's company affected him, his wife, and his two children, all of whom had not only missed their flights but also sleep and food. The man shook his head in disgust when the agent phoned her supervisor.

Dan moaned, "Yeah, no one's leaving for a while." He nodded at the television's weather map smeared with degrees of blues and a swath of pink stretching from Wisconsin to southern Missouri and into western

Pennsylvania and New Jersey. Breaking News flashed its red block beneath the anchorwoman. "It's a big one. At least we made it to the airport. My sister said they're preparing for it, too. And Chicago's getting slammed, which means we're not getting out of here any time soon. Two more inches in less than an hour." Dan kissed her cheek. "The Big One," he said, lowering and grumbling his voice. "Hey, you should sit up." Dan rubbed her knee. "Bad for your back."

The seat shifted as Vanessa slid up and glanced at her husband. She drank from a water bottle and turned her head to the large window overlooking the runways in the late afternoon light, which had become truncated a little more at this time every day. "I want to go back to California," she mumbled.

"Did you say California?" he asked, pausing in the middle of an email.

"Yeah, I did."

"It was a good trip, wasn't it?"

She smiled at him.

"Big news that day. It makes sense that you keep talking about it."

Vanessa stared out the window and wanted to ask him to clarify "it" in his sentence. Did he mean her first trip to California was successful because she, Dan, and the team secured another potential client that would fatten MetaBrand's portfolio? Because she ignored her morning sickness and focused on business, not her body and the headaches that had been increasing—the headaches that a doctor told her were related to hormonal imbalances? Because she had set aside everything that had changed inside of her and everything she had hoped to see outside of her everyday life—the ocean, the hills, the redwood forests, and new mountain ranges? Meeting rooms, formal dinners, and handshakes regulated the three days she, Dan, and the team were in San Francisco. The laptops and the Internet connections did not let go; clients did not let go. The PowerPoint slideshow stuttered like a movie at the end of its reel. She felt as though an impermeable and invisible dome had fallen over her as her work restricted her to a four-block radius; her reach was limited. She had wanted to be alone in the hotel room, but she was inside this dome's center without any exits. Or did Dan mean the upcoming appointment with her OB-GYN? That big news? Or was he implying that she would always associate California and its light with decisions that required climbing further and further down into an obscure space that seemed endless? Her wanting to ask him for this clarification drifted away as quickly as it had appeared. The light she saw at the airport had already reached and left the house where they were supposed to fly; the Atlantic side was ready for darkness and the incoming snow. And although her in-laws' house waited thousands of miles away, flying there would not equal the feeling of getting away. The day on that side of the country had started to end, and the air, driven from the Pacific over the California mountains that she never saw and the Rockies that she has lived near for years but doesn't visit anymore, will reach the East Coast and fall as snow while the next day's light begins its cycle again.

Workers stuffed in fluorescent winter coats and jumpsuits puttered about the runways. Long trains of yellow baggage carts passed the terminal's window. Vanessa reminded herself that this is where they are right now, not where they are going. Letting out a big breath and pushing her shoulder-length hair back from her face, she said plainly, "I don't think I want it."

"What?" Dan asked, his elbows on his khakis. Before reaching down at his feet for a bottle of juice, he fished out peanuts from a bag sitting on his leg. "The Anderson project?" He kept his eyes on the radar. "Let me get through this quarter and into the next one. I'll get Dave and Brian to hire someone to help you. We need you at the front for now. You can work right up until it's time. NorCal will still be there, unless it breaks off from an earthquake. The other Big One." He deepened his voice again while bobbing his eyebrows. "We can go back and do all the stuff you talked about when Anderson is over. And we'll have more to celebrate...professionally and personally." He kissed her forehead and watched the swirl of grays and whites on the television's snowfall map.

"The baby," she whispered. Her mouth pressed against his dress shirt. "If I am pregnant, I don't want it."

"Are you serious?" The plastic peanut bag crunched in his hands. "Or is this because of...what? The Anderson project?"

"I didn't know until now. I've been thinking about this so much."

"You've been thinking about this so much?"

"Yes."

"But you didn't know until now."

"Yes."

"At the airport?"

"I've been wanting to talk to you, but you seemed a little more excited than I was. And Anderson has taken over everything."

"I am excited about it."

"Anderson, or...?"

"Both. I'm excited for both. We've talked about this."

"I know, but we just went ahead without really talking."

"Talking about what?"

"Everything...money, space, work."

"All that is in place." He flipped his phone facedown onto his leg as she held his other hand.

"I don't think I want it." Her voice was firmer and calmer than the last time she said it to him.

"If you're pregnant."

"Yes."

"OK, well..." Dan took a deep breath and sent his eyes up and down the waiting area before returning to the TV. "We're not going anywhere." Dan tipped his head at another Breaking News banner flashing red at the bottom of the screen. "The storm is now stalling smack dab over where we need to fly through. I think we can cross off getting there by tonight. We'll be here instead...all night."

She scooted closer to him and crossed her ankles over his. She looked at the desk where the family had been. No one was there now, not even an agent. Dan stared at his phone, and although his shoulder propped her head and their ankles intertwined, and although she and Dan waited together in the silence and the falling light, waiting to be in other places, she felt untethered and pushed into anonymity with him. Time had stopped for them in that room, and yet it continued shortening around them with the crowds moving but not leaving, the clocks on the flight screens steadily ticking forward, the air outside tumbling toward dusk.

After several minutes of silence, Dan said, "Here's something we won't miss."

"What?"

"The amount of crappy food we won't have to eat at Traci's."

"Such as?" Vanessa laughed.

"Such as the stuffing she makes. That thing is like eating wet, clumpy oatmeal, and it always clogs my plumbing." Crossing his hands over his stomach, he mimed a flatulent sound.

"Or your aunt's pumpkin pie," Vanessa added, gripping her jaw.

"Oh, the sugar," he grimaced. "My teeth hurt after one bite. I think she adds sugar into the ice cream. But it is fun to say, 'I've had enough of my aunt's sweet, sweet pie.'"

She chuckled with him.

"But, it's not always my family," he continued. "There was your dad's chicken fingers that one Thanksgiving...that frozen bag from the store."

"Hey!" Vanessa bit his shoulder. "That wasn't Thanksgiving. That was when you first met him."

"He had those baked beans, too."

"You made a joke about beans to him. *Beans*, Dan...to my *father*."

"I thought he was going to string me up like the gringo I am. I swear he said he was going to kill me in Spanish."

"He didn't say that," she teased. "He said he'd get some cholos from around the corner to do it for him."

Dan flipped out his phone. "We've been here for five hours. It's getting dark."

The mountains in the distance had darkened into purples and navy blues; the sky behind the crest smoldered underneath gray tufts of clouds.

"What about our plane?" Vanessa asked.

"Not happening. Neither is standby." Dan looked at the airline's desk again. Two agents, including the woman from earlier, stood behind it. Both agents cradled phones to their ears while furiously typing on computers. Another family hovered nearby; the father jabbed his brow with his fingers. Dan switched his eyes from desk to television and back to desk. "You're right. We are stuck."

❋

The driver's dreadlocks thumped against the headrest as he turned his head to talk. "Flight got cancelled, huh?"

"Yup," said Dan.

"You're not the only ones," the driver continued. "Our switchboard has been lighting up like a Christmas tree the past couple of hours." He flew past another car; streetlights blurred as the taxi increased speed. "Your airline didn't give you a voucher for a hotel?"

"We live here," Dan said.

"Nice. Airline gonna take care of you somehow? Get you to where you want to go? Maybe tomorrow?"

Vanessa and Dan looked at each other. The highway's lights blinked one by one between them.

"We wanted to go home," Dan answered.

"Right on." The driver hoisted a gloved thumbs-up to them. "Screw 'em, right? They have so much power nowadays. And one day before Thanksgiving! Man, oh man. Maybe you guys can get a good meal tomorrow without reservations. We're pretty lucky. Not much snow this year, at least not at this elevation," the driver said, not bothering with his turn signal when he veered onto another on-ramp. "Up higher, though, they're getting some. We usually get a little something for Turkey Day."

"I think we sent it packing for everything east of here," Dan grumbled.

The driver laughed; his dreadlocks bobbed with his head. The taxi's engine thrummed.

"We're just thankful we can get out," Vanessa raised her voice. "Being stuck in an airport is not how we want to spend our time."

"No doubt. It's a nightmare. You know, there's that good Caribbean joint downtown. Best jerk in town. They might be open tomorrow."

Vanessa looked at Dan, who smiled back at her.

"There's also Thai House off the Sixteenth Street Mall. That's downtown. And Sal's Pizzeria…downtown…and La Luna…downtown. Pretty much all the good stuff is downtown."

"We know," Dan said. "We work down there." He turned to Vanessa and lowered his voice. "La Luna… We could get burritos, margs, and chips and guac. Bring it back home. I could catch up on some email and then we could watch some movies."

"Let's do something we've kept talking about but haven't," she said.

"Because of work?"

"I didn't say that."

"You don't have to."

"Dan…please…not now. We called a truce back at the airport, especially if we're going to be stuck here for the holiday."

"OK." He rubbed her knee. "Such as?"

"Something different this time of night."

"OK." Dan typed on his phone. "Not the mountains. It's a little dark for that now." He swiped down the screen a few more seconds. "I don't know."

Vanessa leaned toward the driver. "What do you think is open this time of night...something cool and unique."

The driver glanced at her in the rearview mirror and said, "The telescope is really cool. The old observatory."

Vanessa gleamed at Dan. "I remember hearing about it when I was in grad school. It's supposed to be awesome. I tried to go once, but it was closed for renovation." She pulled out her phone and thumbed through search results before clicking one. After a few minutes of scrolling, she said, "Let's do it."

"Really? You don't want to stay in?"

"I want to be out. I don't want to be stuck in our house for the rest of the night, before the holiday. We're actually not working these next three days...at least I'm not."

"I do have that check-in with Dave on Friday."

"Fine. But if we're going to be out tonight, then let's be out...really out."

"No hole-in-the-wall Mexi food and binging on rom-coms?"

She shook her head no.

"Change of plans," Dan said to the driver. "Take us to the observatory."

"All right. You got it."

The driver rolled his wheel to the other lane, corkscrewing them down and up and then into the direction from where they had come. The taxi exited the highway and rumbled along the road headed to the observatory; the bright grid of downtown dwindled behind them. The car slowed, transitioning to a two-lane road winding and dipping among thickening trees. The taxi swerved and then coasted. The matte night sky widened and dropped from its black vault once the trees along the road disappeared.

Vanessa leaned against the back seat as though it reclined, as though the metal springs under her and Dan's seat bent with the weight of their bodies. Their spines, their shoulders, the bases of their necks settled in like two animal profiles pressed together in the cold night. They held hands in the back seat, as though the past wasn't dragged into the light with them or into the present. Their bodies swayed with the car and the road—this feeling of floating but not falling.

❋

As the taxi drove off and its taillights faded into the darkness, Vanessa and Dan walked down the sidewalk leading up to the wooden front doors, one of which was open. Bright, warm light poured into the arched portico. Two small lanterns, hooked like shepherds' staffs and affixed to the corners where the portico blended into the rotunda's balcony, washed the portico, the lawn, and the front steps in a diluted cherry red and enhanced the rotunda's squared-off sandstone blocks. Shadows pocked the blocks' rough surface and lengthened the wide edges of each block, intensifying the weight of the Victorian building, sinking it further into the ground. The rusticated blocks contrasted the smoother stones that finished the top, near the metal dome, under the black sky.

Standing between the first step and the portico and in the fusion of the soft red and pale white lights, Vanessa and Dan looked up. The smoke-gray metal dome was turned one-quarter to the right; the galvanized shutters were propped open. The same warm yellow light pouring out from the front doors glowed inside the dome. Dan pointed to the second floor's windows; his breath curled in the cold air. Vanessa saw the great telescope inside angled like a whale pushing itself up and out from a ghostly wave.

Unbuckling her coat, Vanessa stepped through the front doors and looked at the first floor's walls. Its curved outer wall was mustard yellow; its curved inner wall mint green; dark-stained quarter-rounds and door casings trimmed both walls. A chalkboard, gilded-framed paintings of mountain landscapes and luminous valleys, and galactic images of nebulae and constellations hanging from wood rails wrapped around both outer and inner walls. Beneath a photo of the Horsehead Nebula, at a small desk that reminded Vanessa of elementary school, a woman with a friendly, wrinkled face, a brimming smile, and a headful of white curly hair said, "Hello there, how may I help you?"

"Hi," Vanessa answered, laughing to herself and thinking more of elementary school when she saw that the woman, her denim pants hiked up to her belly button by a red-and-white-striped belt, wore a white t-shirt emblazoned with Mile-High Star Gazers Club. "We want to see the telescope." Vanessa removed her gloves and stocking cap.

"I'm sorry, dear, the last group has started, and we close at ten." The woman tapped the large digital clock on the desk with her pencil.

"Do you mind if we look around the building?"

"Of course not. Here's some information." The woman offered two brochures. "Inside are things like public nights, membership, and the history of the place. The observatory was built in 1894 and is registered as a national historic landmark. Astronomy classes are still held here on the first floor." She pointed to a room beyond her desk. "It's a tight fit in there, but they're not here for the...*space*." She closed her eyes at her own joke; Vanessa giggled with her. "Second floor is offices, archives, and of course, the observation chamber, which as I said just took its last tour. You folks local?"

"We're stuck here for Thanksgiving," Dan jumped in, keeping his back to them while he surveyed the floors and the walls. "The snowstorm out east." He threw his brochure in a metal trash basket and then looked at his phone.

"Oh, I heard about that. I have cousins in Iowa. They're spending their Thanksgiving playing in the snow."

"Our flight's cancelled, and we wanted to stay out," Vanessa said. "Too many headaches. It's such a clear night. And this just sounded like a good place to get away for a while. Day before Thanksgiving, you know?" She turned toward a marble bust of the observatory's first director and his quote inscribed on the base: It is better not to know so much than it is to know so many things that are not so.

"I don't blame you," the woman said. "You should have come earlier, if you could have. But the stars'll still be here tomorrow. Enjoy yourselves."

As the woman returned to reading her book, Vanessa and Dan walked toward the staircase and passed a tall cuckoo clock with its hands clicking on nine-thirty. The little wood doors at the top opened until the woodsman, with a small axe and a bundle of firewood on his shoulder, appeared from his dark hole, jittered toward the middle of the clock's track, and met his wife in her dress and headscarf, who, on the opposite side, had popped out of her dark hole and teetered toward him. As their wooden bodies bent toward each other, the gears spinning, the chimes hammering out the time, the kiss between them was a parable.

Trying not to laugh as each step squeaked, Vanessa and Dan walked up the staircase that curled around the rotunda's inner wall. They stopped briefly on the landing where a giant iron wrench leaned in a corner.

"It feels like we're in Willy Wonka's factory," Vanessa said. She heard scraping on the wall behind her and spun to see that Dan had moved and then reset the giant wrench.

"I hope that paint and plaster wasn't from 1894," he chuckled.

"Are you going to leave it that way?" She stared at the faded yellow scratches in the wall.

"What do you want me to do?"

"Leave an apology."

"To who? Granny Clampett downstairs? It's probably for the tenured science professor who will never, ever retire." He grinned at her. "My big ol' tool got in the way again."

"Funny." She glowered and turned her back.

He grabbed her arm. "Hey, I'm trying here." After several seconds of silence, he spun toward the door.

Vanessa waited until he left the room. She shook her head after inspecting the wall's damage. Hypnotized by the three chalk-white marks across the giant wrench's handle, she rubbed her hands over them and, before joining Dan, snapped a photo with her phone. Something inside her had told her to hold onto the image—that it could be needed later; that it had no value now but would in the future when she wasn't expecting it; and that the weight was not in the metal, on the rough surface, or in the three marks but in a presence not yet entirely formed. She stuck a small note on the desk: Sorry for the scratches to the wall that time we were here.

Up they went one more level, reaching the observation chamber and the dome room. The door was closed, and as Vanessa reached for the brass knob, a group of five teenagers threw it open and burst out, laughing and talking. One of the boys bragged to his friends that he "totally saw UFOs and aliens." Before the heavy door swung shut, Vanessa stuck her boot in between its edge and jamb. Come on her face and eyes motioned to Dan.

Fifteen feet above the wood floor, the telescope loomed in a room painted a velvety crimson. The pier on which it rested looked like a matte-black trombone with its bell facing down on the floor. Perched between the telescope's bottom and the top of its pier was a black square that resembled a faceless clock. Copper and brass gears, wheels, tubes, dials, and metal tanks congested the black square. Evenly spaced fist-sized gauges and wheels orbited down toward the eyepiece—a monocle— extending from a copper cylinder. The inside of the dome was charred, and its metal ribs arched toward the aperture.

"This is so steampunk," Vanessa said.

Dan chuckled. "You like this?"

"I do." Her voice faded as she continued looking up.

He shook his head. "It's like someone took the smokestack and engine from a train, blew it up, tried regluing it, and slapped a periscope on it."

"I know," she replied flatly. The feeling of being inside a dome settled upon her again, but the dome with the night sky and the telescope to see the light waiting there was vastly different than the one she had felt in California. There, that dome was invisible, impersonal; it trapped her. Her movements and decisions under that dome were dependent on closures and reminded her that all things in her life were frozen in the present and demanded answers from her. But this other dome, the one under which she now stood, with its metal and wood, was physical, opened outward; this other dome she came to of her own volition and, when she entered it, provided space where light could fall around her without her having to ask for it.

"I'm sorry," a voice yelled above them, "but we're not allowing any more viewers." The grad student leaned from atop a creaking platform next to the telescope and its ladder attached to the track curving under the bottom lip of the dome.

Vanessa moved toward him; her boots clicked and echoed on the wood floor. "We just want to look. This place is so great."

Wrinkling his face, the grad student turned back to the telescope and a father and daughter standing near an eyepiece with him on the platform. For a few more minutes, he rambled on about constellations, star lumens, and planets before walking down the platform and moving toward the pier. To the right, he rotated one of two wheels under a wood shelf centered on the pier, on top of which rested three small clocks and one large gauge. As he turned one of the wheels, the telescope swiveled up and stopped when the large gauge's hand reached sixty degrees.

"I don't want to fight," Dan whispered.

"Me neither."

"But part of me wishes that's me."

"What? Run a telescope?" She turned to the ladder and then, hearing the commotion on the platform, looked up at the grad student and the father and the young girl standing on her tiptoes. Vanessa imagined what the excited girl saw—capsules of light holding steady before breaking open and falling down, light from light, aging, a movement so small and distant that, Vanessa knew, the girl would have to go away for a while and then return when she was older and ask if anything had changed since she last looked, wondering if the source of the light was still there after she had been gone for so long.

"No. Not that. You know what I mean."

"How do you know?" she asked quietly.

"I just do. It's time. Career, beautiful, successful wife who's always leading the way...now a family. We have the house. Your dad never visits, and my family, no way will they stay with us ever again. And once MetaBrand is sold..."

"Which'll be when?"

Dan exhaled heavily. "Before I met you, I thought I'd rather be a big brother or uncle figure. My sister's kids, my friends' kids...not necessarily a dad-dad. But I want to be a dad and keep everything else in place. I want both."

"I just don't know. It's...so far out there."

"What do you mean?"

"I can't put my finger on it, but it's like..." Vanessa peeked at the dome's open shutters and the telescope. "It's like trying to pick out clothes for the next two months based on the weather."

"You've changed your tune."

"I'm not sure anymore."

"Why?"

"We're so..."

"We're so what?"

"I wanted the middle-class life, Dan, not the rut. I didn't know what all of this would take."

He shuffled closer to her. "And now you want to stop? You wanted *this* but without *that?*"

"I don't want happiness. I want *meaning*." Her syllables droned under the starry sky.

Dan strode through the door, stood in the hall, and checked his pockets for his phone. His loafers tapped on the wood floor as he moved away from Vanessa and the telescope. He swiped his phone on and placed it to his ear. The grad student and the father and daughter continued laughing and talking. Vanessa imagined the Pacific Ocean, the very thing she had hoped to see firsthand when she was in California but never did. And she thought of a point perched on cliffs, not a beach, overlooking the waves, as though this kind of point would always be found that close to the ocean and in no other place or time defined by any other landscape. It was the same kind of point that had recently appeared in her thoughts and daydreams—those moments holding everything in place, briefly allowing her to find footing in the world, the minutes and the hours not slipping away from her, slipping so much and so far away that they accumulated into years. She thought of someone else with her at this point, as though she had called this someone or this someone had been there waiting or had known to be there without her having to say anything. At first, she had assumed it was Dan, hoping that he had taken personal time off to meet her, but then she wondered if the someone was one of her parents, a stranger, or someone else. Under the dome and the telescope and the stars, no one stood next to her. But at this point overlooking the ocean, she approached it straight on, the ocean rising to meet her, the cliffs speckled with dark greens, this point without walls and with unlimited space and extending into time; this point, this anonymous someone with her, this Vanessa at this moment waiting alongside coastal flowers and trees and the tides of the ocean rolling endlessly against the horizon.

Walking back into the chamber and holstering his phone, Dan smiled at Vanessa, who smiled back; neither his nor her smile clarified anything other than silence. The soft hum of a generator somewhere in the round room clicked on. She wanted to leave but couldn't. The father and the daughter thanked the grad student. The aperture shutters clanked as they closed. Like a tower falling in slow motion, the telescope silently leveled out with the light that it had collected inside for anyone to see while standing on the ground.

9

"Didn't want to live with your dad?" Tim chuckled as Vanessa opened her condo's front door. A motion-sensitive nightlight on the second floor flicked on in the darkness. For a moment, the two of them stood still in the opening.

"Nope," she answered, trudging up the stairs. "I couldn't live with him. He'd know all the secrets and bad habits I'm trying to hide as a grown-up. I need my space." She slid her keys and purse onto the kitchen counter near her laptop. "Besides, he's a whole different kind of homebody. Ten-mile radius is about all he can handle now. He's not in great health." She closed the blinds over the sink until the red, blue, and green holiday lights strung on the handrails of the neighbors' balconies faded.

"Sorry to hear that."

"Nothing serious. Just, you know, all those years of hard labor, not eating properly, and the stress of the bakery. The recession didn't help anything. And Mom…"

Tim checked the bottom of his boots before stepping onto the hardwood floor. "Yeah, I'm sure it's still tough for him and you this time of year."

"But you know, he shuffles about, gets in his car, and goes to the grocery store or down to Yolie's for some real Mexican food. Same thing every Thursday night. Pupusas pollo topped with more pollo. Extra red sauce and cilantro on the side. One ice-cold Pacifico. 'Pacifico,'" she grumbled in her father's voice. Vanessa caught her breath and rubbed her forehead. "But basically, he doesn't want to cook anymore. He's probably ready to retire from the store."

"It'll be all yours."

"No way. Working there again as an adult is bad enough. Working there as a teenager was bad, but now that I'm older…" She opened a cabinet, pulled out two squat glasses, and braced herself on the counter. "I forget what I was saying." She stared at the blinds and the smudged colors behind them. "Oh…he rearranges the store *after* his employees have done it for him. He undoes all this work that they do because 'they don't do it right.' He reads his paper and his books. He still tinkers with woodworking, some metalwork here and there. No television for him. Even when I was younger and we had finally bought a newer one, he never bothered watching it." She grabbed a foggy bottle from the refrigerator. "He would sit next to me and watch whatever it was I was watching. He was not a big fan of MTV. He'd watch it with me for a few minutes, then go to his recliner and read. He read anything and everything. Still does." She unscrewed the bottle cap. "None of that machismo stuff for him. Books and music. Cultura. Become a better man with your head, not your fists. His favorite is Octavio Paz, and he loves Dickens, Montaigne, Gabriel Garcia Marquez." She started quoting a poem in Spanish, paused to clear her throat, and opening her eyes, finished the line.

"What does it mean?" Tim asked.

"'One day I'll see you in another sun.'"

Nodding his head and smiling, Tim leaned onto the counter that separated the dine-in area from the kitchen. Two star-shaped magnets held a photo on the refrigerator door—a black-and-white of Vanessa's parents the day they were married. Nestled under a crown of white flowers, her mother's hair was pulled tight on top of her head, and her father—baby-faced except for long sideburns; his hair feathered over his ears—wore a black jacket and white shirt and smiled at her mom. Between them they held a bouquet of white flowers. The date was handwritten in pencil below the photo. When Tim took one of the glasses from Vanessa, the kitchen's light accentuated the wrinkles near his eyes and highlighted the gray whiskers in his black beard.

"Ice?" she asked.

"Sure."

She spun toward the refrigerator and cupped her hands under the ice dispenser. "I've become more and more forgetful. Little things. Keys, days of the week. I want to say things, but at certain times, I can't. And my hands and legs will sometimes lock up or just, you know, not work. What am I? Old?" Vanessa filled the glasses with the cinnamon whiskey until the crushed ice soaked it.

"Cheers." Tim clinked his glass to hers and sipped. "I know what you mean. I've had some more aches and pains, too, as the years add on. I think you really can do more when you're younger…not worrying too much about blowback."

Vanessa massaged the top of her head and the base of her neck. She drank more than half, gasped, topped off her glass, and moving into the living room, sat at one end of the couch where she popped off her shoes with her toes and curled her legs under her.

"I remember this time of year when your mom decorated the store with so much Christmas stuff," Tim said. He laid his hoodie across the other end of the couch, rolled up his shirtsleeves, and slid next to her.

"The poinsettias, the garland, the nativity scene…empty until baby Jesus arrived."

"That's right."

"She put out those great luminarias."

"She…" Vanessa broke into laughter until she snorted and covered her face with her sweater. "She used the real deal the first year, but then the fire department found out what she was doing. The whole store looked like a ball of fire on the inside. It was so bright and warm in there. Somebody must have called about it. They show up, the guy's really nice to her, explains it, explains it to me, I explain it again to her, she's at first OK with it, but then she's so defiant and stubborn…because that's my mom. And then she blows it off. She keeps lighting them. The fire department keeps coming by and telling her to stop, and they're so nice and patient with her but firm. I can see her standing in the doorway just waiting for the sun to go down, and you know, it's December, so it's getting dark at four in the afternoon. She preps for the next day and, as soon as the sun is low, lights those luminarias. Fire department guy comes back. Back and forth they go, my dad and me stuck in the middle, we're laughing the whole time, asking her to see it from the point of view of the fire department. You know, we just got this store, don't want to lose it, and my mom is not having it. She says, 'Why can't I? It's tradition.' So, she keeps at it. Eventually, the same firefighter returns…same guy…and he has this sad look on his face and tells her one last time, 'Ma'am, please, I don't want you to get in trouble over something really simple.' 'Mamá,' I say, 'por favor…' 'Flora!'…my dad's getting angry. She gives me this nasty look, like I betrayed her. My father is trying to be firm with her, but he's dying with laughter, and sure enough, she lights them again and the city fines her. 'No mas, Flora!' my dad yells because the money, you know, makes it all clear to him, but he would laugh about it when he took me to school. She was so mad. She had to use the plastic ones with light bulbs. Oh, she hated that. She was more mad about the cheap plastic ones than anything else. The money and the fines didn't matter to her. She wanted that real light…the kind you can feel." Vanessa stared at the fireplace and wiped her eyes and mouth with her sweater. "Want some music?"

"Yeah, sure," Tim replied, crunching ice. "Well, it's nice that you got your own place."

"It all came with a price." Vanessa swiped through her phone's songs and pushed Play. "I don't have a whole lot now. Besides, I don't want a whole lot anymore. I had that. There's no reason to keep stuff you can't ever take with you. It's never really yours to begin with."

"I know." Nodding in agreement, Tim walked over to the fireplace mantel and pointed to an elegantly dressed skeleton couple linked arm in arm. "Where'd you get these awesome calacas?"

"Oh, some random guy gave those to me. I don't even remember his name."

"Creeper?" he asked.

"You have no idea," she answered with a smirk.

Laughing out loud, he moved down to the books with their spines arranged from red, at the start of the mantel, to blue by the back patio door. "Color coded?"

"They just ended up that way." She threw her hands up. "I swear."

"Hmm…sure." He squinted at her. "Totally not ambitious Type A at all." He sipped from his glass and, dipping his head and shoulders down, pulled out a dark green book with bright white letters. "Steinbeck. Nice."

"One of my all-time favorites."

"We should see some old, black-and-white movies some time."

"That'd be nice."

Tim pulled another book off the shelf. "*Where the Light Takes Its Color from the Sea*," he read aloud before turning the bright cover toward her. Silhouetted trees, ocean waves, a sky thinly rinsed in pink and blue watercolors, and an abstract sun faced her.

"Yeah, it's about California, mainly Nor Cal."

"Nor Cal," he repeated, grinning. "Talking like a local already."

"It's gorgeous up there. All those cliffs and valleys and the sky and ocean air. All I know is that I want to swim in the Pacific. Not just see it but be in it. It would mean a lot."

Tim opened the book and read a passage about living in an area where, within a few hours of travel, a circuitry of coastlines, forests, and mountains burned off the clouds of modern life and recharged elements of living. He stared at the page with its corner turned down and, after several seconds, looked up. "'Going to California.'"

"What's that?" Vanessa asked.

"The song by Led Zeppelin. It's playing now. The timing...funny."

"It is."

"When will you go?"

"Soon, I hope. I feel it coming."

"Good," he said, closing the book and setting it back in its place. "Maybe we can go together someday soon."

Vanessa closed her eyes and smiled at him.

"I remember when we had that 'music expert' come in one Sunday school," Tim continued. "He had that list of songs we shouldn't listen to. 'Stairway to Heaven' was one of them. I think number one, in fact. 'My sweet Satan,'" Tim garbled, mimicking the song played backward, as he shook his head.

"'Imagine,'" Vanessa added, laughing with him.

"Yes. Well, you can't say there's no heaven or hell."

"I wasn't about to give up my CDs," she said. "It took me many hours working at the bakery to buy those."

"Then or now?"

"Both," she chuckled.

Tim sat down, closer to her, and wrapped his arm around her feet. "We were young. There was a lot of learning back then, a lot of trying to teach us how to navigate good and bad. But yeah, like we've talked about, it ended up feeling a lot like obedience at times, that it was all watered down to being good and nothing else. It did seem that we would be punished rather than loved. If you did well, you were rewarded. If you messed up, which we were always being reminded of, you were punished. Or worse…that we're just doomed to be bad, that there's no other choice. But, that's where I find myself wanting to be…in the middle."

"The middle?"

"Yeah. Between being aware of God and knowing I mess up. There's room there to move forward. I don't know everything."

"Or move backward."

"No, you're right. Choice, right? Choice to move in either direction. But moving forward like someone always pursuing something greater than the self. Sometimes we end up substituting ourselves for

God…a lot of times, actually. I know all about that. We forget that God has already put us where we need to be."

Vanessa nodded.

"I get that now, working with the teens at my church. Being older and wiser, I really get that. You want to give them the right tools to evaluate, not simply scare them into submission. Fear and judgment are so much easier and less demanding than love…so, so much easier. You don't want to be a dictator, but you have to have something strong to follow, to choose between. It's not much of a church, in my opinion, if it asks us to hand over everything *only* for the sake of authority…we're set up from the start to fail. There's no grace or love there. Choices."

Vanessa inhaled and slid closer to him. She started to speak but then stopped. A word pulsed inside her. "Timshel," she finally mumbled after it echoed in her head. "*Thou mayest.*"

Tim stared at her. "Yeah."

She closed her eyes and, turning his face to hers, kissed him. "I've missed you, Tim."

"I've missed you too."

She kissed him again and rubbed his arms. "Do you want to get the kitchen light?"

He smiled at her but didn't stand up from the couch or move to the light switch. He pulled her hands from his stomach.

"What?" she asked.

"I want to be with you at the right time with this…more than just this."

"Meaning what?"

"It's early. We're still figuring things out between us." Tim kissed her cold hands. "We can't right now because we're not committed."

"Not committed?"

"I mean married. We're not married. I'm still that way with all that."

Vanessa quickly rolled in her lips and nodded. "OK...sorry. No, no, I understand. I'm sorry." She wiped her eyes.

"Don't be, and don't apologize. It's not that I don't want to." He lifted her chin with his finger and kissed her. "It's not like women are throwing themselves at me left and right."

"I don't know," she laughed, her tone rising. "Some of those teenage girls at the haunted-house were really giggly around you."

"Yeah, 'cause that's what I need. I trashed my own studio and now have teenage girls on me." He pulled her closer.

As they hugged, she said, "That reminds me. I'll do it. I'll help you."

"You will?"

"Yes, but *only* the branding. I'm not getting you out of hot water with your church or with the money. I'll look at your website and get some ideas for advertising and promotion. OK?"

"Thank you." He kissed her and interlocked his fingers with hers.

She inhaled and exhaled deeply. "There's one more thing."

"What's that?"

"I want to tell you about some things in my life...one of my secrets."

"OK."

She inhaled and exhaled deeply again. "I had cancer...and had surgery for it almost a year ago."

"Vanessa..."

"Brain cancer."

"*Vanessa...* I'm so, so sorry." He kissed her forehead.

"It destroyed everything at the time...my marriage, my job, my life. That's why I'm back. I had to start over."

Tim pulled her closer to him. "Are you OK?"

"I'm still in the watch-and-see stage. I did chemo, meds, all that. I get scared at times. I've been getting more headaches and feeling sick. I get really, really tongue-tied and mess up with words and things I want to say, like I did when I had it, and it's all been happening more, but I don't know if it's coincidence, something else, that I'm just messing with my own mind, getting old. I don't know. Part of me wants to go to the doctor, part of me doesn't. Part of me knows I should, but if I go looking for monsters under the bed, I have a feeling they'll be there."

"It's OK," Tim said. "I'm here for you...whatever you need. And to be fair, you've been under some stress. Maybe your body is getting used to everything that's happened in the last year. Plus, you've been hanging around me and coming to the shop more, so maybe you're getting some fumes, and the timing of it just feels like something bigger. I get headaches, too, when I'm there. The lights, the fumes the system can't get. And, look, I'm definitely a horrible speaker. I get really locked up and tripped up all the time. It happens."

"Thank you," she whispered to him. And Tim kept talking and stroking her hair and holding her hand, and as she watched him form another sentence in his mouth, a shadow from the past passed over her, and she assumed his next words would be "Let's pray" or "I'll pray for you." But he leaned toward her and said, "I'll always be here for you because I love you." And it sounded like he said those words from a distance, as though he said them through a metal tube between them. She rubbed his chest and closed her eyes, hoping to erase the guilt of her assumption. A phosphorescent-white light burned under the dome of her skull, and she saw it, felt its small burn, and something in her fell further down while she simultaneously felt something lifting her up out of her body. And as she and Tim huddled closer, she whispered to him, talking over him, but she was unaware of what she said, her words sounding nonsensical at times to her own ears, but in her mind she believed she told him more secrets: her loss of faith when her mother died; her and Dan; her fear of relapsing; her fear of facing what had been and what may be. She told Tim these things as though she held them up for any scrap of light to shine through, that there were no shadows to fear. "I think I'm getting sick again," she believed she said to him, feeling the hard knot of the unknown in dark space, and she thought that she let this slip out of her because of the alcohol or maybe because the fumes from his shop lingered on his body or that maybe her body's chemicals were conspiring against her. The end of a year had fallen apart, but the pieces remained dangling over her in hot and cold and in shadows and lights—all of this working in conjunction, lifting and settling, pushing and pulling, opposite but equal forces, two different bodies pressing against a gate where the cycles of the sun are the brightest.

10

Vanessa pointed toward a breezeway connecting several restaurants, clothing stores, and a pharmacy. "In there's fine. Just drop me off in there. Please."

"Here? It's a shopping court, Essa," her father said. "The church is another block down around the corner. I can see it from here." His chapped hands folded over the steering wheel as he leaned his body into it. The truck rattled and creaked at the stoplight.

"I'll walk. I want to walk. It's so nice out." The late-summer light animated each storefront's fonts and colors facing her.

"Essa, the church is up *there*. I'll drop you off there."

"I want to walk. Please, Dad, go do your errands for Mom." She pulled long black hairs off her jeans, reapplied another layer of makeup and lip gloss, and glanced a few more times at her face in the side mirror, tilting her head side to side and up and down. The pimple in the middle of her cheek had not magically disappeared in the last thirty minutes of their drive from one side of town to the other.

The light turned green, and Roberto pulled in front of a fabric store. The corroded hood of what was once a midnight blue truck faced a concrete hill that sloped down into the church's main property. The chassis squeaked as he set the parking brake. Tools and debris in the bed slid toward the cab.

"Thanks." She hopped out, slammed the door, and pulled down her yellow shirt at the hem, which tightened and enhanced her shape for a moment. She looked at her dad and was about to ask him if she looked OK, but his face formed an expression that she had seen from him before, especially when she went on dates with Jacob—not an expression of disappointment but one suggesting that she wear a turtleneck and a much thicker sweater buttoned over the top of it.

Her father nodded. "You look very nice, Essa. Seven?"

"Later…a little after. I'm sure there's a phone I can use. It's a church," she said, distancing herself from the beat-up truck and looking over her shoulder several times. The sun cast a red tint on her hair.

"OK, have a good time. Bye. Te amo." Roberto blew an invisible kiss to her as he had done when she was younger and headed off to school, but she didn't catch it. She waved him off and let the invisible kiss fall between them, something she had been doing more and more within the last year, and which, she knew, made her father feel old and out of place. The truck's guttural exhaust pipe rattled down the concrete slope. Her father rumbled out of sight and turned right onto the street, the blinker not switching off. She walked toward the church.

A burger shack and its orange-brown roof stood alone at the leveling-out point of the concrete slope. As she approached the large windows, teenagers sitting at the booths threw their heads back while eating, talking, and laughing at the same time. Vanessa wondered if this was the place to hang out before youth group. She wondered if Tim was tangled somewhere in there. She wanted to go inside and be there with them, not needing to know their names, but wanting to laugh with them, smile with them, take a hamburger, an order of onion rings, and a cola off a tray as she sat with them in the middle of a booth. She imagined what they were laughing about: school, football games, television, movies, music. Maybe they were talking about God. Vanessa smiled to herself and kept moving toward the church and the lantern-like lights inside its windows.

Built widely across a dark green lawn and a sprawling parking lot, the focus of the church's shape was the sanctuary and its gray metal steeple towering up, giving the illusion that, with the clear blue sky behind it, its peak was higher than the hospitals or the businesses scattered around it. The sanctuary's limestone and white trim accented the many A-shaped entryways in front of the flat, broad building attached behind the sanctuary. Architectural arrows drew attention to the tip of the cross on top of the steeple. The landscaping on the property had also been manicured into these arrow-like shapes pointing up. Blocky newer buildings expanding from the sanctuary intensified the footprint, as though this colossal structure had tumbled from the sky and its massive jigsaw-puzzle pieces had fallen into place.

From the outside, the church reminded Vanessa of some of the old churches she had seen in books and encyclopedias during research for an eighth-grade paper on *The Hunchback of Notre Dame*. Compared to Vida Nueva and its rural, shanty-town setting, the church soaring in front of her might as well have been a grand medieval cathedral complete with peasants, crypts, bats, and a stake in the courtyard to burn a witch. A small bell glimmered inside the steeple, and Vanessa hoped that a mysterious, misunderstood outcast rang it every hour.

Once through the front doors and into the creamy interior, she glided across the floor and flopped in all the chairs and sofas. The leather squeaked under her body as she shifted, crossed her legs, uncrossed her legs, and stood.

Turning up a set of carpeted stairs with gold handrails and through another large set of wooden doors with deep inlays and metal hardware, she found herself inside the sanctuary—massive, hooded, and deep like a conch cut in half. Rows of pews flared out from the raised stage, upon which a clear plastic pulpit stood. Chairs for the choir sat behind it, and steps in front led to the flat floor of the congregation seats. The silver pipes of the organ flanked the choir, rising high into the ribbed ceiling. A tall stained-glass window nestled between the pipes; a teal-blue cross hovered in the center space. With the sun setting, the stained-glass window shimmered like water. Rays of light, cartoon-like with their thick black lines built into the glass, shone forth from the top of the cross, and Vanessa floated into this space like Esmeralda had run through Notre Dame's wood pews, under the eyes of stone saints and out of the many shadows cast by votive candles until finally reaching sanctuary. The image had stayed with Vanessa: protection could be given to anyone entering a holy space; anyone, even vagrants and pariahs, could be safe inside the house of God.

Closing her eyes, she felt calm, sinking into the silence and the colors of the sanctuary, but the space overwhelmed her, and the sounds she heard inside this bubble were further away than what they were; the sanctuary pushed out everything toward an edge and kept it all pressed out. She felt the opposite effect when she swam. Floating near the bottom of the pool, the water, swaddling her so tightly, increased the sound of blood pumping in her chest and through her ears. Hearing her body and its rhythms, she knew she was alive.

"Hi there, may I help you?" a voice said behind her.

"I'm just looking for the youth group," Vanessa answered, spinning around and facing a short, lean man with liver spots peeking through his silver hair. Wrinkles sagged around his lips and jowl and near the crook of his nose. With his slacks hiked up to his stomach and wearing a dress shirt, he looked like a grandfather.

"It's in the other building, the youth-group building," he said, smiling. "You have to go back out." The man's swollen knuckles shook in the air as he pointed to the main door. "Turn right out the front here, then walk along the sidewalk. You'll see two buildings. One is the wedding chapel. Don't go in there. There's a rehearsal. You want the rectangle in between. There's a large parking lot. It's probably full now with cars and kids. You'll see a door facing the parking lot. There's a gym inside. It's big and metal. You can't miss it. You'll probably hear the music before you see it."

"Thank you."

"You're very welcome. I haven't seen you here before. Are you new?"

"I am."

"Well, welcome. It's so great to have you here." He smiled at her, waved, and sitting down at the front of the stage, fished through a black bag until he pulled out a wrench. He lifted a panel off the bottom half of the organ and reached inside.

"Thank you." She looked at the sanctuary once more before heading outside.

The metal edge of the youth-group building shone between the wedding chapel and a pergola covered in flowers and vines. Cars streamed into the parking lot, several blasting music, and teenagers poured out of the cars and into the building. Vanessa knew a lot of the songs from the radio and her friends at school. The group of kids from the burger place walked over, and they were still laughing. As they slid past her, they said hi and smiled. Vanessa waved at them, hoping they might bring her into their group, but they kept walking.

A live band with drums, a guitar, a keyboard, and a singer surprised her when she walked into building. Teenagers ran around, shrieking and laughing. The chaos reminded her of school right before a class bell rang or at lunchtime when kids flooded the halls and lockers, except that here, the crowd's faces shocked her a little more. She dodged a flailing arm from one of the air-hockey tables before bumping into the tight packs of girls chatting and boys throwing a football. The gym was bigger than her high school's gym and certainly would not be found in any of the parks or community centers near where she lived. A complex structure of metal frames supported the roof, and as she looked up, she saw several basketballs lodged up there. A few of the lights were out too, the metal hoods dented, but the gym was bright.

The younger boys who weren't playing pick-up basketball in one half of the court drank sodas and played their handheld video games; several pimply and bony ones sat against the concrete walls or in the bleachers. The girls giggled, flipped their hair, and stretched out legs that, to Vanessa, looked like they swam in private pools, soaked up the sun on a boat at the lake, or rode horses. Many of the girls wore outfits that she had seen in magazines or when cruising the mall with her friends. If she wanted similar clothes, she would have to buy cheaper versions at another store. The women at Vida Nueva wore dresses from thrift stores or Wal-Mart, if they could even afford those. Vanessa sucked in her tummy, held it for a few seconds as she walked by, but then let it out. She crossed her arms over her chest. She smiled at some of the girls; several smiled, waved back, and introduced themselves. After saying hi and chatting with a few of them, her assumptions broke away, and she opened herself to the new momentum pulling her. And as she started to turn and walk deeper into the gym, she slammed into a dark-haired boy and instantly recognized his face and toothy smile.

"I thought it was you. You came. I can't believe you came, Vanessa. I'm so happy to see you." Tim hugged her.

Blushing, she replied, "Yeah, me too."

"I came by the bakery the other day, as soon as I got back to town, but your mom said you were out helping your dad with his work."

"She told me. Yeah, I was."

"How was it?"

"It was OK. I'd rather hang out, but you know…"

"Where did you have to go?"

"It was just this office."

"I had to help clean the rec room here at the church," Tim said. "I never gagged so much before in my life. Old, soggy chips. Salsa in the carpet. Stains. Napkins everywhere. *Used* napkins. Kids these days." He rolled his eyes. "How was the rest of your summer?" He wiped sweat from his face with his shirt.

"Busy. Same ol', same ol'. I babysat and worked in the bakery and read. Helped my dad. That's about it. Swam with my friends at the pool."

"The bakery…my favorite place." Tim's eyes glistened. "June and July were so fun hanging out with you. I'm so glad that we got to do it."

"Me too. We had so many more customers after you stopped in. You must have told everyone you knew."

"I totally did. I told you my mom knows everyone."

"What about you? How was the rest of your summer? Did you help out any other churches?"

"We went to the Appalachians in Tennessee for a big mission trip in August. Just got back a couple of weeks ago, actually. And I mowed lawns *every day*. It's so awesome you're here because I was actually going to stop by the bakery this week, now that things have settled down. I was going to ask you if you wanted to come to this and, um, hang out. I guess your mom passed on my message."

"She did."

"Did your mom finish the wall? I still want to sketch those drawings...the Aztec symbols."

"No, not yet. She's been swamped with orders."

"Not mine."

"Maybe," she laughed with him. "But yeah, you should come by. You totally should. You'll want coffee and sweets, I'm sure."

"Most definitely."

"That's all you need, right?"

"Yep." Tim puffed out his chest like a superhero until it was less spoon-shaped. "It was great hanging out this summer."

"It was."

"Um, I was thinking, um, if you wanted to..."

A basketball slammed into him.

"Tim-o!" a voice yelled on the other side of the court.

"Chris, hey," Tim mumbled, throwing a mop of hair back from his red face.

The ball dribbled to Chris. Vanessa snickered to herself when she saw Chris with his short curly black hair, coarse and Afro-like for such a pasty white boy. His biceps were defined, not large, but very little fat around the veins running down the middle of his arms. He was shorter than Tim, and he wore shoes stamped with the silhouette of a basketball player, that she knew were expensive because several of the boys at her school became envied and god-like when they paraded them up and down the halls, in the cafeteria, and around the plaza during lunch and after school.

"You done?" Chris asked Tim, glancing at Vanessa and rubbing the soles dry with the palms of his hands.

"Yeah, I'm done," Tim's voice wavered.

"Dude, come on. We got time for one quick five-point game. Last one." He stared at Vanessa. "Hey, I'm Chris."

"Vanessa."

"First time here?"

"Yeah."

"Awesome. You wanna play?"

"Oh…no, thanks."

Chris leaned in and whispered to Tim, who blushed before glancing at Vanessa.

"No," Tim mumbled, wrinkling his greasy face.

"Cool. Well, see you in there. Nice to meet you." Chris nodded to them, mainly to Vanessa, before changing his shirt and swaggering out of the gym with his friends.

"He and I are…we know each other here," Tim said. "We go to different schools. He's a jock there and here, and I'm not…really. Anyway, I had a great time hanging out with you this summer."

"Me too."

"I can stop by…after school."

"Yeah, that'd be fun. I'd like that."

"And, thanks."

"For what?"

"Um, coming here tonight and for, you know, hanging out this summer. I said that already. I mean, I know you didn't have to come here…or hang out with me this summer."

"What do you mean?"

"No, I mean, doesn't your church have a youth group?"

"No, not really. I don't go that church anymore. My parents thought it would be a good idea to go to a new place. I wanted to come and see you."

"Cool." Tim looked down at the sweat pooling under him. "I'm really glad you came." He glanced up at her, and she blushed. They looked around the gym. The noise and the action had started to move, and herds of teenagers had trampled into the hallway outside the gym.

"Time to go?" she asked.

"Yeah. Sit with me."

She followed Tim into the hall until they reached a group of kids who pulled them in. They smiled and introduced themselves, laughing with her, hugging her. They all walked toward a door. The room on the other side was dark, save for colored lights spinning around and the live band breaking down their set, amplifiers and microphones humming in the air. The room was wider than it was deep; several metal pillars supported its low ceiling. With the flood of teenagers, noise, and pulsing lights and darkness, the room could have been mistaken for a basement club.

Welcome Back, Real Life! glowed the fluorescent orange banner in the dark. Several more teenagers bumped into Vanessa, all welcoming and hugging her. As she approached the back of the crowd near the small stage at the front of the room, she and Tim were separated. She stood by herself in a green light that somehow had stopped spinning and landed on her. But the girls and the boys around here kept swirling like froth in a green sea, and although she wanted to be with Tim, for a moment she wondered if coming here was a stupid idea; for a moment she wanted to leave the crowd that orbited around her and to slip from the slow pricking of time and strangers whom she may never meet again.

A coldness bit her arm. "Hey," Tim said, his voice cutting through all the other noise. He pressed an icy can against her elbow. "I was trying to get your attention over there at the snacks. I know you like Coke. Is that good?"

"Yes, thank you," she said, smiling at him and wanting to stay.

"What do you think?"

"I can't believe this. There's so many people here."

"Yeah. Back to school is always insane. I mean, I hate to sound this way, but the first few weeks, especially this back-to-school party, is huge because it's free food and drinks and music and everyone brings their friends, and they bring their friends. Ken's over there. He's our youth pastor." On his tiptoes, Tim craned his neck past the crowd. "See the guy who has on the t-shirt, jeans, and a blazer? Looks like Keanu Reeves a little bit?"

Vanessa craned her neck over two boys with baseball caps on. "Are his ears pierced?"

"Yeah. He's awesome."

"I've never seen a pastor with earrings."

"He was in a rock band for a while."

The lean, tall, youthful-looking man smiled as he greeted several teenagers with hugs before stepping away from the crowd and onto the stage.

"What does he play?"

"Guitar and piano, and he sings. In fact, he's getting ready," Tim said, staying on his tiptoes and stretching his neck more.

"Hey, Real Life! Welcome back!" the microphone echoed as Ken slung an acoustic guitar over his chest and tightened the black strap, which was decorated with a large silver cross.

The crowd erupted.

Ken smiled, and his teeth and earrings glistened under the stage lights. As he strummed his guitar, his hair dangled in front of his face. He would stop, strum again, stop, and then adjust the microphone or tune his guitar strings, and each time, he winked or fluttered his fingers at the people around him. He closed his eyes for several seconds, and when he opened them, he stared at a point in front of him and began to sing a slow ballad.

As Tim sang along with the voices surrounding her, the song moved Vanessa, not because she knew the song but because the lyrics had nothing to do with sin or salvation, heaven or hell, or anything that she had heard Calderon fire from his mouth. The simple pleas for a place of acceptance washed over her. At first, she was frightened by the song's repetitions overcoming her, but she surrendered to the sounds and the voices as they swelled from the blue light and haze at the front and rested inside her before gathering her again and slowly lifting her up and out. Several of the kids around her raised their hands, closed their eyes, and cried, and she felt that she had reacted too harshly, judged them and this place too quickly; that they must be feeling the same things she was feeling; that they were momentarily less alone here because they had a place in the world that they could call their own. She glanced at Tim who had his eyes closed while he sang. She lifted her hands slightly; her mouth moved with the song's chorus repeated by Ken and the crowd. Tim opened his eyes and smiled at Vanessa.

The youth pastor stopped strumming his guitar but remained at the microphone, his eyes closed, his right hand in the air, cocked at the elbow, the green pick glowing in his fingers. The music had stopped, but Ken and the crowd kept singing. After several repetitions of the chorus, he opened his eyes, stopped singing, and said in a tranquil, waking-from-sleep voice, "Oh wow, you guys." He faintly strummed his guitar. "God is awesome, you guys. God is so, so awesome. Beautiful, beautiful, everyone," he said, wiping sweat and tears from his face, handing his guitar offstage.

Laughing and wiping their own eyes, the crowd whistled, cheered, and hugged each other.

"What a song, what a day, what an evening!" he said louder, the microphone amplifying his energy. "Look at y'all. So much love out there. I can feel it up here. Look at my hands…shaking. I feel God and the Holy Spirit present right now. It's so powerful, you guys. It's really so, so powerful." His laughs thumped through the amplifier and the light that had changed from ocean blue to a soft, natural light. He adjusted his hair over the collar of his blazer before pulling down his white t-shirt. He removed his blazer, which brought on whistles and hollering from the crowd. Chuckling and shaking his head in response, Ken paced back and forth along the stage with the cordless mic.

Their knees touching, Vanessa sat cross-legged next to Tim. They smiled at each other.

"Hi, y'all!" Ken offered the crowd a big bow. He tucked his t-shirt into his jeans and adjusted his silver belt buckle. When he lifted his arms, the fabric around his underarms was wet. "Let's just jump right into it, OK? Ecclesiastes 11:9 says, 'You who are young, be happy while you are young, and let your heart give you joy in the days of your youth. Follow the ways of your heart and whatever your eyes see, but know that for all these things God will bring you into judgment.'" Ken closed his Bible. "I'll never forget the first time I read those words. I was on the road with my band, near Austin. My band, by the way, was called Heart Surgeon," he said with a change of pace and tone in his voice. "Let me repeat that for you, in case you didn't hear me correctly or if you want to buy our discontinued music. *Heart Surgeon*." He grimaced in disgust, egging on the crowd's laughter. "Anyway, we wanted to stop at this hotel near where we'd be playing that night. We wanted to drop off some things. Checkbooks, clothes, *manners*. You know, stuff rock stars don't need."

The crowd laughed and smiled.

"One of the guys was from around there, went to high school there, and he knew some friends who were still around. He calls them up, they come over with, I mean, everything you can imagine. Food, beer, booze, drugs…and, of course, *women*." Ken pulsed his eyebrows up and down and raised his hand until his wedding ring shimmered. "And at that point in my life, I was starting to question my life, my own place in this world, wondering about God and heaven and hell. I knew what was right and wrong in my heart, and yet I also *willingly* took hold of sin, and in turn, it took a hold of me, and I sure as hell didn't want to end up in the wrong place, excuse my language."

The crowd laughed.

"I sat on this old, mangy couch on this guy's back porch. I don't even remember who this guy was, but he was a buddy to a buddy to my buddy in the band. You know how that is. But I do remember two things about that night." Ken pointed his left finger in the air. "*One*, the fireflies glowing outside in the backyard. Don't ask me why I remember them, but I do. I have my own personal reasons why. It has a lot to do with my life and who I was at that time and what I *thought* I wanted. I've spent many minutes contemplating why such a beautiful thing of nature affected me so, right then and there. And *two*, this girl who was kissing me up and down my neck." Lowering the mic, he said, "Not you, honey. My beautiful wife over there."

The crowd turned toward the back. The dark-haired woman sitting in a chair reminded Vanessa of some of her teachers with their approachable faces and welcoming demeanors, but she looked nothing like the images of a rock 'n' roller's wife.

"I've improved since that time," Ken chuckled. "Love you, honey." He puckered his lips at his wife, who puckered back. "Anyway, I had a fifth of whiskey in one hand, several beer cans at my feet, a joint ready to be lit in my other hand, and this girl…and those fireflies glowing and getting me to look *out there*. And, guys, I just *felt numb* all over." He stiffened on stage like a corpse. Scratching his whiskers, he continued, "I needed *direction*. But more importantly, my actions were going to be judged in the eyes of God. Which direction was I headed in? Which way, you guys, did I want to go? I didn't know. I thought I knew, but I really didn't. That's how it is. You *think* you know. You think you've got it all figured out. You start out, and then, WHAM!" Ken clapped the microphone with the palm of his hand.

The crowd jumped and laughed.

"But then you find yourself in these situations that make you question the direction you were on. Like those fireflies, you have a *purpose*, not just floating around aimlessly...to have this guiding light *inside* you. A different kind of direction." His voice lowered and softened as he held up his Bible. "That night, I thought, 'What am I doing? What am I doing with my life? Where am I headed? But more importantly...*why*? Why go one way versus going another way?' Meaning and direction. I need to be pointed toward something bigger than my own little desires." He smiled and paced along the stage before stopping on the left side. "I went back to the hotel room before the concert, after this party. I actually called a taxi because I wanted to be alone, and there was no way, *no way*, anyone from that party could have gotten their act together and driven me. And when I got back to the hotel room, I randomly opened this little Bible I had with me. I'd been carrying it around on that tour after my best friend from high school had accepted Jesus into his life. This verse, y'all, this verse was it. Random guiding light...but not really." He paused and looked into the crowd.

Vanessa felt that he stared at her.

"I felt a connection. I felt a power in my heart and in that hotel room. I felt renewed. *But* I had to return to the life in front of me. You can't run, and you can't always take a new path, but you can change your direction on that road. Can't avoid things. Can't avoid what's in front of you. See, I had a job to do, be a musician, honor contracts and the tour and studio time and all that. A newly forged Christian in a secular band, guys. Me. I had a new light guiding me, one that was inside of me the whole time, starting a teeny-tiny glow. But the direction I was heading in, the direction I was being *led* in, had nothing to do with that kind of music or lifestyle." He chuckled as he shook his head. "We wanted to be the next big rock band. Radio. MTV. Come on, not going to happen, especially with that name. Heart Surgeon."

The crowd laughed.

"See, rather than *falling down* with that world, being part of it, I needed to be lifted *out* of it. I needed to find what would *lift me up*. Direction. Pointed *up*. Being responsible for my own actions and choices. Jesus. That's what lifted me up. You see, the world matters to God, and you in the world, your place in it, matters to God, too. Let's pray, y'all."

Vanessa closed her eyes and listened to the prayer. In her head, she saw her father and mother and the city park near the bakery where she liked to read or watch the ducks paddle across the pond. She saw Tyler Herrarra, who, she knew, liked her and knew she was off and on with Jacob. Spending time with Tim over the summer and deciding to come here, she worried that her girlfriends would continue teasing her, would call her vendida—a coconut, brown on the outside, white on the inside. She saw Tim in her head, his gangly arms and legs, and his mop of hair. She saw her school. She saw her parents. She saw everything in her head but the things she was supposed to see during the prayer.

"Amen," Ken said.

A hundred teenage voices replied, "Amen."

"OK, y'all ready?"

The crowd whistled and hollered.

"We have a special presentation from our very own Tim Baxter!" Ken extended his arm toward the middle of the crowd, where Tim took a deep breath and waved to everyone. He blushed when he made eye contact with Vanessa, who beamed back at him.

As Ken stepped offstage, a projector screen lowered in front of the crowd, and the room's only light was a floating square. Vanessa glanced at Tim. He kept his chin steadied at the screen, and sitting on the floor, he had rolled himself into a cross-legged ball and had wrapped his arms around his knees. A video player clicked on behind them, and the screen scrambled from blank, bright white to black with The Screwtape Videos looming in red gothic letters and, on the very next screen, By Tim Baxter – With Apologies to CS Lewis.

A fly-like creature walked into frame and sat at a table in a dining room with a large sliding-glass door behind him and, on his right, a brick room-divider and fireplace. "Good morning, Uncle," he said. Gray and black paints caked his human-shaped hands; blood-red polish coated his fingernails. The camera panned to the left and passed over a family portrait of Tim sitting with his brother and his two young sisters, all wearing matching Fourth of July t-shirts.

The uncle unfolded a newspaper—"*The Devil's Times*" was glued over the real newspaper's title. The nephew stuffed a napkin in his collar. As the camera pulled back, the uncle was dressed in khaki pants, a navy jacket with gold buttons along the cuff, a light-blue dress shirt, and a tie patterned with maroon and gold squares. His long claws clinked a fork and a knife. Yellow eyes highlighted his demon head. Behind him, two little girls paraded into the scene. They sat their dolls on pink chairs and placed a teapot and cups on a small table in front of the backyard's playhouse.

The uncle and the nephew debated the pros and cons of popular culture and media. "It's our duty to always remind humans to be obedient to their idols," the uncle said, his voice squawking as the teenage actor tried to sound diabolical.

"We're so winning! No one can stop us!" the nephew yelled, pumping his fist and buzzing the camera's microphone.

"Actually, you can be stopped," a man's voice said off-camera.

The uncle and nephew stared at each other. One of the uncle's fangs popped out.

Ken walked into the frame with a Bible in his hand and a guitar over his shoulder. He started to play his guitar and sing. The uncle and nephew covered their ears and moaned. Zooming in on the nephew, the camera shook violently, and the screen blurred until he disappeared in smoke. The youth pastor smiled at the camera and, like a rifle, pointed the head of his guitar at the uncle. Covering his ears, the demon shivered and, in the next scene, turned into sawdust sitting in the chair. A plastic bag held by human hands and covered in sawdust quickly left the scene.

A Bible verse appeared—Romans 12:2. Credits rolled. Holding their dolls up high as they slid down the playhouse slide to their tea party, the little girls in the background froze in the clip as the words rolled over them.

"Give it up for Tim, y'all!" Ken yelled once the whir of the video player stopped.

The crowd cheered and turned toward Tim.

Vanessa covered her mouth while laughing and watching him blush and smile.

"Thank you," Tim said, slowly standing up. "Um, thank you to Pastor Ken for letting us do this and being in it, and to, um, Scott and John for being in it. My parents for the house and, um, for not being in it. But apparently my little sisters were in it. And, oh, um, thanks to Video Plus, Lisa's dad works there. He was a big help. Thanks for letting us use your video equipment." Tim waved and sat back down in a swarm of high-fives, smiles, and hugs.

As the crowd thinned from the youth-group building and moved into the parking lot, Vanessa waited until she could stand next to Tim. "You're famous now," she said, leaning against the metal handrail. "It was so cool what you did. You're really talented."

"Thanks," he said, blushing and acknowledging more hand slaps and praises that passed him. "There were some mistakes." Tapping a notebook and shaking his head, he became serious.

"You can fix them the next time. I think it was all awesome, and so did everyone else. You wrote and directed that and made all those creatures?"

"Yeah, it's this thing I like to do. I remember the first time I saw *Legend* and was floored. I really love movies."

"I haven't seen that. But I love movies, too."

"I remember we talked about that. Your abuelita liked all those old movies."

"Yeah." Vanessa curled her hair behind her ear. "Have you made other movies?"

"Mostly with my friends. Home movies and this one project for tenth-grade English class last year. My buddies Abe and Bobby and I made this serial killer movie. We had the main character, Fred, be this crazy killer who uses a hammer, a saw, and a nail gun, but during the day he's a normal guy...like, an office manager. But when he hears this certain song, he transforms into the serial killer."

"Like *Jekyll and Hyde*."

"Exactly. We found this creepy children's sing-along song at a thrift store. We played it on this record player that Bobby's mom has. I don't know what it was, but it was creepy. Out-of-tune piano and these children singing."

"I totally would have let you borrow my dad's record player."

"Yeah? That'd be cool. Anyway, um, the story is that his dad played this song when he was drunk and smacked around Fred."

"That sounds horrible. This was for English class?"

"Just wait. So, Fred grows up and controls his pain by killing people. That song releases him, I guess. Makes him feel better." Tim shrugged. "So, yeah, it's like *Jekyll and Hyde*. But the last scene, where Fred kills his dad, is totally taken from 'Tell-Tale Heart.' He chopped him up and put him in the floor of the room and hears the beating of his heart. And *that's* the English-class part."

"I love that story."

"Yeah, me too. It's a good one. But, we got a B-plus."

"A B-plus! I bet it was awesome. Why?"

"Mrs. Overstreet said it was gory and showed literary influences but was too disturbing to watch. The themes were too adult, I guess."

"That's lame."

"Yeah, I know. It's OK. She told me after class that I showed a lot of talent with the special effects."

"Nail gun?" Vanessa scrunched her face.

"That was a fun one. I took one of those Styrofoam heads you sometimes see with wigs on them. I painted it, put some flesh on it and hair, of course."

"Flesh?"

Tim laughed, "Yeah, fake flesh. Then I had Abe shoot the gun into it. We had this cool worm's-eye view, from the back of the head, looking up at Abe…Fred. I was off-camera, but I pumped fake blood, and you could see it trickle out from the cheeks and temples. Pretty cool."

"Disgusting."

"Thanks. We had so much blood. I made buckets and buckets that day. That circular-saw scene was pretty fun, too. And whenever the song came on, I made up Abe's face with lots of scars and bruises and dark skin. Ever seen *Jekyll and Hyde* with John Barrymore?"

"No."

"We should see it. Um, anyway, it was like that. Simple but effective. I gave him this big scar from one lip up to his cheek." Tim hooked a finger in his mouth and pulled up.

Vanessa squished her nose.

"Is that your dad?" Tim nodded toward the parking lot. "He's been sitting there ever since we came out, and he's been looking at us every now and then."

Turning, Vanessa sighed. "Yep, that's Mr. Ochoa." She waved at the truck and its rusted top sticking up among the shiny hoods of cars and SUVs.

"I guess that means you need to go. Tell him I said hi."

"I will."

"It was really nice to see you again. I'm so glad you came."

"Same here. I didn't know what to expect. It was pretty powerful, and I'm really glad that you were here."

Tim looked at the concrete floor and then at her. "I glad we got to hang out this summer. I would have done it more if I didn't have that mission trip." His blushing intensified his pockmarks.

"Me too. It was fun."

"I want to come back to the bakery and hang out with you and sketch that wall. The Aztec Wheel of Time."

"I'll get us some good coffee and marranitos, the gingerbread I told you about."

Tim twisted on the balls of his toes. "We should go out sometime...hang out at some place other than...the, um, bakery. A movie. We both like moves. See one...a movie...together."

Vanessa smiled. "I'd like that."

"There's, um, *The Island of Dr. Moreau* with Val Kilmer or *Bordello of Blood*. Or *Independence Day* at the dollar theater."

"How about *A Time to Kill?*"

"The courtroom thing?"

Vanessa laughed and nodded.

"Hmm, yeah, OK, drama. OK, sure. That'll be good." Tim cleared his throat. "See you next Sunday?"

"I think so."

"There's Bible study on Wednesdays, if you want to come to that too. I go to those. They're fun. Different house each week."

"OK, sounds good. See you soon."

"Yeah, definitely."

They moved in to hug, and as they got closer, her father's truck rumbled and a group of kids burst out of the building.

"There he is. Man of the hour!" Chris hollered with several girls and guys following him. "We're getting something to eat. You're in, right?" He looked right at Tim, who looked around. Vanessa stood at the truck.

"I said I'd call you when I was ready," she huffed, slamming the door shut as she glanced at the teenagers.

"I got here early." Her father pushed his ball cap back and looked at the crowd. "I was out, getting some supplies for the store. Did you have a good...?"

"It was fine," she quickly interrupted.

"What did you do?"

"Sang, talked about God, watched a cool movie Tim made." She watched Tim merge with the teens piling into Chris's Mustang.

"That boy from the bakery?"

"Yes."

"I thought I saw him. Your mom said he came in every day this summer." His smile broadened under his mustache.

"I know."

"Sounds fun. You did all that tonight?" He put the truck into drive, the gears grinding.

Before Vanessa answered, she stared at where she had been. After Tim's movie was over, one of the college-aged leaders counted everyone off and broke them into small groups. Vanessa was in the sevens; Tim was in the eights, but he sat across from her group so she could see him. It grounded her, made her feel more like warm, soft flesh than cold, hard stone overlooking the air. The leader asked her circle if any of them found it difficult to follow God's unique plan for each of them, to be in but not of this world, to follow a guiding inside light. Most of them found it challenging but said their hearts would always be tethered to the right Bible verse, pulling them back. Trap doors and false starts are all around, they acknowledged. They leaned forward for prayer, thanking each other for coming and sharing, hoping for better days out there, welcoming Vanessa, who smiled and felt overwhelmed again, like a clock changing direction, brought on by this circle that leaned forward on tiptoes, their arms linked across their backs, ready to jump into a new moment yet standing still in one place. "Yes," she answered her father.

"Bueno." He tapped her leg and pumped the truck a little gas. "Your mom has dinner ready. Hungry?"

"I am," she said, watching the Mustang rumble out of the parking lot. A caravan of cars stuffed with kids followed behind it. Her father's truck turned the other way. They were all headed in different directions.

11

But where? Where's the middle ground? she asked herself. Answering her own question was taking her all day. Tim's website glowed in front of her. She compared her scribbles in the margins of the printout of the FAQ page to the original source; neither of those answers helped her. The day slouched toward its end, the late-afternoon light dropping. The wind picked up. Shadows of bare tree limbs shimmied on her bedroom's wall like water. Vanessa looked out the window. One neighbor, stuffed in a coat, gloves, and stocking cap, waddled out of her condo and bantered with another neighbor who, in his t-shirt, shorts, and gloves, had returned from a run while steam lifted off his shoulders and bald head. They laughed at each other before waving goodbye. The neighbor across from Vanessa had not taken down the holiday lights and garland framing the balcony door. Beer cans and red plastic cups littered the balcony. The year, even though it was new, had shrunk a little more, its surface lower, its core softer. She returned to the FAQ page.

Why does a Christian company and artist make violent and demonic images?

Good question, and a fair one too! We're not making these products to glorify violence, evil, or Satan. We make these things to remind us of all the evil like this that exists right in front of us every day, because without them we wouldn't be led back to Christ, our rightful home.

Notes scattered around her and on the floor. She stopped typing because the winter light glared on her computer screen. Rotating her laptop on the mattress distorted her vision. Standing up made her woozy. She pulled the laptop to the edge of the bed and knelt, but the aches in her back and chest flared. She returned to her original position. In a matter of minutes, the sunlight would disappear behind the complex.

She rearranged her notes and uncapped her pen, striking through *NIGHT'S WATCH SFX PRODUCTIONS* on the About Us printout. She underlined a note about a new company name on her notepad, starring it and adding *#1* next to it but then realized it was already a major bullet point on another piece of paper that she had lost the other day. She massaged her hand. Underneath the stack of possible images, color palettes, and other drafts, the paper lay like a black-and-yellow wing folded in a white landscape.

About Us

Since 2009, Night's Watch has had the great pleasure of working alongside many individuals and organizations all across the USA committed to quality faith-based entertainment. We operate as a full-service SFX production company for stage, film, television, and live events, offering support from installation to performance to de-installation. We provide special effects makeup, prosthetic application, and prop fabrication to all facets of the film and television industry. Night's Watch SFX stands 100% behind our products. We take pride in offering product support and assistance to guide you through any project. We complete orders with quality and fast delivery. Discounts always available for churches and faith-based organizations. We also welcome inquiries from other interested parties. Thank you, we can't wait to work with you!

When she reached Contact Us and saw Tim's name in the email address, a pang fell from her head and a pang rose from her heart; she stopped reading. The burn in the middle of her chest faded. "Who's *we*, Tim? It's just you. It's *your* story." Nodding, Vanessa grabbed her pen.

How long have you been doing this?

Tim Baxter, the owner and creative director, has been making masks and prosthetics since he was in junior high. He saw *Legend* and *Aliens* and was hooked after that. He's self-taught but has received certifications from the special effects industry.

After striking the paragraph, she pressed her back against the wall of her bedroom. The coolness sank into the base of her skull. She read aloud what she had written, edited, and rewritten over the past several days, tackling each of her bullet points and the major areas she wanted to address—images, styles, fonts, media platforms, content. Theme was key, the hub to the spokes, the content around which everything else rotated. She flipped through her notes and the photos remaining on her laptop, ending on one from years ago in Denver. Warmth surged inside her and connected the shore of the present to the never-ending horizon of the future. Staring at the laptop's screen, she mumbled to the air, "I want it to be honest. No tricks." A second surge rose in her, more powerful and warmer than the first. The ache in her hands dissipated as she typed quickly.

Whether polishing a set of fangs, adding another layer of shellac, or balancing faith and career, Tim Baxter has never lacked imagination. He has always pursued the colorful and the unexpected while never forgetting where he came from and what matters most to him. Influenced as a teenager by classic monster movies and 1980s horror and science fiction films, he spent hours honing his skills and unique vision in his parents' home. Baxter's foundation was laid in school as well as in church, where he produced videos for the youth group, an opportunity he considers a blessing and the chance to acquire a workshop mentality. Developing his talents and vision organically, outside of Hollywood and New York City, has also been a vital part of his process; it has allowed his creative sensibilities to shine and reflects the vibrancy of his eclectic portfolio and the growth of his spiritual journey.

Since his formative years, Baxter has been thrust onto the stage as a rising star in the special effects industry. The Tulsa native has gained a reputation for creating potent content and working with a keen eye and an open heart and mind. He has provided immersive environments for Christian haunted houses seeking an authentic, raw, and real expression of modern life and its relationship to Scripture. Partnering with faith-based production companies big and small, he has found his imagination stretched and his faith invigorated. His work has received strong, positive responses and accolades from industry leaders, collaborators, and fans, proving that Baxter's talents impact everyone who comes into contact with them.

Baxter has embraced the triumphs and challenges of working exclusively for faith-based organizations, and he is ready to push himself and his newly formed company into the mainstream world of entertainment. His experiences in special effects production and Christian culture qualify him to build a bridge between these two markets. Providing solutions for all clients and their needs is a privilege for him. Baxter has established relationships with his clients that go beyond prosthetics, glue, and paint. Regarded as real, authentic, and transparent, that connection with people sets him up for the next stage of his career where one thing is for certain: Tim Baxter always delivers a vibrant product that is entertaining, memorable, and of the highest quality. He loves sharing his talent with people, and standing in the intersection of art, faith, and commerce, he and his company are poised to become a crossover sensation, his gifts transcending boundaries and making him a household name. This is only the beginning.

Her eyes clenched; her fingers and knuckles tingled. The winter light slid itself between two end units of the complex, sealing the walls and the air between them. And then an answer hit her as quickly as the other content had hit her. *What I make is not all serious, and it's not all silly. It's a little bit of both. But the reason I do what I do is what matters the most. And when I return to that, everything falls into place.* When Tim said it to her months ago, she told him that this was his starting point and that he had to move with it before it vanished.

She quickly typed and then reached the bottom of her to-do list for the day. Most of the list had been crossed off, except for *Follow-up w/ Dr. – 2 PM the 6th.* Staring at those words, she added underneath them *Print off T's Portfolio and News.* In the darkness of her room, she sniffled while glancing at the laptop's clock; her eyes watered. She read Tim's answer again but stopped because of her headache or the light or because she lost her train of thought, the hour of fog and mist seeping into the bays of her body. Massaging the base of her neck and tightening her sweater, she read the answer again and cried because it had been given to her and that she had to write it before it drifted away, because it had drained any energy floating in her that could helped capture and steer it.

Her eyes drying, her breath calmer, she stared at the quote and all the work she had done, hit Save again, and then moved the folder to the desktop, just in case it took her another day to find it buried in her computer, open it, and do this all over again. She had spent New Year's Eve deleting files that she no longer needed, nearly emptying the computer of all that it was designed to hold. She slowed over the words *his newly formed company.* Vanessa thumbed through her sketches, notes, and ideas. She found the Bible verse that she had drawn stars around. She had found the name of Tim's new company in that verse. She had forgotten that she had already found it. It took her all day.

✸

The driveway leading to Tim's house lengthened more than Vanessa recalled when she had been over by herself. The previous day's ice storm had pulled down some small branches of the big tree in the front yard, and the salt melt that Tim used on the driveway and sidewalk remained as white swirls crushed in the dark concrete.

Roberto idled behind Tim's car, the headlights exposing the loss of red paint on the trunk, and commented about the model and make and that it probably had a carburetor, which reminded him of the old truck and its carburetor that required him waking earlier than usual on cold winter days in order to start it. "Wasted so much gas just sitting there," he chuckled. "And I didn't get warm."

Cold slicing through her coat, gloves, and scarf, Vanessa barely heard him. She stared at the wipers scraping the February air from the windshield, the heat of the car turning it into frosty pearls that glistened on the glass, her body fully aware of time melting and sloughing off. She gazed toward the brick house. Tim's shadow stretched across the living room's wall.

Roberto kissed her hand and turned off the car. "Come on, mi corazon."

His smile snapped her from her haze and nausea.

Keeping an eye on their footing as ice crunched under them, they walked up the sidewalk. The curtains of the large front window were pulled open, and silhouetting the couch in front of the window, a warm yellow light filled the living room. Tim's shadow on the wall shortened, lengthened, and shortened again as he moved from the kitchen, where steam curled around the corner, and into the living room. Roberto and Vanessa huddled in the cold under the front door's small roof. When Tim saw them and smiled, her breathing swayed.

"Hey! Come on in." He finished pulling on his blue fleece and extended his arm toward the living room; the glass to the screen door fogged up as soon as he held it open for them. "Mr. Ochoa, sir." He patted Roberto's shoulder. Baking bread, the smell of cooking pasta, and an old house greeted them; the weight of the evening pulled them all inside.

"Hello, Timothy. Thank you for having us over." After removing his gloves and shaking hands, Roberto handed Tim a bottle of red wine.

"It's the perfect time for all of us to get together." Kissing Vanessa, Tim said, "Hi."

"Hi," Vanessa replied while hugging him and glancing at her father, who nodded at her. Her right thumb and forefinger twitched.

"Have a seat." Tim motioned to the couch under shelves of books, comics, role-playing games, and action figures. "Drinks? I have Pacifico, Roberto."

"That would be great. Thank you."

"Wine?" Tim asked Vanessa.

"Please." She tucked her greasy hair behind her ear and tugged her sweater from her chin, the red turtleneck amplifying her swollen pale skin. She wore no makeup; her eyes were baggier, her face and body stringy in some spots, lumpier in others.

"Cheers."

"Cheers," Roberto and Vanessa replied.

"How was everyone's day?" Tim asked.

"We got a Facebook page now and a Twitter account for the store. She's been handling all that," Roberto said, smiling at Vanessa as she stared at the wood floor and sipped her wine. "She's much better with that than when she was a teenager."

"She's a good employee?"

"She's late, she complains all the time, she wants this, that." Roberto chuckled. "But I can't fire her. You should swing by and buy up all our coffee and sweets, just like you used to do."

"Do you still have the Aztec symbols?"

"We would collapse from inside if we didn't."

Leaning back in the recliner, Tim said, "I finished some mockups for a digital series I'm working on. Iraq and Afghanistan vets return home and deal with PTSD. I'm designing flesh wounds for flashback sequences."

"He's the lead-effects guy, Dad."

"Congratulations."

"Thanks. It's a good gig. This same company also produces a Western, and it looks like I'll be contracted for that, too. I feel very blessed. Vanessa is helping me rebrand myself." Tim grinned at them. "Should we give her her birthday presents?"

Roberto nodded as his thumb circled his beer bottle.

Tim sprang from the recliner and flicked on the light in the second bedroom. Movie posters—*Metropolis*, *King Kong*, and *Pan's Labyrinth*—hung over the desktop computer alongside production stills, sketches, and a printer. He returned to the living room with two brightly wrapped presents.

"You didn't need to," Vanessa croaked.

"This one's from me." He tapped the larger one and kissed her cheek. "Happy birthday."

She peeled open the floral paper; the gold ribbon twisted around her finger before spiraling to the ground. "*La Perla*."

Roberto's eyes lit up. "Ah, that's a classic. Pedro Armendáriz and María Elena Marqués. Steinbeck. Good stuff."

"You said it was one of your favorite movies based on the book."

"I did," she mumbled to Tim, wiping her eyes and clutching the DVD. The memory of her saying that to him was unrecognizable under slower blood, cold swirling in her body, and the small lights pulsing behind her eyes.

"The other one's from your dad and me."

The second present was no bigger than a deck of cards; a silver bow looped over the printed flowers on the box's edges. "A thumb drive," she chuckled. "For me or the store?"

Roberto smiled as Tim plugged the thumb drive into his laptop and, pivoting the computer toward the open space of the living room, pushed play. Small speakers on the shelf above the couch crackled.

After several seconds of popping and scratching, like an old record, the microphone thundered, and a tentative but deep male voice spoke, weaving in and out of Spanish and stilted English. *Hello…hello…OK.* The microphone thumped again. The voice whispered to someone close by. *I will, yes. Uh, hello. My name is Roberto Luis Ochoa, and I am thirty-years old. I am the proud father of Vanessa Rosa Ochoa, who is… How old are you, Essa?* The voice of the young girl giggled and spoke faintly. *Eight. Wow, you are getting so old. Me too.*

"Oh my God." Vanessa quickly covered her mouth.

I have a story of when I was a young boy, Roberto's younger voice continued, clicking and popping. *I got scratches and cuts all up and down my legs and arms when I wandered off by myself near dusk near the tiny village where I grew up. I followed my oldest brother to the river. He told me that I couldn't go where he went, but I did anyway. I waited until he left, and I could see the top of his head walking down the road. My younger sister was playing close to the road, and she said, 'He said he's going to the capital, and we're not allowed to go with him.' 'Well, I am,' I told her. So I followed him far behind so he wouldn't see me. When he stopped, I stopped. When he moved, I moved. I trailed him until I looked up and he was gone. I thought I saw his footprints and followed them, but they led me to the river and the brush. I went through the brush, but they scratched me. I saw the river. It was dry and low. The drought was so strong that year I could have walked across. I thought my brother had tricked me and crossed to the other side. But it was near dark, and I was cold and hungry. I walked back through the brush again, and the thorns scratched me again all over. I got home late, and my father, your abuelo, spanked me and gave me no dinner at first. I told him I was sorry, and he made me wait for dinner. He pulled my brother out, and at first, my brother laughed at me and told me he had watched me from afar at the river. His face and body were scratched, too. Our father told us how foolish we had been. He cleaned our scratches and fed us dinner, telling us, 'Those thorns will teach you a lesson,'* the younger Roberto laughed.

The mic thumped as her father handed it off. *Hi, my name is Flora Maria Ochoa. Before that I was Flora Maria Guardado. I am Roberto's wife and Vanessa's mother. I am twenty-six years old.*

Vanessa's hands shook in her lap; cold spread across her body.

Listen, someone, someday may ask you who you are and where you are from. Don't let anyone scare you. You are an American. Flora cleared her throat. *I love the old stories of the old days. Your abuelita, my mother, had so many she liked to tell. If I had gone to university, I would have studied history because I love it so much. A lot of people these days don't care for these old stories, but I do. I think they're important, even if they're not all true. Your abuelita was an amazing woman. Mestizaje, that mixed blood of hers. She told lots and lots of stories. My grandmother, your great grandmother, and your great-great grandmother knew many stories, many things that are forgotten or considered foolish these days. They were very smart women. And they loved the church, but they loved those old stories too…maybe a little more than the church.*

Vanessa saw her mom smiling while she held the mic.

I love those old stories too. They remind me of some of the stories you've been reading, Essa. The books your papá will pick up for you. Talking animals. Magic. Miracles. Good stories. Old stories about the old days. Her mom cleared her throat, and Vanessa saw her mother's eyes staring hard on the horizon as she waited for the story to flow from her. Flora paused many seconds before speaking again. *Abuelita always started her stories with 'When I was a little girl…' or 'A long, long time ago…' and you knew she was about to tell something about maybe a saint or La Virgen or maybe something Father Aarón did that week. She always had tales about him. She liked Father Aarón quite a lot, but she knew he liked to drink too…a lot.* Her mother chuckled. *But she enjoyed the old tales, and I did, too. Your abuelita knew many things. Her hair was black like a raven. She squinted all the time, especially as she looked up into the sun when she spoke. Her voice wobbled when she spoke, but her words were clear. She used her hands to emphasize certain words or things in her stories. She was short, but she had a presence about her, and we all knew when she had entered a room. When I was a little girl, I would sit close to her on the floor and become lost in the stories she told, often looking at her while she talked. She wore average clothes, not too large, not too small, just right for a woman of her age and size and where she stood in the world. Plain, solid colors, dresses, panty hose, but she had a shawl draped over her all the time. It didn't matter if it was summer or winter. That shawl was draped over her. Your father started calling her Josef, especially when he felt ornery.*

Roberto grinned.

One day I asked him, 'Why do you call Nanna Josef? Her name is Josefina,' and I scrunched my face at him. I did not like his joke all the time.

'Escudo de muchos colores,' he said. *Her shawl was like a rainbow, just like Joseph's, and she wore it all over the town, especially to the movies. She loved those old movies. I know when my father died she wished she'd run into Pedro Infante.* Flora chuckled. *She would wear her long gray hair rolled at the top in a moño, and she would wear old lady shoes with taconcitos that tick-tacked on the pavement.*

After a long pause and crackling on the microphone, her mother said, *I want to tell you one story about Coyote. The Aztecs believed Coyote the trickster was the god of music, dance, and mischief. There is Coyote who helped us cross, then there is Coyote who is a trickster. Your abuelita and her abuelita knew all about Coyote the trickster, and this is one story they liked to tell.*

A long, long time ago, in the beginning of this world, there was no such thing as Death. And there were so many people that Earth had no room for any more. The chiefs held a council to determine what to do. First Man rose and said he thought it would be a good plan to have the people die and be gone for a little while, but then they could return, if they wanted to. As soon as First Man sat down, Coyote jumped up and said, 'I don't like that not every living thing doesn't have to die. Birds come back to the people, flowers come back to the people, even people can come back to the people. They have no other place to go. I propose we make a new rule. Any person who dies is dead forever, and no one can ever see that person again.' The council disagreed. First Woman asked, 'Who does not want to see their loved ones again, like the birds or the flowers?' Coyote pointed out that this world is not big enough to hold all the people, and that if the people who died came back to life, there would not be enough food or water. But this was not enough, and the council voted to keep people from dying. Well, Coyote did not like this. So he decided to trick us, because he can't help himself. He is who he is. He convinced First Spirit to walk down the Lonely Road. Coyote had covered the end in smoke so that First Spirit would not see the cliff dropping off into the Land of the Dead.

Coyote set up two hollowed-out stones for First Spirit, one filled with food, the other water, and he said, 'Eat and drink, for the journey up ahead is long.' First Spirit thanked Coyote and continued walking until he fell off the cliff into the Land of the Dead, never to return again. Once he saw what he had done, Coyote became afraid and ran away. But he can't stop himself from doing this over and over again with each person on Earth. Coyote tricked us into eternal death, but he did not take responsibility. Coyote is everywhere. You just have to look around.

Paper rattled close to the mic, and her mom spoke softly. *And this is an old Aztec poem. 'We will pass away. Do we really live on Earth? Not forever on Earth. Only a brief time here.' And always remember, your mouth speaks of what your heart has inside.*

After the recording stopped, Vanessa wiped her eyes.

"Remember the Delgados?" Roberto asked. "You used to play with their youngest daughter."

"Yes," Vanessa whispered, seeing them stand outside the old RV down from Vida Nueva. Invisible hands pulled her deeper into her memory; the right side of her body trembled as those two little girls from the past laughed and played with her and their cheap plastic horses in the dirt and weeds. "But I can't remember her name."

"Danielle was the youngest. Estrella her sister and their brother Eduardo. They let us borrow that tape recorder from their English teacher. Your mom and I told stories on it. I gave them to Tim." He nodded at the thumb drive resting like a black jewel in the computer.

"You can put them on your computer or your phone," Tim said. "Wherever you are, you can listen to them."

"Thank you," she stuttered.

"Happy birthday. Te amo. I love you," Roberto mouthed, wiping his eyes under his glasses and standing up to kiss and hug her.

"Happy birthday," Tim joined in, holding her pinkie until she jumped at the sound of a timer beeping. "We're on in five," he said, heading into the kitchen.

Vanessa braced her palms against the seat of the chair. She wanted to stand up, but her muscles had not yet contracted. She grimaced and pushed herself up. Wobbling at the top, she nodded at her father, who nodded back and retracted his hands to help her. "I'm going to wash up."

"Are you...?"

"I'm fine," she cut him off and gingerly walked into the bedroom. The torso, resting in its bloodied and burned tuxedo on the other side of the door, frightened her. She tiptoed around giant plastic mushrooms, camouflaged helmets, a set of fallen fangs, and Styrofoam steps meant to look like they had been chiseled for an ancient city. The metal table in the middle of the room was very cold as she balanced against it. She grabbed a plastic folder from her coat. Before leaving, she looked at the poster of *Metropolis* with its gold paper, heavy black ink, and the two Marias split down the middle with a lightning bolt: one slept in her original flesh form; the other one was transformed and wide awake.

Sweating profusely, Vanessa made her way into the bathroom and quickly turned on the faucet to muffle the sound of her vomiting into the toilet. She splashed cold water on her face and held onto the sink's porcelain edges until the bathroom stopped spinning. She knew she was taking a long time before dinner, but she believed that her father and Tim could wait because the turkey she had prepared wasn't quite ready. She smelled it; she saw it shimmering in the oven because she believed that it was Thanksgiving again, and she had spent all afternoon preparing it for her father, Tim, and Dan, who would be joining them as soon as he flew in from Houston, where he had courted another high-profile client for MetaBrand. She froze, believing that she heard Dan arrive in the living room. Vanessa looked at herself in the mirror. The puffy, pale face with heavy, matte eyes staring back at her told her that the night was not Thanksgiving and that no turkey waited to be carved or stuffing to be served. She cried because she stood in Tim's house and because it was February with its bare trees, dead grass, and gray colors—everything frozen until spring. She trudged toward the small table under the kitchen window where Tim, her father, and a large bowl of chicken alfredo waited.

Tim blessed the food, saying how thankful he was that all of them could be together for the first time in the new year and on a very special day. "Thank you so much for how our paths crossed."

Roberto nodded gently.

"I have something for you," Vanessa said as they began eating.

Tim raised his eyebrows. He finished chewing and loosened the strap on the folder that she handed to him. An envelope, a piece of paper with designs printed on it, and a business card clipped to the paper sat in his hands. The designs on the piece of paper and the design on the business card matched, but the paper's designs were larger and identified the fonts and colors used in the designs as well as the names of the files. A large black wrench outlined in white lay in the middle of the smoke-gray business card; three white claw marks scratched the middle of the wrench. Above the wrench, stylized in Victorian-era font:

Not of This World SFX Productions
Tim Baxter, Owner

Tim's eyes widened as he looked at Vanessa, who smiled numbly. "What is this?"

"Your new logo. I'm still working on your website. I've got a few things left to do, but your story's in place."

"The colors, the font..." He flipped through the other papers in the folder. "You kept this." He pointed to the phrase *Tim attends Solid Rock Church and thanks everyone there for the opportunity to do this as a career.*

"It's who you are." She handed him a list of contacts, conferences, and upcoming events.

"Face and Body Art International? Professional Makeup Conference and Expo? Comic-Con?"

"You have a lot of work to do. People need to see your gift. You need to share it. Open the envelope."

Roberto kept his eyes on his food and folded his hands in his lap.

"That's a whole lot of zeroes." Tim stared at the check in front of him.

"It's my investment in your new company," she said. "You can only use it to branch out, cut yourself free a little. Market."

"*New* company?"

"MetaBrand sold."

"I can't believe this. Thank you." He hugged and kissed her.

"There's more."

Roberto wiped his eyes and nodded at Vanessa.

"What?"

"It's back," she said calmly.

"What?" Tim asked, looking at Vanessa and then at Roberto whose chest rose and fell rapidly.

"My cancer's back."

"Vanessa..." Tim touched her hand.

"It's much more aggressive than the first time. My survival rate, even if I opted for surgery, would be less than three percent."

"What do you mean *if* you opted for surgery?"

"I've decided not to do treatment or surgery. I'm still young enough that the rest of my body could hang on even though my brain is disappearing. I could suffer in a whole different way. It's not just my body. Who I am is slipping away."

"But that's... No. No," Tim's voice rose. "Roberto, tell her..."

"We have talked so much about this. Day after day, night after night. Every time we are together. She has weathered so much. I want her to be happy. I want her to have a life she wants." He looked at Vanessa. "She is not only mine. She is also her own. Mi pequeño sol. My little sun."

"But there are other options. A second or third opinion."

"Tim..."

"MD Anderson in Texas. It's close. I'll pay for it." Tim tapped the check.

"I would have to do it all over again. For what? A percentage? I'm going to go to California in the spring. That's where I want to be. I want to be close to the ocean...in it. I just want to go, Tim. I just want to go to this place I couldn't before that was so close to me and was taken away. I have to go to it."

"How will you get there? Drive? Fly? What happens if something happens to you on the way?"

"I've thought about this."

"You could go to California and have treatment. I'll go with you."

"But that's not living, Tim. It's machines and medications. I don't trust the physicians for my care. I don't want to live that way."

"You've known about this?" Tim looked at Roberto.

Roberto cleared his throat. "Yes."

"Is this why we're all having dinner? So the two of you could gang up on me?" His head rotated between Vanessa and Roberto. "I can't believe you approve."

Roberto dropped his napkin on the table as he scooted his chair out and stood up. "I should let you two talk in private." His weathered hand squeezed Tim's shoulder, and shuffling to Vanessa, he wrapped his arms around her. "Te amo. Te amo," he whispered, kissing her and heading for the living room.

Tim turned to Vanessa. "Why did you keep this from me?"

"I didn't want it to stop…us…this. I haven't been busy at the bakery. I stopped working full-time there earlier this year. I handle very little now. I've slowed down, and it takes me a while to process things in my head. I fainted at the bakery in the middle of morning rush-hour one day. I have to have a pencil and pad right next to me to talk sometimes. I have to write it down right away or else. And even then, I sometimes can't write. I lock up. I think I'm writing, but after a few seconds I'm not. I want some control, some meaning that's mine. It's not how I want to live, but I can't seem to escape it. I have to go with it, give myself over to it." Across from her, the basket of fruit on the kitchen counter burst with colors like birds in a cage; her body wobbled before she spoke again. "He went away."

"Who?"

"Dan."

"But I'm not Dan."

"I know, and I'm thankful for that. He'd be there by my bedside for hours, day in, day out, night after night. He'd work there for little bit, but then, it all went away. He started coming in less and less, said he was needed at work. He'd check his phone more. Soon after I got home and began recovery, it was too much. Maybe he saw me with no hair and this huge scar across my head and being fragile. I added more weight from the medications. I was fat and ugly.

"Vanessa…"

"It's true. I was not in the best shape. I told him I felt ugly. I told him that more than I told him how much physical pain I was in. I kept coming back to my appearance whenever I talked to him, that I felt I had to come back to that. I realized that's all we had between us. He could provide but not care for me. He got tired of being responsible for someone who wasn't returning on investment. He got tired of picking me up off the floor. We made time for each other when it had something to do with our careers. Why would we talk about anything else? All this comfort and immediacy. But it all went away." Her hands twitching, she stared at Tim. "He said he'd stick with me. He didn't. I affected his career. I needed… I looked to him for…what?"

Tim reached for her hand.

"After my colleagues found out, the work started drying up. I started getting fewer and fewer projects. All the ones I had floated away from under me. Fewer and fewer calls from clients and contacts. They started going to my colleagues. Looking back, I regret telling them. I had become The Cancer Patient. I didn't want to be that transparent. They claimed I wasn't productive anymore, which…they were right, to some degree. I was so livid at the time. The nerve of them defining what was productivity or who was productive." Spit glistened in the corners of

Vanessa's mouth. "After a while, my only correspondence with Dan was between our lawyers. But I actually want to talk to him. I'm no longer mad or afraid. I want to talk *to* him. So much had been lifted from me…so much." She looked up, as though she had lost her breath from being underwater, her hands paler from rubbing the back of her neck. "I gave him everything he wanted. The house, the cars, the boat, land for a cabin in the mountains. I don't care about those things. Everything except the sale of MetaBrand. I wanted liquidity. That's all. Liquidity and time."

"And you got it." He rubbed her palm.

"I did, but it took so much from me. Something told me to reach out to you this past summer. I wanted to see you again. I needed to. I had no choice, it felt like." She let out a long breath. "I'm dying, and medicine or surgery can only do so much. It could go on and on. My father is getting some of the money, too, for the bakery." She looked into the living room where Roberto sat on the far end of the couch; the pattern of the chair next to it reflected a little field of lights. Her father nursed his water and slowly flipped through the pages of one of Tim's movie-production books. "I didn't want to say anything until I knew what was happening to me, until I knew what I wanted to do. It came to me, settled on me the way things do sometimes. I wanted to see how one plus one adds up to two, not some other number. I wanted to know where I could take things. I didn't want this to dictate my life." Her pale hands raised in the air. "I've read about terminally ill people, and a lot of them, not all, go on these wild, lavish trips or buy cars or buy drugs. Not me. I just want to go to California…the cliffs and the Pacific. That's it. Nothing else. OK? Nothing else. Just something so simple." Her eyes watered as she looked at him. "There's this state park outside San Francisco. I've only seen pictures of it, but it's beautiful. I came so close to it once, driving with Dan when we were there for a tech conference. He talked about going, but we drove past it in so many ways." Vanessa shook her head as her brain throbbed. The memory faded and she remained quiet, but the ocean rumbled inside her. "I worried so much about piddling stuff, like my 401(k) or my appearance. My parents lived in fear every day, every night. I did too. For many years we lived in real fear. Every day, a knock on our door made them jump. Anytime a cop car drove by, anytime an unmarked car with dark windows drove by. They decided not to have any more children, for fear of losing them or not being able to support them. Their papers had not come in as quickly as they hoped or as quickly as Calderon promised. And then, we were granted amnesty because we had been in this country at the right time. They were good people to be given that opportunity. I was born here. I'm as red-white-and-blue as they get," she said, smiling and seeing the large American flag greeting the bakery's customers and a Mexican flag on the other wall opposite the Aztec Wheel of Time that her mom painted. "But it was still a very long process. All that red tape. It was like watching my father chase a very quick cat. Every time he'd move in for something, *whoosh!*" Her palms slapped apart. "That cat would take off in front of him. Gato rápido! Such a quick cat. He eventually caught it. Not more money, but everything turned out all right."

She saw the star-shaped cells in her brain's image, the doctor pointing out where they had metastasized and would extend over the next several months, maybe a year or more. "But then it was fear, real fear. I used to lay awake at night, worrying that it would come back, and then when I found out it had, I worried more, but then I imagined I had a box under my bed. And I actually believed at one point there was a *real* box under my bed because I reached for it. I imagined putting my worries into that box and then stuffing it under the bed. That worked for a little while, but then I pictured a cloud, and I put my worries into that cloud, way up there, high above." Her eyes fluttered up. "And I watched it swirl above my head. I was floating on my back. And then that cloud slowly floated up and away.

"There was a massive tornado that destroyed the small neighborhood where we lived in the trailer. But Calderon's church was spared. I remember the elementary school where I went was damaged, the monkey bars twisted over, the slide with branches in it, some windows broken. I think that was the time my parents were most scared. The tornado was one thing, but FEMA came. Only a handful of Calderon's flock was legal, not my parents at the time. I remember seeing my father shake, sitting on the curb. Someone called them mojadas. I had never seen him so scared in my life. He clutched me and my mother so hard that his hands left bruises on us. He would not stop kissing us. He had this big hat and a flannel shirt, his boots and jeans, and a little utility knife he clipped to his belt. He had a mustache, and my mother hated it." Vanessa turned toward Tim's living room; her mother stepped from the hallway, the second bedroom's door closing behind her, glided over the wood floor, and brushed her father's face and hair. "She said his mustache reminded her of hombres violentos. He was always up at four in the morning and didn't come home for dinner until after six. He'd eat, play with me, then quickly get ready for bed. Many times he danced with my mother in the middle of the trailer. She'd make him champurrado, and he would stop dancing at the right moments and take a swig from this cheap coffee mug she got at a pulga." Her father stood from the couch in Tim's living room and greeted Flora; their bodies swayed in the darkness with tiny stars glowing around them. "They are so close, touching, one of his hands on her waist, the other holding hers between their chests." Vanessa tightened her eyes and craned her neck as far as her muscles allowed. "Dad. Papá. What is your favorite Bible verse?"

In her vision, Roberto stopped dancing with Flora, who kept her face on his shoulder. Vanessa's father turned to her, sitting in the kitchen with Tim, and with his graveled voice replied in Spanish, "Matthew 25:35. 'For I was hungry and you gave me food, I was thirsty and you gave me drink, a stranger and you welcomed me, naked and you clothed me, ill and you cared for me, in prison and you visited me.'" Her father tapped his heart.

"Calderon gave hope. 'Como un rayo,' he said to me. Like lightning." Vanessa glanced at the kitchen's cracked ceiling. "He took us *all* in." Her hands circled invisible things falling around her.

Roberto looked up from his book and into the kitchen.

"Dominicans, Venezuelans, Nicaraguans, we all ended up celebrating Thanksgiving, Easter, Christmas, the World Cup, the Super Bowl, and of course, Día de los Muertos. Because who doesn't want to celebrate the Day of the Dead?" She stared at the small lights fluttering on the refrigerator and then at Tim. "How do some cupcakes sound? Or maybe some cochas or elotitos? How could you say no to this, right? La casa de mi madre. The home of my mother." She looked down; her hands were empty and held nothing sweet to offer Tim.

Tim began to speak but stopped.

"My father chases that elusive cat, the health inspector, the tax man, the refrigerator repair man who never shows up, some employees from the church who steal from us. Calderon tells us to forgive them. How could we not, right? And then, we have to get rid of it. Leave. They had this plan, talking about taking what was theirs, about the heavy tithes, about falsos espíritus. All those false spirits. Lavender..." Vanessa smelled it in the frosting pressed into her mother's apron. "I saw you that first time at the store and felt this need to go to youth group, even though I knew it was way out of my league. The first thing I remember was seeing a lot of clear-faced white girls with nice bodies and cars. I had none of that. It didn't matter. I liked my curves, but I really wanted a car. I felt that I had no choice but to go, to see you. My heart was pulled that way. Ah," she sighed, giggling, "you were a pimple-faced nerd."

"I still am," Tim said, laughing with her.

"I didn't have the right feelings for you. I couldn't give you the right feelings. And I can't give you those kind of feelings now." She swallowed as he nodded in agreement. "You made me feel safe and cared for, but I was so stupid, followed these other feelings. It doesn't matter. None of those boys from my high school have amounted to much. Some got into community college or the big state schools. One got in at Arkansas only because he played baseball. Jacob got arrested for stealing. But the ones who really stood out, the ones who are lawyers and business types, they're a handful. Three out of how many?" She looked at Tim for an answer, but he only shrugged. "I stayed in touch with them because we were the ones who didn't party or get into trouble." She stacked her knife and fork on her dish. "I couldn't tell you right away. The bakery is still around. All because of you, right? Your big mouth. My life has never stretched out before me like a straight road. There was a point when it actually got straight, but it wasn't right because somebody else gave it to me. There were no bends, and no bends that were my own. It was too perfect. There's a bend in it now, and I want to do something about it."

Tim stared at her and then closed his eyes.

"I love you because I have no choice," she said.

191

"I love you, too," Tim echoed. "I love you, no matter what happens to you or what you become."

As Vanessa stood up, she wobbled at the table; blood rushed between her head, heart, and legs. She stacked all the dirty dishes from the table and carried them to the sink. After several minutes of silence, Tim stood up. The chairs scraped the kitchen floor. He flicked on the light over the sink and turned on the hot water. Vanessa dipped her hands into the suds and steam. For several long minutes they washed dishes and said nothing as water ran and so much slipped between their hands.

"It's not about surviving," she said, to which Tim could only embrace her in those hours that had become pearl-like, harder, moving over them, emptying themselves into one source; hours that do not have the last word; hours that wait to be found and, when they are, lifted between two fingers into the oncoming light.

12

Vanessa knew the room well, a plain undecorated room, save for the large flat screen television attached to the longest of the four walls, the other walls slick and plastic-like, the power cords snaking up through a hole in the ceiling tiles. Executive-level personnel held their meetings here, and all of them sat at a long, narrow table in the middle of the room. During business hours and meetings, the flat screen was used for teleconferencing with clients on both coasts; the white backdrop of the walls erased anything resembling Colorado, Denver's downtown, or the size of MetaBrand.

After six on Friday evenings, after the bulk of the third-floor staff had left, sports, news, and the occasional viewing party of the most popular television shows took over. Vanessa didn't pay much attention to storylines, the scores, or the news, but she cheered, gasped, and judged with her colleagues, sharing frustrations and victories, big and small, that happened during the week or since they all got together last. Dan sat next to her, draped an arm across the back of her chair, tossed back fried okra, and washed it down with a beer, smiling all the while. He even sat aside his phone or laptop for the hour or two that they were there, pretending that the work that brought them all there, inside that warmly lit cube, was malleable and could be detached after certain hours and certain days.

Today she sat in one of the swivel chairs flanking the sides of the table with its conference phone flattened like a black starfish. A pen and a small yellow notepad bearing MetaBrand's logo waited for her. Three flights up, the windows overlooked cars and people weaving on downtown streets and sidewalks. Although she had seen snow, rain, sunshine, and the blaze of autumn trees, she always associated looking out the windows with spring light, no matter the season; she always thought of spring, nothing else. The summer could be blistering, or people on the sidewalks below could be bundled in thick coats and moving quickly through winter, but she would remember them when they strolled in jackets and through the returning colors of flowers and trees and the butterflies fluttering across the blue sky. She could see spring in the extremes.

And today Vanessa looked out the windows facing downtown because it was late spring, nearly summer, and the light coming in through the windows warmed and splashed a lively color on her face—a needed color, especially after she had to walk past the open offices and cubicles of her staff and coworkers, some smiling, some nodding, but all of them staring at her as she hobbled toward the conference room. She was the last to arrive for this afternoon meeting that was no longer a circulating rumor.

Her chair squeaking as she coughed, Vanessa feared that suppressing her cough would worsen it, so she let it out. She placed one hand on her head near the pain's source, the pink scar and where the staples had been, and brushed what new hair she had over it. Her hands flopped in her lap while her breathing relaxed. And although four of her colleagues, including Dan, surrounded her, she sat alone in the room.

None of the four sitting at the table looked directly at her, and she was very much aware that she looked like a ragamuffin wearing mismatched colors slipped in among starched shirts, slacks, and varying tones of business blues and blacks. Dave sat at one end of the table, where he always sat, putting him in a straight line to the television; Wendy from HR, notepad nearby, sat across from her; Jane, another executive, sat next to Wendy; and Dan sat with a corner of the table pressed into his ribs, his body angled away from the rest of them, one leg crossed over another, both arms folded across his chest. Vanessa stared at him. He would not look her way. He checked his phone until the meeting began. Trees blossomed in pinks and whites on the other side of the window behind him.

"Thank you for coming in, Vanessa," Dave said, as he scooted his chair to the table and adjusted his glasses. "We appreciate it." He maintained eye contact with a document in front of him. "And I can't tell you how glad we are that you are up and about and recovering..."

"That was months ago," she snapped. "You sent me a card and made a hospital visit. Just get on with this."

"We all want you to be healthy," he continued, leaning forward. "That's the first and foremost thing. Your health is so important to us."

"Oh, for God's sake, Dave." She pressed her head into her hands.

"It's true, Vanessa," Jane said, smiling and trying to touch Vanessa's hand across the table. "We're so glad you're better. It's so great to see you."

Vanessa stared at Jane's face with its heavily packed makeup pulling down the folds in her cheeks.

"We all think it's great that you want to work again...to come back to us." Dave clasped his hands together. "When we heard that you wanted to pick right back up where you left off before your surgery, we were ecstatic. Dan says..."

"Dan?" She spun toward her husband, who refused to turn from the window.

Dave cleared his throat and then looked at Wendy before continuing. "The reality is, Vanessa, that while we want to help you *personally*, with your health, we do need to talk about your professional contribution." He tapped the palm of his hand on top of the document. He looked at her for the first time since she had entered the room.

Vanessa rocked back and forth in her chair. Numbness and sensitivity cycled through her head and body.

"Vanessa, as difficult as this may sound, given the timing and..."

"And?"

"We're asking you to vacate your position for the good of the company. Executive staff has talked, and we'd even be willing to keep you on a temporary basis so you can transition out for a month. It would give you time to work, not as you wanted, but it'd be work."

"Transition out? Meaning, I train someone who would take my place."

"Yes." Dave's face brightened. "That's definitely one of your great qualities and strengths, something we've all commented on over the years. You have so much institutional knowledge. We wouldn't have made it this far without you. You can continue setting the bar high for us and your successor, who has big shoes to fill."

"And if I refuse?"

Dave glanced at Wendy and then at the document under his fingers. "We don't want it to come to that. We want to work with you while you off-load."

Vanessa's head throbbed as she stared at Dan, who chewed the nail of his left thumb and, when he was done, brushed his slacks as he switched and crossed legs, swinging his shoe like a metronome. She could tell that he was bored but didn't mind being there, sitting in the same room with her and their colleagues, not because of the emotions over the last several months or her declining health, but because none of this would affect him in the long term. This—sitting here, being in this meeting, facing her—was something added to his calendar that he needed to cross off in order to move on to other things during the same day.

"You will, of course," Dave continued, "sustain the percentage of ownership that you have, and once we're sold, you can reap the rewards of a decade of work here. We're very close to making that happen. It's going to be fantastic. All our work and *your* work, Vanessa, will..."

"The answer is decided?" Vanessa interrupted. "I can't think about this?"

The table fell silent.

"Is that right?" she asked louder.

"Yes, it is," Dave answered.

"You made your decision long before this. Why drag me in here today?"

"Because we wanted to talk to you in person," Jane said. "To see you."

"You called me in, set this up, *after* you had a client meeting...*after*...just like any other day. It's four in the afternoon. You've just finished meeting with someone, probably the Waterhouse project because that thing won't get off the ground without me, and you're trying to figure out how to do it without me." Her eyes tightened and then reopened. "You called me after a meeting...to hold another meeting about me...with me in it." She laughed and then stopped.

"We've already all voted," Dave said.

"Of course you have." She stared at the back of Dan's head.

"We know you're angry," Dave continued, "and we know…"

"Anger doesn't begin to cover my emotions right now. Do you know how exhausting it is just to come here? It takes a little longer these days. Coming here…*that* in and of itself is like running a marathon." Her eyes blinked. "I have zero energy, even if I told you I was excited to work. That's all I have. Work. I'm the one who has to do all this. Or has he lied about that, too?"

Dan turned toward the table and stared at its surface.

"We know, and we thank you for coming in." Dave said. "We know you have much more important things to focus on. Your health…"

"Please stop." Vanessa wiped her nose with the sleeve of her sweater that hadn't been washed in weeks. After a few seconds of silence, she cleared her throat. "I quit."

"You quit?" Dave asked.

"Yes, I quit. I'm not transitioning into a temp worker after ten years of being here. That's actually more of an insult than being asked…told…that I need to vacate my position. I quit." She sniffled; her hands shook in her lap. "You thought you called this meeting to ask me to leave, but I came here, to this meeting, to quit." Her pale face softened. "I quit."

The group at the table shifted in their seats.

"OK…" Dave pushed himself off the arms of his chair before settling back down into it. He glanced at Dan, who nodded. "You are still required to surrender all institutional knowledge before leaving. And that would happen even if you transitioned out as a temp. And when we promoted you to executive staff, you signed a non-compete clause, which lasts for a year after you vacate your position."

"Fine. I'll hand it all over to the next person. But I want it clear on my HR report that I'm not stepping aside or becoming a temp. I quit. I'm handing you my resignation, effective today."

"OK," Dave said. "Vanessa, I know these last few months have been extremely challenging and difficult, but the company is on track..."

"Stop. Just stop. I know all that. I was on the executive committee, Dave...this group of people in front of me. But that's not the case now, is it?" She looked around the room. No one answered her.

"We need to focus on your health...on getting you better," Jane said. "The stress here at work, in your position, would be detrimental to your recovery. We don't want that."

"Stress? You can call it for what it is. You don't have to dance around it like you did the day I took leave and in your get-well cards and hospital visits. Poor Dan, right? Poor Dan having to deal with his deadweight of a cancer-wife. Poor Dan with all this potential, all this equity and time in the company, and now he has to deal with this thing pulling him down and keeping him back. It's so sad that she's sick, but we're *so, so* close to being bought out by one of the big boys. She got us this far, and now she's holding us up. Can't have that." Vanessa quickly stood up and braced herself on the back of her chair to keep from falling over. She glared around the table at each one of them sitting in the same positions that she had found them in. Only Jane made eye contact with her, but as soon as she did, she returned to looking at the wall across from her with squares of sunlight on it and dust shimmying in the air.

Vanessa heaved open the door to the conference room, an action that shortened her breath, but out she went, propping it open with the weight of her body leaning into it. She promised to focus on the end of the hallway, where the light became fuzzy and gray and where the red door on the left would lead her back to the stairs and eventually to the parking garage. At first, she believed she could walk quickly past her coworkers and back through the narrow alley of cubicles and offices with their doors open, more of those doors opened now than when she had first shown up for the meeting, but after five steps, her leg muscles and back tightened and required more energy from her to keep them moving. She slowed down in the maze of cubicles.

For a brief moment, she felt lost; all the surrounding walls had dissolved into a blackness winding its way into her stomach. Shuffling through the sounds of typing on keyboards and ringing phones, she tilted her head higher, chin pointed at the end of the hall, as though she were entering quicksand. She kept up the appearance of marching forward, even if sinking was now the only movement.

Two coworkers she didn't remember became quiet when she reached them at the end of the hallway. One stood in the doorway and, turning toward Vanessa, cast her eyes up and down. The other sat at her computer and stopped talking while she stared at a ghost lost among the living.

✺

The garage door humming behind her and vibrating the glass cabinets in the kitchen forced her to open her eyes. Bracing herself on the countertops, she looked down at a peeled but unsliced banana and two pieces of bread shredded from a knife caked in peanut butter. She had started this sandwich minutes ago but stopped because she had forgotten what she was doing and why she was doing it at all, lost in a house filled with memories that she was trying to relocate. As soon as she came to, the smell of the ripe banana—brown and black and soft under her hand—nauseated her. She slid the rotten food into the trash bin. After several long, heaving breaths, she managed to avoid vomiting.

A car door slammed, and the door to the garage opened behind her. The air pressure and the temperature on her neck and face immediately changed. Dan's shoes clacked from the concrete of the garage to the stone tile of the kitchen; the echoes shortened and compacted as he approached her, one foot in, the next foot in, the door to the garage whooshing as it sealed shut, and then two more steps to the small wood desk standing at the edge of the kitchen, where he rustled through mail. They said nothing to each other, but for a brief moment she felt the urge to turn to him and welcome him home, kiss him and ask him how his day was, as though the purple and red clouds over the mountains and Dan's cologne could convince her that another time and another place tied her and Dan to the weight of old emotions. But the images of those days fell around her and then continued rolling off her, shedding any confusion, until her mood was stripped of anything amiable, leaving behind a smoldering indifference.

Vanessa shuffled to the living room and, easing herself onto the couch, wrapped one of the blankets around her. Dan set aside envelopes from the mail and placed his keys on the counter as he always did after work. He wrinkled his nose at the smells lingering in the kitchen and spotted two moldy apples in the fruit basket; black had sept from the avocados nestled under them. He shook his head as he set down his laptop bag on the floor, leaning it against the island, and glanced at Vanessa who, eyes locked on him, didn't budge. Opening the refrigerator, he clanked and pushed around and found a beer. She knew the bottle was tucked behind expired turkey slices and wrinkled peppers. The smells hit her again. The image of decay trailed behind. Her eyes clenched, but his actions, his cologne, and the space between them, from opposite points in the house, remained intimately tethered to her. She didn't know where the future began, where the past ended, or what lay spiraling in the middle. *What would you like?* she caught herself wanting to say to him, her heart thudding because the thought had emerged so naturally and without any resistance and she didn't know if she wanted to stop it. Dan turned on the faucet and splashed cold water on his face. He dried his face with paper towels, throwing them away after wiping the countertops. He walked out of the kitchen, rolled up his sleeves, and stood at the end of the leather couch in the first-floor den where Vanessa had made a bed. She watched his eyes stop on the mounds of Kleenex and medication bottles circling her. He took a deep breath and placed his hands on his waist. "I'm here to get some things. I won't be long."

Saying nothing to him, Vanessa rolled onto her side, faced the couch's back, and lay very still under the blankets piled on top of her. She stared at the chalky streaks of sunlight on the leather.

After several seconds, Dan exhaled. "I know today was tough. I know you think we're all out to get you...that we don't care about you. That I'm cold and heartless. But you leaving the company is what's best for the company and for you. It's not only about the company. I want you to know that. You'll cash out big time. That's how close we are, and how much all those years of putting in the hours will pay off. It's all yours. It will be the cherry on top, showing how far you've come."

She imagined him looking at the abstract painting hanging over her and the couch, its creams and grays caked on the exposed, unprimed canvas, degrees of red dragged across them. She remembered when they had bought it, hung it, and ate underneath it for the first few months after moving in, until eating out or bringing food home became more convenient and required less of their time and less of them.

"I'm not going after what's yours." He sat in the leather chair adjacent to the couch, which became animated with his weight. She listened to him shift in the seat and breathe heavily. "I will make sure my lawyer doesn't go after what's yours. It's not even an option...not on the table. You've earned it. I want you to know that." In her head she could see Dan lean forward onto his elbows, resting them on his knees, as his starched shirt slid across his slacks, sounding like a small blade unsheathed. "My lawyer is willing to concede to some of your requests." He leaned back, and he twisted his body to determine where she hid under the covers, in the dark mass on the couch, where her face and eyes could be seen. After several long seconds of silence, he sighed. "I just can't keep this up anymore. I panicked the day you were diagnosed. I didn't know what to do. I didn't know what to do with myself because everything I wanted was falling apart in front of me."

She rolled to her other side, facing him, and through a small opening in the blankets watched him open his arms and hands to the air. The room darkened as the sunset bled deeper into the sky.

"I got the great job, I got the fantastic city, the beautiful wife, the beautiful house. It all cracked that day. I wanted to be by your side the whole time...and I was. You know that, right? The headaches, the memory loss, the depression, the yelling, those doctors telling you those headaches were because of work and stress and the baby...the big fainting spell you had at work...the surgery, the chemo...all those things. I thought I could see you through them all. But I couldn't." He stopped talking to swallow. "Because I don't want to." The beer twisted in the palm of his hand; condensation dripped down the neck and broke on his fingers. "I saw you in that hospital bed, right after surgery, and your face was like it had been in a fistfight...all those bruises and you were swollen. And your shaved head with that massive scar running down your head. Those stitches. That wasn't who I married. And everyone said the surgery was successful, but they weren't a hundred percent you were in the clear. And I just sat there in that dark room with that breathing machine beeping every second, and I said to myself, 'I'll have to do this again?' I felt so scared and sad. Vanessa, I..." He wiped his mouth. "If we had had that baby and this happened, it'd be...a baby without its mother." He paused. "I forgave you for that. I just want you to know that, too."

Curled inside the blankets, she was motionless and quiet on the couch, the light on the black leather and the blankets longer, sinking deeper across her body, the sunlight marking the outside of her body with translucent stripes. The ceiling fan above her turned slowly.

Dan wiped his mouth again. "I couldn't go on. I *can't* go on. I don't want to spend my life doing this or living this way. I have a life, too, you know. I had a life in place before I met you." He lowered his head and ran his fingers through his salt-and-pepper hair. "You know, if this had happened when we were both old, then, yeah, I'd understand. I'd feel different. Someone else would take care of it all. But in your mid-thirties? We shouldn't be living like that. It frightens me. I have a life. I'm in good shape...healthy. I don't look my age. I'm successful. I have all those things. I can't just throw them away this soon. I put them on hold for those few months, but I realized I can't do that." He reached into his pocket and pulled out his car keys. "It was good to see you today. It was the most energy I've seen you have for a long, long time. It was like the old V. Your memory was clear, and you spoke just fine." He looked away from the couch. "I'll continue to stay away, sleep in the hotel, until our lawyers figure out what's best for us. I'll let you know when I need to be over here. I'll probably text. I still have files in the spare bedroom. We'll work it out. I promise not to come over late, probably just after work and on my way to work. OK?" He said these things as he stood up and stared at her, coiled tightly under the covers. Holding the beer next to his slacks, he cleared his throat and looked down at the rug under his loafers. "I wanted to see you today up there. I know you may not believe that. But I wanted to be there, to see you, to show that..."

The covers shifted, like a stone coming to life, and, underneath, her throat cleared. "Dan?"

"Yeah?"

"I paid for the parking garage today. I had to turn in my parking pass with my ID card after I resigned."

Dan nodded to the voice on the couch before he left the room. "OK. I'll have someone take care of it."

✸

"I need to come home, Papá," she whispered into her phone.

"Come home, Essa? Why? What happened?"

"Dan and I are over...officially."

"Ah, I'm so sorry."

She imagined him sitting on a wicker chair in the sunroom leading to the back patio of his new house, wearing pleated jeans and tennis shoes, a nice shirt, his shins angled back behind his knees, heels off the ground, his chest angled up and out, trying to stretch higher and higher, one hand stirring a spoon in his afternoon cup of atole, lost in the steam of the thick brown drink, the other hand holding the phone.

"Yes, you need to come home. You can use the office. I'll get an inflatable mattress today when I'm out."

"Oh, Dad, you don't have to do that. I only need to stay there for a little while, until I find my own place." Wiping her cheeks, Vanessa shifted in bed and rocked her shoulders over a pillow to alleviate a nagging ache.

"No, no, it's no problem. I need to stop by the store today anyway and make sure an order of flour came in. They've been unreliable the last two times. Bastards," he said with an inflated Mexican accent.

Vanessa giggled, which loosened a black haze floating in her head. "You get 'em, Dad."

"I've been after them for a month now. They don't have their act together. They couldn't get out of a room even if I showed them the exit sign."

"It's good to hear your voice, Papá."

"Yes… I'm very sorry about Dan…and your job. I think it's very cruel and inhumane what they did to you. Very cruel, especially the timing."

Vanessa clutched the phone closer to her mouth as she nodded to herself. "It's less exhausting now. I'm better. My spirit is up, better than what I was when that all happened. I'm still in pain and still slow, but it's gotten better. At first it was unbearable. I actually feel better. I don't think I look it, but I do feel better." She patted her puffy cheeks and eye sockets. "Time helps."

"You had a lot done to you, Essa. Come home," he spoke with a soft voice. "I'll make sure the house is clean. We can have pizza when you get here."

"Simon's?"

"Where else?"

"I can't believe they're still around."

"They are. They're a little bit different than when you ate there last. They've upped the image. They're fancier now. Square plates. More fancy pasta dishes. Red wine. Racks and racks of it. The Americana photos and chucherías...all those knickknacks gone from the walls. Candles and linen napkins and fine paintings."

"No more sports while eating?" she teased, blocking the light in her bedroom with the crook of her arm.

"Nada. The mayor ate there not too long ago. A grand reopening. I was invited but didn't go."

"*Dad.*"

"Well, Essa, Simon Zanetti insulted your mother's polvorónes during that bridal fair."

"That was years ago."

Roberto chuckled. "He said his grandmother's cannoli recipe was far superior."

She pictured her father shrugging and frowning, trying to be serious but letting his good humor rumble underneath and eventually surpass his grudge. She could see him brushing his mustache with his thumb and index finger and lifting his head into the summer light pouring onto the sunroom.

"I'm just teasing. He came in the other day to the store, said he hadn't seen me in a while, which was nonsense because he cut right to the chase and told me about the grand reopening. Zorro gris astuto," Roberto said, chuckling until he coughed. "Sly fox."

"Mom always thought he was handsome. Hombre guapo," Vanessa cooed.

"Well, your mother always did have good taste in handsome men."

"Si, papacito." Vanessa heard him step outside, and she saw him standing still on the small back patio, the door open behind him, a noise or a change in the weather calling him outside.

"Do you need help moving your things? I don't know if I can get away from the store. Gus won't be back until school starts in August, and Tina can't come in until...oh, I don't remember."

"No." Feeling worse on her back, she rolled up in bed. "The lawyers agreed to my use of a moving company. I guess Dan's paying for it, or it's baked into the settlement...something like that. Thank you, though."

Roberto paused and became serious once again in his tone and rhythm. "Did you get anything, Essa, out of this? The house? Money for your recovery?"

She licked her lips and looked out the living room's window and at the mountains, the yellow flowers sprinkled against its base, and the fields in front of its slope. "The cars, the boat, the cabin in Aspen will be sold off and split. The house, when we sell, will be split too. I'll get half. But it's really his. I don't want it or any of those things. I just want out. I'll get the check once the company is sold. It'll be nice to have, but what I really want back is time."

"I know. You'll get it back somehow."

"I hope so. The money will be a Band-Aid to all this, but it's over. I'm free. And that's what I wanted." She wiped her eyes and turned on her laptop. There was a silence on her end as she looked down and away from the gray screen bursting into a bluish light, her mind not moving forward but falling backward onto memories held together by synapses firing in hazy circles. Snapping back to the webpage loading in front of her, she said, "I should get going. I need to research moving companies and set up a time for them. What energy I have, I need to spend it on that."

"OK. You can stay with me as long as you need, Essa. It'll be great to have you closer to home."

"I'll get my own place shortly after I'm there. It'll be best." Seeing the bakery and his home in her head, she smiled and closed her eyes. "It will be great to be closer to you again, Papá."

After a short pause, Roberto said, "The temperature has dropped quickly. The sky has turned black. We are under a tornado watch."

Vanessa swiveled her head away from the window. "That's one thing I do not miss about that place." She imagined that her father lowered the phone from his mouth to look up into the sky and stare at the seam where black spread like ink over blue. Sitting up in bed, prompted by his voice, she looked higher into the bright window centered in the master bedroom, in front of her bed, and saw the sky darkening where he stood. She saw this change in the sky and weather while looking into the crisp blue shining behind the peaks and troughs of the mountains looming outside in her own sky.

"Esto también pasará," he said. "This too shall pass."

"I know it will. You sound like Mom."

"Buenos días, mi niña hermosa."

"Buenos días, Papá, mi corazón."

Waiting for the click of her father hanging up, Vanessa set her cell phone on the pillow next to her and stared at the search engine box. She took a deep breath in and typed *Denver moving companies*, but after the results returned, she opened a new window and logged onto her email account. She felt tired, but memories of where she had been when she was younger and where she was now returning flooded her. An intuition opened its wings and flickered over a path inside her. She typed *Tim Baxter*, the year that they graduated, and what she thought was his high school. Several hits returned; none of them was the Tim she was looking for. She stared at what she wrote, feeling that something was wrong, a place misaligned with a time, but she couldn't specify. *That high school is mine, not his.* She shook her head, avoiding eye contact with her reflection on the computer screen. She took a few minutes to concentrate on where he went to school but then flipped back to the moving companies.

After providing her contact information for a price quote, her hands pulled back from the keyboard and then exploded back onto it, adding *special effects makeup* to the original search. She scrolled through the results and lost her breath on the website for Night's Watch SFX, operated by a Tim Baxter who looked like a bearded twin of the Tim she remembered. She clicked Portfolio, diving into a macabre lineup of monsters, oddities, and horrific scenes that weren't found in handheld home movies; scrolling through demons, angelic and nightmarish creatures, ripped-off limbs and burnt faces, mangled torsos, all featured in videos, movies, and haunted houses around the country. Vanessa clicked About Us and was certain that the Tim in front of her was the Tim she knew. A few years ago, he had been at a Denver comic convention. She clicked the link; several photos from the event included one of Tim proudly standing next to a small table and a sign with Night's Watch in black block letters amongst a sea of booths and larger, glossier signs in an expo center. He looked so happy; she laughed at his beard and red flannel shirt, tight like a balloon in the waistline. In another picture, Tim had his arm around a famous actor who, in turn, had his arm around one of Tim's full-size demons with its pink crystalline wings spread behind its beetle-like arms and claws.

Pulse racing, she sent the homepage link to herself. She closed her email account but, after sitting in bed for a few minutes, logged in again. In that short span of time, four new emails had appeared in her inbox, including one from the moving company and spam from a divorce lawyer promising, "The first divorce is always the worst, but the second doesn't have to be." She reopened the Night's Watch page and clicked the email listed under Contact Us. She drew in a deep breath.

Dear Tim, she began but then stopped to cough and drink water with her afternoon medications. The cursor blinked. Pressing against the large plush pillows, she erased the greeting and started over. She closed her eyes and typed.

Hi Tim,

I can't believe it's been so long since we last saw each other. Time flies, doesn't it? I wanted to reach out to you to see how's your life and what you've been up to over the years. I'm using your work email. Cyber-stalked you—guilty :) Wow! It looks like you've really hit it big with the makeup and the special effects you've always loved. You've always had a real gift for that, and I'm glad to see it paying off.

I've never forgotten you or our times together or the memories we made. I had brain cancer earlier this year and had surgery for it, and I hope everything is all right after it.

She deleted the last sentence.

I've had some health issues, but I'm better now.

She deleted that.

Getting old is no fun.

She grumbled at the screen and massaged the base of her neck, closed her eyes, and imagined that her head was as light as a balloon. Her phone buzzed. *Home later* Dan texted. She tossed the phone back on the nightstand but checked it again to make sure she hadn't cracked it with the force of her throw.

I'd like to have you back in my life again.

She grimaced at how that phrase sounded and watched the ceiling fan spin.

I'd like for us to be in each other's lives again.

She struck that.

It will be so good to hear from you. I can't wait. Here's my cell number if you want to catch up by phone. It would be great to hear your voice.

All the best,

She shook her head.

Yours,

No.

Until then,
Vanessa Ochoa

Her name without Miller after it made her cry. She typed *Hi there! Blast from the past* in the subject line before sending the email. She closed her laptop, which she placed next to her, on her left, in the spot where Dan used to sleep, the heat of its battery the only warmth in the bed.

✳

On a Thursday afternoon, she woke to the sound of her phone buzzing. Vanessa assumed it was either Dan or her lawyer, and she ignored it. It buzzed again: a voicemail from a number she didn't know but an area code she did know. It wasn't her father, who barely touched his phone, and she doubted it was any of her high school friends who preferred keeping in touch through email or social media, when they stayed in touch at all. Rolling onto her back, she pushed Play.

After a long stretch of silence and static, a voice said, *Hey, Vanessa. It's Tim. Tim Baxter. I got your email the other week. Sorry, I've been in Texas and Louisiana doing some consulting.* There was another long silence.

Anyway, yeah, I'd love to catch up. It's, let's see, four central time. I'll be in the shop until six. This is my personal phone. I'll have it next to me if you want to call back and talk. It'd be great to hear your voice. Bye. The message clicked off.

She hit Call Back on his message but then quickly hung up. She swiveled her hips and legs out of bed. The floor was cold. She let her toes spread across the carpet until she caught her breath. Clutching the phone, she pushed herself out of bed and opened the curtains over the main windows. Sunlight warmed her body. She dialed Tim's number, and when he answered, she flopped down on the edge of the bed, nearly missing it with adrenaline and nausea pulsing through her.

"Hey, Vanessa." Tim's voice was warm and soft and still had a tinge of adolescence under its tone.

"God, is it really you?"

"Nope, not God…just me, Tim."

She laughed with him and wiped her eyes. "How are you?"

"Busy. But good. It's so good to hear your voice."

"Yours too. Are you at your shop?"

"I am. It's almost quittin' time for me."

"What time do you usually quit?"

"Depends. If I'm in a good groove, it could be late. But I like my schedule. In at nine, out at five."

"That's so great." She braced her free hand against the bed and pushed herself up. "I saw the pictures on your website. They're amazing."

"Oh, good. Thank you. Yeah, staying busy with it all."

"It's so great, Tim. Doing what you love."

"Yeah, it is. Super blessed."

She smiled to her shadow across the room.

"So…what's up with you? Denver, huh? I was there not too long ago."

"I saw that."

"Too bad we missed each other."

"Yeah… I've been here since grad school."

"Grad school? Wow. In what?"

"Public relations and marketing."

"Really?"

"I know, right? I bet you thought accounting."

"Well, you were smart enough that you could do anything."

"Yeah, it got me out of there."

"Good. I wish I could get out of here sometimes."

"You said you were just traveling."

"Yeah, but that's for work, and it's paid for by the church."

"Well, that's not bad. It's still travel."

"True. I can't complain about that."

"What's it for?"

"Haunted houses."

"Haunted houses?"

"I designed and fabbed a lot of their props and costumes and shipped them there, but honestly, they need to be installed a certain way."

"The Tim Way, right?"

"Yep."

As Vanessa stood in front of the bed, she found a patch of sunlight on the carpet, window-shaped, stretching at an angle so that the shadows formed an exaggerated X. She stepped forward and inhaled deeply before speaking again, but before she could, Tim jumped in. "Hey, sorry, I actually should get going. The timer on one of my masks went off." Machinery clanked in the background. Tim cleared his throat. "It was great talking to you. Now that I have your email and phone we can keep in touch with each other. Maybe someday we can talk in person."

"I'm moving back," she said quickly.

"What? Really?"

"It's a long story. I can tell you in person."

"That'd be great. I'd love that."

"I'll be in touch soon. I'll be there soon, actually."

"Yeah, I absolutely want to see you."

Vanessa smiled and put one foot in front of the other, orbiting the X shape on the ground. "I'd like that too."

"Let me know when you get settled in, and we'll get together. My busy season is starting to peak, but maybe you can stop by and see what I'm working on."

"A haunted house?"

"Yep."

"I'd like that."

"OK." A sound beeped on his end. "I need to run. We'll talk soon. Bye, Vanessa."

"Bye, Tim." She turned off her phone but kept walking in a circle, drifting in the wake of the intuition that had opened its wings inside her and then quivered away. She gazed around the master bedroom and felt like a guest allowed to stay for a little while until it was clear that it was time to leave. Nothing had changed in appearance—where she ate, dressed, and slept day after day; where Dan's and her things remained in their places. Their home built with memories would return to being merely a house, as it was before they moved in years ago. The scar under her hair, its shepherd-hook shape running down behind her ear, the two sides of skin pushed together, like dirt in a field, had re-sealed, the mass underneath it removed, leaving behind a hollowed-out shape along with the marks of time that it took for those things to appear and then disappear. She remembered this as she completed one more circle around the sunlit room.

13

And when Vanessa woke in the morning, so much depended on April and its colors, opening like a window from one season to the next, and this dependence could be seen not with the calendar or with a clock but with the weather and its greens and flowers rising, blue skies deepening, and the rains keeping all this cycled together and tumbling one after another. She sat on the edge of the bed and dug her feet into the carpet, toes up and then down, grounding herself deeper; her fists clutched the sheet and blanket. Placing her hands beside her hips, she was ready to push off but did not have the strength yet to leave. Her legs twitched, her arms shook, her neck tightened with frustration—but no movement. She sat there waiting for her brain to reconnect to her muscles and bones like an echo coming back to the source. Her body, an exaggerated arc scribbled in blank space, leaned forward slightly. Her mind remained foggy, distorted, tender, left behind in her sleep and the hours that had passed; part of it caught up to the body that was awake but moved in pain and, when it could not move, sat in pain; and part of it cast invisible lines into the open waters of the future.

Shivering, she rubbed the sleeves of the thermal top she slept in and then massaged her scalp, slowing down through her pixie-cut hair, over the soft patch of skin, and the scar sealing the middle-right of her head. She stopped on this area, circled it a few times with her fingertips, and then glided away from it because it had not changed since she last felt it. Relaxing her toes, Vanessa stood up, wobbled. Her nausea and headache reminded her that today was the day and that the ocean and its consistent promise of waiting for her had not been broken. She closed her eyes and breathed in and out for ten counts; she did this again until she felt stable. She mumbled every now and then until the headache and nausea were less intense, as though she had control over them and the words scrambling in her head.

She shuffled into the bathroom and, after turning on the lights and opening the vanity's drawers, looked away from the mirror until she dried her face with a towel, dabbing the white splotches that had formed on her skin; dabbing the extra weight that puffed out her cheeks and throat; carefully dabbing around her eyes, where the skin had sunk the most and where lack of sleep had spread its black wings. At a mirror years ago in Denver, long after the hospital and surgery, she cried every morning and night, when all the things in her life that she wanted to hold onto shifted and forced her to hold onto some of them but let go of others.

Standing in front of the plain mirror in her unfurnished condo, she could see another Vanessa standing in front of the larger, multi-paned mirror in her old home in Denver where she would apply or wipe off makeup inside the rows of lights. She saw a face she hadn't expected to see at this age. The makeup she had layered on all those years ago never made her look younger; it only evened out the wrinkles, shortening their shadows but not eliminating them. Today, though, leaving her body and her face for what they were—limited and stark—she stared at herself and, for the first time in weeks, did not cry.

One pair of shoes, two pairs of pants, a few t-shirts, and her hoodie were all that remained in her closet. Buying new clothes did not matter to her anymore. She grabbed her running shoes, the gray hiking pants, a shirt, and the purple hoodie. Vanessa thought about Tim and her father as she double-checked her backpack. She stopped in the doorway and turned around. She wanted something, but she couldn't remember what it was or why she wanted it in the first place. Several seconds later, she moved again and hobbled downstairs for breakfast where she made coffee and opened the bag from the bakery, pulling out two day-old payasos, eating one before she scrambled eggs and microwaved sausage. She smiled as the pink, brown, and white frosted her lips. She was awake and nearly full.

*

"No baggage?" the agent behind the counter asked her.

Vanessa shook her head no and tapped the backpack. "That's it."

Continuing to type at the computer and sliding a tag toward Vanessa, the agent replied, "Let me at least give you one of these, in case you want to check it at the gate." After the ticket printed, the agent pointed her long cherry-red fingernails over Vanessa's left shoulder. "OK, one-way to Denver. Everything is on time so far. You'll head that way, go up a flight of stairs, and see security. Once you're through there, you're at gate twenty-three. OK?"

"Great, thank you," Vanessa said, nodding.

The first thing she did after passing through the scanning machine and security was check that she had slid the ring back onto her finger—the ring with the piece of wood floating inside that her father had given her, her only ring now—as well as make sure that her phone turned back on. She wanted to make sure that the files Tim had created for her birthday present still worked. Once the phone came on, she saw a text from him. She inhaled deeply, smiled, and shut off the phone, hoping that the long walk in the bright passageway would ease her head and her stomach.

Flopping into a seat near her gate, she covered her mouth with her hand, and as she scrunched her face and closed her eyes, she wiped away tears and saliva with the back of her wrist, quietly thankful that she was sitting by herself in the row of seats. She had promised herself not to cry in public, especially at the airport, or on the plane, or in the line for security, where all eyes would shift to her. But now she struggled to keep her promise.

When the seat next to her rocked and a man sat down, plopping his feet on his bag, Vanessa sucked in her lips and blew her nose, sniffling away any excess. He paid no attention to Vanessa, who at first wanted all the sights and sounds to go away and for the room to crumble like old wallpaper until she was left alone on a bright floor, the sunlight breaking through. But as she looked at the lines of people gathering near the doors of the jetways—the colors of their clothes plucked from fields that grow this time of year—she wanted to hold on to it all, briefly, before letting it go. "It always returns," she mumbled to herself, staring outside the window at a blue sky that had not changed since the last time she saw it. Composing herself, she cleared her throat and smiled. The room around her quieted. She opened her phone, found one of the audio files, and clicked it. Vanessa listened to the recording long enough to confirm that the voices on it had survived and were coming with her.

When her flight was announced, a headache ballooned, her stomach re-knotted, and electricity rushed up the back of her spine because it was time. *Please don't faint here, please don't faint here*, she thought, as she handed the ticket to the man checking in passengers. She wiped sweat off her top lip and walked down the jetway, stopping every few steps to regain her balance and clear her vision. Vanessa was relieved and impatient with the line outside the plane's door. Standing and waiting, she could calm herself, but this also meant that she was in neutral—that the endpoint hadn't moved in closer and that it remained out there for her to reach it.

The line bumped up a few passengers, she lost her balance slinging the backpack on her shoulder, and she had to brace herself against the jetway's wall. No one stared at her, and no one helped her. She smiled at the attendant when she took her seat, buckled in, and reminded herself that her one goal for the next two days was to stay intact until the ocean.

Vanessa's seat was two rows behind one of the wings, and when the overhead speaker buzzed with the captain's voice announcing their long descent into Denver, she leaned forward and to the side in her seat and pushed up the window shade. The late-morning sun had rotated behind the wing, backlighting it like black bullets and small torpedoes, blinking with lights that cut across the blue-gray clouds.

The plane tilted again, diving a little bit more, and the same clouds, which had earlier masked the sun and the wing, turned white as the wings shredded them open. The blue sky returned; the land rose up with squares of tans and browns, transparent greens glazed over them, a few patches of remaining snow, the scar of a long river running through them, connecting them. Waiting for the plane to land, Vanessa shivered. She breathed deeply, returned her eyes to the landscape, and focused on believing that everything above, around, and under her was new, as though she had never seen it before and that all the business trips in and out of Denver over the years of living here were breaking apart— something else shining through—as though she were starting over but on her own at the time of her choosing.

On the outskirts of the runway, the land divided into large squares and rectangles—no circles or ovals; no sense of rotation; only compartments and hard-cornered sections with dirt roads between them. Lighter colors defined the borders: the brown of winter's end over here and the greens of spring coming in like moss over there. But closer in, crossing the highway, the buildings on the fields multiplied, more of them clumped together, yet the fields ruled the space, huge blocks of them, spanning wide and reaching the mountain range. Some of the fields were flat and tan like leather, and some of them were dark green with gold scumbled over ochre ground.

The first time she experienced this she had flown out of Denver for a meeting in Seattle along with Dan, who fidgeted until the flight attendant signaled that electronic devices could be used. Glancing between him and the scenery, she thought that he was dedicated to his work, as she was becoming to hers, and that once things settled down at their new home and at her new position, he would put aside his laptop and ask her to go for long drives in this landscape, where they would be alone with a different kind of time that was only theirs, trying to be closer and intimate again, as they were early on, under a sky that could fall as snow or stars without warning.

✺

Throwing in her backpack and closing the door, Vanessa rattled off her old address to the taxi driver as though she was headed there to stay—headed not to a house but to home to fix a hot cup of tea as soon as she walked in after the two-hour flight, where a stack of mail waited for her and where she would open windows and shades and take the lights off the timers. She spoke the numbers and street name so nonchalantly that she didn't feel the need to watch the city go by on the highway, as the western suburbs, with their shops, big-box stores, and the mall with its IMAX theater, passed.

She bit her thumbnail, massaged her temples, and keeping her head turned toward the window, pretended to ignore the scenery and the associations increasing with it as she moved closer to the house. She recalled how many times she and Dan drove this way in complete silence, often with her driving so Dan could take a phone call or send an email; how they never hiked on the trails by their house that wound through horse ranches and along the foothills. At the end of every day with him, all she had were diminishing words, stunted promises, and a feeling of something slipping away from her.

The taxi turned south, and she saw the mountains and the lake, sparkling blue in the clear air, and the gold and green fields sloping up and down around it. Her throat cinched, her vision blurred, and Vanessa thought that she was having another spell, but she knew the neighborhood's stone and concrete entrance was just around the corner. Colby. When she had first heard the street name, she had assumed that it was named after someone important to the area—maybe a pioneer or a prominent prospector; maybe the area's first doctor or educator—but Dan quickly set her straight. "It's a college in Maine. All the street names around here are named after prestigious colleges or universities on the East Coast." He half-circled his left finger in the air. "Yale is over there...Harvard, Dartmouth, Columbia back along the park."

"No NWSU?" she giggled, pulling her long hair across her shoulder and over the seatbelt.

"NWSU?"

"Oh, come on. My alma mater. Northwest State." She looked at him, waiting for him to catch her joke.

"Right, right," Dan laughed with her, parking the car alongside the For Sale sign.

Vanessa smiled back and shifted in the leather seat, using the button on the side to power her up a little more so she could see the house that he drove them to. It was perfectly spaced between the other large houses; the street was wide enough for two large vehicles to pass. The hazards on Dan's car blinked. She was glad that the windows were tinted, and she hoped that at least other one person in this neighborhood had a last name ending in –ez or a vowel and that they owned a home, not cleaned it or looked after the children and the meals, not occupying it but living in it. She stared at the manicured yard and imagined Dan mowing and watering it, his shirt draped over the front porch's lounge chair, his pasty white skin streaked with zinc oxide in the sun, a cold beer and a mountain sunset waiting for them when he had finished. But Dan hired a professional landscaper weeks after moving in, and whenever the crew came around, Vanessa kept herself indoors, ghostly, wanting only to pass invoices to Dan from the foreman who had light brown hair, his last name Jensen, his crew full of men who looked like they could have last names ending in –ez or a vowel.

Dan had driven them there before dinner so they could see what the house was like at dusk. She stared at warm lights intensifying the texture of the brick as well as the color of the two garage doors and the siding that reminded her of a bluebird. "We definitely can get another car." Dan pointed to the second garage door. "Maybe a boat."

Vanessa looked at the driveway with its four large, perfect squares of concrete and a smaller, narrower sidewalk peeling off the main one and curving like a handle between the lush green lawn, a rock garden, and the mailbox. "It's so new that the trees are tethered in the ground," she said.

"Dining room, I bet." Dan nodded to the bay window snug under the second story. "Built three years ago." He flicked his finger across his phone's screen. "Five bedrooms, four-thousand square feet, stainless steel appliances, double oven, fireplace, vaulted ceilings, mountain view, hardwood floors, *finished* basement...and it's ours." His eyebrows bobbed over the ghost-blue flame of his phone. After texting the realtor, he patted her knee, a motion he did when he had already decided something. "A lot of the area's big tech people and their families live here. My boss...our boss...Dave lives two streets over." With his wrist cocked on the steering wheel, Dan leaned back in the leather seat and surveyed the large houses along the streets. "We can drive around and check out Yale and Princeton."

Vanessa stared at the house in front of her with its clearly defined bright walls and its shape eclipsing the sky, the setting sun, and the mountains that she had hoped to see up close and in person. A fear coiled inside her, and she knew that to maintain such a house and the lifestyle tied to it would require a different kind of sacrifice than her parents had made when they came to this country. Dan punched the keypad on his phone and laughed with someone on the other end. "No, it's fine. Let's stick around here," she said, having nothing else to say to him as new expectations loomed over her.

Sitting in the idling taxi that had taken her from the airport to where she used to live and realizing that nothing in the neighborhood, since she left, had changed or could change, Vanessa remembered what that different sacrifice had been, and for a second, before going up to the front door, she wanted it back.

Given that the day was a workday, she didn't expect anyone to be home, but she knocked anyway, two successive times, firmly. She stepped back from the door and composed herself, closing her eyes and conscious of her breath and her racing heart. A smudged shape, a red top, the face becoming lighter and brighter, filled the front door's etched glass. The door slowly cracked. A woman's face turned pale, and her eyes widened when she saw Vanessa; her hands quickly ran up the door to cover her mouth. Her sandals clicked on the doorway's polished floor, and the door opened wider—too wide for an unannounced visitor on the other side. Looking like a lone red flower standing amidst stone, wood, and plastic, the bleach-blonde woman stared at Vanessa, standing in the shadow of her old home.

"Dan's not here," the woman said plainly. "He's on a business trip and won't be back until next week. I'm sorry." She wrapped her arms around her midsection; her small jawline tightened under the tone of her voice.

"Of course he is," Vanessa muttered, her head throbbing. Breathing in deeply, she continued, "Please give him this for me." She handed a letter to the woman.

"I will. Do you want...?"

"No," Vanessa cut the woman off. "Just make sure he gets it."

The taxi driver honked, and Vanessa motioned to him.

"Yes, of course," the woman said softly, nodding. She cupped the letter like a small bird.

Turning to the taxi, Vanessa felt the woman gawking as she slowly staggered down the sidewalk and the perfectly squared driveway, passing the manicured lawn and the mailbox with its flag up. Once Vanessa slid back in the taxi and told the driver to take her to the hotel, the woman slumped away from the door and closed it slowly, staring at the letter as she did.

When the taxi drove out of the neighborhood and onto the highway again, Vanessa imagined the woman contacting Dan. *Your ex-wife was just here. She looks horrible. She left a letter for you.* Depending how long the two of them had been together, Vanessa imagined that this woman had discovered it was more efficient to communicate from a distance than to speak personally to Dan. But Vanessa also knew that it no longer mattered how long it would take Dan to follow up on any part of this moment.

✻

That night at the hotel near the airport, Vanessa cleaned her face with a towel and an almond-shaped bar of soap branded with a name suggesting regality, opulence, and a lavender field somewhere in France. The bar bubbled in her hands like any ordinary bar of soap. The aroma at first interested her but then quickly nauseated her. After staring at her face in the mirror and at the increased swelling, she closed her eyes. The ocean was closer now; only mountains remained between her and the water, mere mountaintops to cross over, the snow crests of the western mountains giving way to the Pacific coast and the mountains there tumbling toward the ocean and the land sliding into the water where it disappeared under patches of silver and blue rolling against the horizon.

Before slipping into bed, she checked her phone. One text. It was from Tim. *Hey, just checking in.* She controlled her breath, closed her eyes, and then shut off her phone. She folded the hoodie, bra, and hiking pants over the desk chair but kept on her one pair of underwear and t-shirt—all that she had brought with her. She pulled herself between the sheet, blanket, and soft bed and lay there in the dark, trying to fall asleep, halfway to where she wanted to be.

14

After school, the eight of them meandered to the fountain in the middle of the student plaza. Rain from a storm that had rolled through the day before pooled in the cracks and dimples of the plaza's red bricks. Vanessa and her friends flopped down on the benches. They flung their backpacks on top of the green metal table or dropped them on the damp concrete. Tanya took her usual spot in the middle. Stephen sat across from his sister Stephanie. Standing away from the table, Eric and Jacob hit each other on the arm and then ran in a circle until chasing each other exhausted them. Carmen raked her hair with her fingers; her loose hairs rippled in the wind while Vivian's eye shadow sparkled under the May sun. Vanessa sat at the end.

"How much longer is Mel gonna be?" Stephen moaned.

"Five hours," quipped Jacob.

"She shouldn't have been messing around."

"Mrs. Gibson did not like it."

"Nah, it was Mel's eye-roll. That's what got Mrs. G's granny panties in a wad."

"How do you know Mrs. Gibson wears granny panties?" asked Vivian.

"I seen them."

"How have you seen them, Jacob?"

"She bent over one day to pick something up off the floor at her desk."

"That's why Jakey sits at the back with the other delinquents and pervs."

"Yo, I've seen plenty of teachers' underwear and bras." Jacob stabbed the air with his skinny finger in front of the table. "Granny Gibson's is no good. But Mrs. Hartzler's the best. *The best.* She wears a black thong."

"A thong, Jakey?" Carmen pulled her hair into a ponytail, the top of her black hair colored cherry red. "The only thong you've ever seen was on some smut show on cable. You've been watching too much TV."

"Stephen watches that stuff all the time late on Friday nights…all alone in his room."

"Shut up, Stephanie."

"We know V don't wear thongs," chimed Tanya, grinning and smacking her gum.

The table laughed while Vanessa blushed and shook her head.

"She's saving it for after prom." Jacob covered his mouth with his fist as he grinned.

Vanessa glared at him.

"You gotta feel for Mel, though," Stephanie said. "She's been working more hours and babysitting her brother a lot."

"Her mom's still sick. I saw her the other day at Albertson's."

"In the liquor aisle?"

"Where else?"

"She still looking into nursing school?"

"Yeah," Tanya answered, "but she's gotta get past Mrs. G first."

Jacob stood up on the table's bench and said in an old lady's voice, "Tell me, class, why did the piggy-wiggys kick out Mr. Jones from his farm?"

"Mel doesn't know. That's why she's staying late!" yelled Vivian.

"Only because Mrs. G didn't call on Jake the Snake." Eric punched Jacob in the thigh.

"Didn't read it, don't care. I just got lucky she didn't call on me."

"Or else *you'd* be in there," Vanessa said quickly.

The table snickered.

Jacob's diamond earrings glistened as he cocked his head. "Who cares about some stupid book and stupid talking pigs?"

"Napoleon and Snowball. They have names," Vanessa chided.

"Of course V read it but never gets called on."

"That's because she would be answering all the time for everyone who hadn't read it." Stephanie swirled her Coke can. "Love you, V!"

"Love you guys too," she sighed, leaning forward on her arms and looking away from the table and up at the sky where a patch of blue broke through the clouds.

"Besides, V's gonna leave us someday soon," said Carmen. "She's too smart."

"You gonna remember us when you leave?" Vivian hugged Vanessa.

"She's gonna be all freshy fresita when she comes back to visit us."

"Preppy clothes." Tanya dusted off her black-and-gray flannel shirt.

"Preppy 'tude."

"Nice car."

233

Vanessa rolled her eyes at their comments.

"Reunion in ten years!"

"If we all make it till then."

"So far not Mel."

"V can spray perfume on letters to Jake when he's in the army."

"You mean when he's in jail."

"Whatever." Jacob pushed his shirt's raglan sleeves higher up his arms.

"Dude, where is Mel?"

"Relax, Stephen. I know you want some Cinnabon, but the mall will still be there when she gets out."

"Who's driving?"

"I'm driving."

"Nuh-uh," Stephanie cut off her brother. "It's Thursday, and that means it's my turn for the car."

"You gotta pay for gas then. And I doubt you have much left after you paid Mom back for that jewelry."

Mumbling something, Stephanie pulled her stocking cap down to her eyebrows.

"One of you has got to drive. I gotta get to the mall today, y'all. I gotta get something for my cousin who's getting married." Tanya's raspy voice dominated the table. "She's going all out, too. Horse-drawn carriage, fancy dinner. It's gonna be bigger than her quince. Max out all the credit cards." Pursing her lips and snapping her fingers, she shuffled her head back and forth between her shoulders.

"Which cousin? Jackée?"

"You know it, Zamora."

Covering his heart with his hands, Stephen leaned away from the table and toward the grass. "¡Ay, caramba! Oh, Jac-kée, Jac-kée," he sang. "I remember that one summer she came to visit, and we all swam in that pool at that house down the street. She blossomed that year. I was ready to make her a woman."

"You were fifteen, and I've seen you in your swim trunks." Stephanie locked eyes with Carmen who dangled her pinkie finger in the air.

"She's still too much of a woman for you," Jacob said, slapping him in the middle of his stomach. "Stick with the likes of Gina."

"Wilkins?"

"Yeah."

"Dude, she's in the seventh grade."

"Exactly. She has a crush on you."

"Tio Anthony paying for your cousin?"

"Who else?" answered Tanya while picking apart the remains of a peanut butter and jelly sandwich.

"One of these days I got to introduce myself to Tio Tony as his long-lost favorite nephew."

"My cousin, Adriana, up in Nebraska, she doesn't even know about quinces, being a woman, wearing makeup, no more dolls," Carmen said. "I told her she could have a Cinderella ball, if she wanted. Boys in zoot suits. Dance cumbias and salsas. She's missing out."

"What you all wanna do after the mall?" asked Vivian.

"Sleep."

"Eat pizza."

"Study."

"V!"

"Movie, y'all!"

"Rent?"

"Blockbuster!"

"No, that takes forever. And I don't want to see *Lost Boys* again, because y'all pick that every time."

"Vanessa and I are going to a movie." Jacob's fingers wiped his faint mustache.

"You mean you'll see a movie and then go to the park and make out."

Vivian, Stephanie, Carmen, and Tanya made kissing sounds and puckered their lips at each other. Vanessa shook her head.

"And the whole time during the movie V will be crying with the characters and saying that it was a timeless story about eternal love and the universal human condition, but Jake will be trying so hard to bust a move on V."

"I heard that." Jacob put Eric in a headlock. "But, yeah, you're right."

"Jake, don't make those poor kids working at the theater clean up after you. They're hourly workers, like you're going to be after graduation."

"If he graduates."

"Sticky floor, Jakey."

"Yeah, those kids work hard for their dime bags."

"Funny. Ha ha."

"No," Vanessa said, refusing to look at Jacob, "let's *all* go tonight."

"Really?" the table asked.

Pouting, Jacob rubbed the palm of his hand over his shorn head.

"Yeah. Let's go see something funny."

"What about studying?"

"I can still do that."

Jacob frowned at Vanessa's answer.

"*Big Lebowski*."

"Again?"

"Nope."

"*Man in the Iron Mask*. It's got Leo." Vivian fluttered her eyelashes.

"*Wild Things*," said Stephen.

"You just want to see two chicks make out." Carmen flicked her tongue at the other girls.

"Maybe V's other boyfriend can give us a suggestion. Qué onda, güero?" Tanya cooed. "What's up, white boy? Which movie?"

"He's a big movie fan, right, V?"

"Timmy!"

"Tim, Tim-a-roo!"

"Tim-o-thay."

"Tim-an-y."

"Tim-may."

"Güero and fresita," the table sang, except for Jacob.

"Yeah, call him up, V." Vivian elbowed Vanessa.

"So much chisme," the girls cooed at the gossip and secrets.

"Uh oh, looks like Jakey don't know everything."

"Hey come on, V, we're just teasing."

"We're just friends," Vanessa said.

The table made kissing sounds.

"Hey, isn't that your dad?"

The table's eight heads snapped toward the street as Roberto's truck rattled to the half-oval driveway and squeaked to a halt near the sidewalk leading to the main building.

"What's he doing here, Vanessa?"

Vanessa watched the driver-side door creak open until her father, dressed in his denim shirt and black corduroys with spots of flour and paint on them slid out. He walked toward the large glass doors of the administration building.

"He brought real food for the cafeteria."

"Finally!"

"We'll all die of bad education but not bad food anymore!"

"He's looking for Jake. He made himself a shank out of a butter knife." Eric mimed cutting his neck with his finger.

"Mr. Ochoa has had enough of Jake touching his daughter," Carmen giggled.

"Cochina," Tanya whispered, elbowing Vanessa. "Such a dirty girl."

Roberto and the principal walked out of the building together.

Jacob's face turned pale. "Shit, he's with Lowell."

"Run, Jakey, I'll distract them." Stephen stood up and pushed Jacob into the open. "He's over here, Mr. Lowell! Jake's over here!"

Both men marched in a straight line, making no extraneous movements or inefficient actions with their bodies. The wind picked up, chilling skin, and as the two men plowed through it, the table grew silent and huddled closer together. Roberto's shirt billowed like a sail; Mr. Lowell's tie flapped to the side of his blazer. Vanessa's father strode with a pace that she had seen before when, his arms hooking down for her and Flora, his shoulders leveled, the angle of his body piercing the air, he had pulled her in one hand and her mother in the other from Vida Nueva and Calderon. Roberto's charge toward Vanessa pushed the school, the parking lot, and the football stadium from her field of vision until his body blocked the afternoon sun.

"Vanessa," Mr. Lowell said, "your father is here to pick you up."

"I'm going home with Stephen and Stephanie after we hit the mall. You said it was OK."

"I'm supposed to take you," Jacob snarled, quickly stopping when Roberto glared at him.

"Vanessa!" her father yelled before calming his voice. "Now...*please*."

Some of the table chuckled; some looked away as Vanessa huffed, snatched her purse, and followed her father.

✺

As he stood up and quickly covered his mouth with his hand, Roberto threw the newspaper on the seat; the waiting room where he teetered reeked of rubber tubing, medicinal cotton, and bleach. Between his shoulders, sweat had darkened his denim shirt, spreading from the center of his back like rings in water. For several seconds, he stood and wrung his hands until he cleared his throat and crossed his arms. Vanessa couldn't tell if he wanted to hide his tears, if he was about to vomit, or both, but she had never seen her father so quickly accelerate from sitting to standing, as though the same source that had first shocked and propelled him to her school now neutralized him. His blue shirt was the only color inside the hospital, where everything was some variation of white.

Vanessa grabbed the newspaper. A story in the bottom right of the front page described a car accident involving a teenage driver, his mom, and a motorcyclist. The teen had pulled into the left-turn lane, nosing into the lane of oncoming traffic on a yellow light as he began his turn, believing that he had a clear space and plenty of time; the motorcyclist in the opposite lane slammed into the car, rolled across the hood, and dropped onto the street, helmet intact, and received severe, but not fatal, injuries. Both the teen driver and his mother were uninjured, mainly because the motorcycle impacted the car's boxy front, crunching the hood, the grille, and the fender, and entirely missed the passenger door. "Rush hour traffic ground to a halt on one of Tulsa's major streets," the reporter wrote. The small color picture, photographed from the rear of the car, showed the station wagon barely damaged, except where the blue and red lights of the police car warped over the tire well; the line of traffic snaked behind it. Neither the biker nor the mother and son were in the picture. The sixteen-year-old, anonymous in the story because of his age, was driving to the grocery store on one of his first outings with his new license. The motorcyclist, taken to one of the other hospitals in town, was twenty-six and a manager at an electronics store in one of the malls, where, his fiancée told authorities, he was headed for his shift.

Vanessa stopped reading because, as intense and tragic as that accident was, all three people involved sounded fine, whereas her mother, unconscious and undergoing emergency surgery because of her critical condition, was not. The nurse who had spoken to her father hadn't appeared again in the hours since they arrived. His arms crossed and pulling the weight of his body forward, Roberto circled the chairs in the middle of the waiting room. Every so often he stopped at the windows.

The newspaper's accident happened yesterday afternoon on a stormy May day. The reporter stood near an intersection that Vanessa had been through many times on the way to the mall, where the motorcyclist worked, and had used the same left-turn lane that the anonymous teenage boy had used, but the story—the people and the places involved—felt strange and distant as Vanessa read it, sitting in the hospital after seven at night. Her mother's accident happened only hours ago, after school, while she sat with her friends in the plaza, killing time, and her knowledge of it came from her father, who boiled it down to a fragment like a headline. But this simplicity narrowed around her when she and her father reached the hospital. Her mother's accident had happened on the side of town where her family lived and worked, but Vanessa did not know the street. Yet Fifth and MacMillan now gripped her mother's name as tightly as it gripped Vanessa while her father stared at the sunset.

She wondered if her mother's accident would be in the newspaper tomorrow morning in the same spot, perhaps, or buried deeper inside, where the advertisements for sales of clothes and the week's discounts for groceries began. Vanessa's eyes closed; her long, thick hair draped over her face. She tried not to imagine the scene that her father had described to her. "A drunk driver hit your mother," he said, hustling on their way from her school. The truck rattled louder than usual when he started it and put it into gear. *Drunk driver in the middle of the day?* she thought to herself, craning her neck at her friends still sitting at the table and assuming all drunk drivers crawled out from shadows and slithered into their cars in the middle of the night while good families and good people stayed in their homes behind locked doors and drawn curtains. On the ride to the hospital, her father remained silent except for deep inhales and exhales and the occasional cursing at traffic and red lights as he sped through areas that he shouldn't have been speeding through. All Vanessa could focus on were the words *your mother*, *accident*, *grave condition*. But as her earlier embarrassment of seeing her father roll into school dug into her as guilt, shock quickly rose around her, chilling her and blurring the edges of her eyesight. She gripped both sides of her hair like a dark shade that would not close.

"Mr. Ochoa," a voice called out. An apple-shaped man with skinny legs and a black goatee wearing scrubs stood on the edge where the hallway's tile floor met the waiting room's carpet. Adjusting the stethoscope around his neck, he held a clipboard in front of him.

Roberto rushed over.

The nurse smiled, but the smile was lips only, curling up slightly, no teeth, and he spoke nothing more than a handful of words to Roberto. The nurse closed and opened his eyes, his head nodding and dropping, and after he smiled his no-teeth smile again, he opened the large door on one side of the reception desk and extended his arm into the hallway.

Pale, Roberto motioned to Vanessa to come with him.

"What is it, Dad? What's wrong with Mom? Dad? Where are we going?" Her rising voice did not extract a response from her father.

The temperature dropped as they followed the nurse, who stopped, turned right, and waited for them to enter behind another heavy door. Their footsteps were the only sounds in an area of the hospital isolated from the other wings and rooms, as though the hallway stretched in clouds or far underground. As the nurse held the door open for them, Vanessa's body quivered, her throat swelled, and her tongue and legs fell numb.

"The driver is fine," her father stuttered, crying and shuffling with her. "He walked away with cuts and scratches...a broken leg and nose. But your mother..." Roberto stopped before entering the sparsely lit room with an empty desk. "Piedad, por favor, piedad. Mercy, please, mercy." Glancing at the ceiling tiles and lights, he pulled Vanessa into the room, his hand never letting go of hers.

"The doctor will be here shortly." The nurse spoke with a deep but gentle voice, stepping out of the room.

Minutes later, the door behind Vanessa and Roberto opened. A doctor pulled up another chair, sat next to them, and nodded with a face softened by sadness. "I'm so sorry, Mr. Ochoa," he said quietly. "Despite our efforts, we were unable to save your wife. We did everything we could. The whole team here wants you to know how sorry we are. When you're ready, come to the front desk and ask for Nurse Richards. He'll find me, and we'll all go together. Take your time." The doctor touched Roberto and Vanessa's shoulders before standing and leaving the room.

Several minutes of silence passed. Roberto uncovered his face. "She was out doing her usual errands. Supplies and groceries for us and the store. That man...the other driver...was driving a huge SUV. Police said he was intoxicated. Destroyed your mother's car like a piece of paper." He looked at his hands with flour smudged on them. "My truck would have survived. It's bigger. She should have been in it."

"Dad, he was drinking," Vanessa whispered.

"She used to tell me, 'I wouldn't be caught dead in that truck.' She teased me all the time about it." His voice cracked. "She hated that truck. She's too small. I said, 'I'll build you a stepstool.' 'No, Berto. I want my own car.' So, I bought her that carachita...that junker. It was so cheap and just for getting around town."

Burying her face in her father's shoulder, Vanessa could see the old Honda Accord crumpled in the middle of Fifth and MacMillan, its hood and driver side smashed, looking similar to the picture of the accident from the newspaper. A month ago she had caught her mother singing in that car. Crying in the chair of the secluded hospital room, Vanessa cringed at the image of her mom rolling into the driveway and shimmying her body under the seatbelt to the song that she and her friends obsessed over that summer. As soon as the tires squeaked, the chassis rattled, and the radio speakers buzzed, Vanessa leapt up from the couch and was about to yell at her mom for being late with the car that the two of them shared and for making Vanessa late to pick up her friends on their way to the mall. But before she marched toward the driveway, Vanessa stood behind the storm door and giggled at her mom sitting in the parked car, trying to rap along with the song, pausing, closing her eyes, and throwing her head and voice into a rhythm that tried to be more Southern hip-hop than Mexican-Spanish and broken English, her voice stuttering and stumbling along with the joy of singing an imperfect result.

✹

The white vertical blinds blurred the Saturday afternoon sun like gauze placed over a light. When Flora's casket had stood at the back of the narrow and deep viewing room, friends, neighbors, and regular customers of the bakery spoke about her, offering their memories and love, and stood off to the side, along the walls, so as to not block the view of her and the line of people waiting their turn.

Roberto's body had acted as an end point for the lilac-tinted casket that hovered between him, the vertical blinds, and the sun working its way down to the right. He mentioned nothing about Flora, heaven, or Jesus; he talked about his love for her, about her love for their daughter, and about their love for the new life, he emphasized, that they had built together as a family of three. And when he finished, he faced the casket, adjusted the bottom of his blazer, faded in the elbows and along the hemlines, and in a voice as steady and clear as he could, quoted a poem to her that reminded how immense, how transformed, and how fully aware of themselves people become by simply closing their eyes and following their hearts. Walking over to the casket, sinking his arms and chest across it, he kissed the top and placed his ear on the lacquered wood, over the small circles of light that had formed on top when the afternoon sun had moved.

After her father motioned to her, Vanessa bolted from her chair to stand next to him. "Te amo, Mama. I love you," she stuttered, looking at the casket and then, unable to say any more, pushing her face into her father's side.

The service ended, and the crowd, one by one, offered their condolences to Vanessa and her father.

"She had a good life," Mrs. Acosta said, draping a long black shawl around her arm. "Todos merecemos una buena muerte. We all deserve a good death." Her dress cascaded silky black down to the funeral home's worn carpet.

"I'm getting some heat for a closed casket and no cross...no crucifix," Roberto sighed. "I couldn't afford *presentation*, they called it. I can barely afford all this." He spread his hands to the room. "They had a price list. It was like checking off groceries. No, yes, no, no." His fingers approved or rejected imaginary prices in the air. "That brings it to over two-thousand dollars. Cut this, cut that to save more money. At least the background music and parking were free." He smiled at Mrs. Acosta.

"Things are different. All these prices and having to let a business handle this. It's like a bank," she said, miming a bad taste in her mouth. "In the old days, it was more personal, less about money. There was a lot of crying...very sentimental. Even my hard-shelled uncles and brothers broke down. Not today." She glared at Vanessa. "What do they think this is? Playtime?"

Vanessa turned around; her friends laughed and talked loudly at the back of the room.

"Black colors, yes, but jeans and t-shirts?" Mrs. Acosta continued. "They look and act no different than when they're at school." She shook her head. "This used to be in a home. The whole neighborhood would stop in. My mother wore black for a year when her mother died. We weren't allowed to do anything noisy in the house. Tranquilo. Everything and everyone tranquil." Her dark eyes locked onto Vanessa before smiling at Roberto. "It doesn't feel like a funeral. We should be sad, not laughing and making jokes. We only see each other at funerals now. They're our little reunions. We catch up with each other, promise to call or check in, but we never do. We go on without really stopping. Then we all get back together again at another funeral. El cuerpo, la comida y pan dulce. The body, food, and sweet bread. The things that bring us together."

Roberto nodded.

"It was my duty to be here," she said, squeezing Roberto's hand and kissing him on his cheek. She hugged and kissed Vanessa before walking away.

Leaning from the crowd of teens he had come with, Tim waved and started walking toward Vanessa, who took a small breath to control a spike in her pulse and to focus on her father. But the closer Tim got to her, the more she felt pulled toward him.

"Hey, Vanessa." He lifted his arms for a hug. His too-large sport coat's shoulder pads slumped forward, while his shirtsleeves dangled past his wrists, nearly to his knuckles.

She smiled and hooked her arms around him. Her eyes closed for the first time that day. "Thank you for coming," she whispered, still embracing him. "You look great." She smiled at the healthier shades of pink around his cheeks; his acne had indeed improved as he had confided to her during winter break.

"Thanks. I'm so sorry, Vanessa."

"Thank you. Me too."

"Is there anything I can do?"

"Bring her back."

Tim smiled the way that the nurse and the doctor in the secluded hospital room had. "I wish I could. She's in a better place."

"Tim..."

"She is, Vanessa. She's in heaven, and..."

"Not now. *Please*, Tim." The words *not now* reverberated in her head and carried off any remains of a world that had become a complex web woven with bargains and if-thens, beliefs and doubts, clear paths and obscured turns. And when those words had finished flying away, a gap opened between an immediate world and a distant world, between past and future, Tim and her, and what she had been told over the years by Calderon and by Tim's church—both of which now sounded like far-off echoes while she waited in the present. Vanessa wanted that gap to be closed, to be bridged by something that had nothing to do with religion, social status, money, or the various lights she was told to carry into the world, illuminating it from the inside for the shadows and the real things and for the lost and the found. Words from Tim or anyone—from either of her two worlds—could not turn her eyes from a darkness falling onto a moment so tangible and fragile that it would break into many pieces with the weight of that descending darkness.

"OK, OK," he responded, reaching for her hand.

She grasped his fingers like someone reaching into a river, feeling how cold and fluid it is, and realizing that a fist can never hold a river that has to reach an ocean.

Throwing his eyes toward the four other youths from Real Life talking on the opposite side of the room while Vanessa's other friends swirled around them, Tim started to speak. "I came with..."

"No, I know," she cut him off.

A girl peered over a red plastic cup and waved at Vanessa and Tim.

"Is she going clubbing after this?" Vanessa scolded. "I mean, I know we're poor brown trash and all, but could she have at least worn something less revealing and more respectful?" Vanessa glared at the hemline of the girl's bright crimson skirt resting high on her thigh. "If she walks over here, I'm afraid she might fall, that thing is so tight. I really don't want her crashing into anything in here. My dad's paying for it all. I don't want anybody getting the wrong idea." She looked at Stephen and Jacob sitting with the rest of her high school friends. She glanced at her girlfriends, at the other kids with Tim, and then at him, and for a brief moment, she still wanted to be someone somewhere different who could accept a love that had no ulterior motive, was given to her merely for who she was, and could move her, if she let it. Her desire to be someone and somewhere different was not about satisfaction in the distance but was about a longing deep inside her, moving her through time and place until she realized how close change had always been.

"I'm sorry we came." Tim stepped away from her.

Crossing her arms, she wiped her eyes. "Yeah, maybe. I got my friends here, my familia..." She sniffed and stared at Tim. "My boyfriend."

He stepped further from Vanessa. "No, I got it. It makes sense." His arms dangled at his side. "Which one is he?"

"You want to know?"

"Yeah, he's a lucky guy to be with you."

She turned her head away from Tim so he couldn't see that she had closed her eyes when he said that and, in turning away, felt that she had surrendered to the present and all its caverns, peaks, and valleys surging in front of her. "That's him." She motioned to the table of her friends and, staring at them, wanted to hold onto the past that shadowed her—the past that was familiar and knew her in ways the present or the future never could; the past that, she knew, would say her name and wait for her, flattening itself once again into one direct path for her to take. "Jacob Padilla. Hey, Jacob!" she yelled over to him, earning a few stares from the older men and women in the room.

Jacob's shaved head lifted from the crowd of high school friends, who gawked and giggled at Tim and Vanessa. "Yo, whad up?" he yelled back, earning the same stares from the same older men and women in the room.

"It's OK, Vanessa. It's a crazy time right now. We can leave. Don't..."

"Yeah, that's him," she mumbled.

"Well… I'm so sorry."

She nodded at Tim.

"I know graduation is next week," he continued.

"Two weeks, in fact. That date is pretty much burned in my head now."

"Mine's next week. Maybe I could come to yours and sit with your dad? I'd really like to be there and watch you walk."

"You don't have to." She looked up at him, her pupils large.

"I know I don't have to, but I'd like to. It'll probably be the last time I see you for a while. You're still going to college and all that, right? You're still going to Northwest State?"

"Yeah."

"Good. You should. You absolutely should. You'll be so amazing there. You're so smart and talented. I'm really excited for you."

"You're going to TCC, right?"

"Yep, community college, here I come." He blandly pumped his fist in the air. "More time to figure out what I should be doing. My dad enrolled me in this after-school program that's supposed to help me figure out what I like to do and how to turn it into a job. I talk to this career counselor every Wednesday."

"Really?"

"Yeah. It's not like a guidance counselor at school. I mean, that person is useless because I can't go to the University of Special Effects."

Vanessa chuckled with him.

"This person helps you with your interests. I took this computer test the first day I was there and answered all these multiple-choice questions. Do I like science? Do I like art? Math? Are you happier working with a team or on your own?"

"And?"

"Guess."

"Artist. Duh, right?"

"You know me pretty well."

"Who else would you be? A banker? A doctor?"

"Not those. My dad would want those."

"No med school like your dad?"

He shook his head. "My mom and dad are supportive, but they always said, 'Make sure it pays the bills first.'"

Vanessa scanned the room. Her father stared into the lower-angled light; Eric and Stephen made flatulent sounds with the palms of their hands but tried their best not to be caught; Tanya braided Carmen's hair, twisting its cherry reds and blacks; Jacob scowled at her and Tim every now and then as his foot rubbed a rhythm on the carpet; and Tim stood close to her, his presence slowing everything and everyone around her like wings settling on the ground after having travelled from a long way away—how she always felt when she was with him. "After-school program," she giggled.

"I know. I sound like a juvey."

"You'll be like Jacob now."

"I guess that means Jacob and I have *two* things in common."

Blood rushed to her head and heart, and closing her eyes, she waited until the feeling of the past tripping the present on its way from underneath her had disappeared. She cleared her throat before saying to him, "I think you already know what you want to do."

"Yeah. My dad's set up an interview with this company in town that produces videos. He knows the owner through church."

"That's good."

"But I don't want to move to Hollywood. I'm not sure I could do it."

"It may be good for you," Vanessa laughed, holding back a comment about him being a sheltered white boy and getting some street smarts were he to move there. "I could probably hook you up with some East LA connections," she teased him. But then she became serious, stared at him, and blocked out everyone else around her—those who could claim they knew something about her, little pieces stitched together that resembled her but weren't really her. "I can't wait to get out of here for good," she said, her mouth neither smiling nor sad, her eyes locked on Tim's.

"For good?"

"Yeah."

"You're planning on leaving?"

"I'm getting out of here as soon as I can."

"I thought you meant just college. Like, you'd go there and then come back."

"No, I don't want to be in this town. I mean, it was Nowhere State, the safety school, or working minimum-wage jobs…waiting for something to pan out. OU would have been nice, but it's too expensive, even for in-state. What are my options? That?" She nodded at her high school friends. "Working at a hair salon? Going to the mall every day? Joining the military? *What?*" Vanessa caught her voice's tone rising with frustration.

Her father paced the room and glanced at his watch.

Vanessa thought of her mother's casket lowering into the ground, the density of it, and the weight of it carried by men her father knew. The casket sunk like a purple petal into the dark hole that had to be dug.

"Before you leave for college, we're having a big going-away party for all the seniors at Real Life. You're totally invited. I could pick you up, and afterward we could go see a movie or hang out like we used to, go to..."

"That's nice, thank you, but..."

"OK. Maybe we could hang out soon. Just the two of us."

"I don't know."

After Vanessa replied, Tim glanced at Jacob, her friends, his friends, and the room holding Roberto and Vanessa in the middle as the sun revolved around them. "OK. I guess it's time for me to go."

"You didn't have to come for everything today," she said. "I know it was a lot. The viewing, the burial...all this. Thank you," her voice softened. "I'm glad you did. I wanted you here."

He smiled and hugged her. "Bye, Vanessa. I'm really sorry about your mom. I'd really like to see you before we each start a new chapter."

Wiping her cheeks and avoiding falling into memories that could decide the next moment for her, Vanessa said nothing to Tim's wish before he left through the same faux-wood doors that her mother's casket had rolled through, her father had shuffled through, and she had followed her father through—all of them merging in the rectangular room with one of its ends facing the sunset, while time outside the room swept down before arching over the four walls stuffed like a box with recollections and what's missing.

"It's time," Roberto said, appearing next to her as suddenly as Tim disappeared. His face was soft, steady.

Time? she thought. *Time to do this again? Time for something else? Something worse?* "Time?" she asked him.

"The funeral home closes in fifteen minutes. We can't stay. I can't afford their overtime."

15

Time possessed her on the flight to San Francisco from her stop in Denver. The end of the day and the beginning of the next stalled in front of her, and yet, headed west, she raced the sun before it set. Moving minute by minute backward in time, slivers from where she had been, she could gain back the time that she had lost from where she had started a day ago. Newer light and shorter shadows would greet her as she headed into an earlier version of the day rising over the waters and the mountains—the illusion of the sun never ending as the world spun on its axis. She was present in and moving between one world leaving and another becoming, the preceding one wilting before the new one replaced it. But her heart ached because the hours that she had briefly earned couldn't be held and were already slipping forward, were meant to slip forward, as the airplane strung an invisible line between two points and would bring her to the endpoint where more days would pass over her. She refused to focus on the things that she was losing and, instead, focused on the many things that waited to spiral out, starting again just past zero.

The landscape changed: seams of the mountains stitched up to the middle; tan Rorschach-shapes on mountaintops, dark greens nuzzled alongside, water breaking it up; the ocean taking in the vertebrae of the land; islands, bridges, boats in the Bay scribbling frothy question marks in the water; and white and gray buildings on the crosshatched peninsula pulled up like mounds and towers of snow. The red of the Golden Gate glistened in the sunlight.

"Never gets old," commented the woman on Vanessa's left. "It's so beautiful around this time of year."

"I know," Vanessa said, before returning to the scenery. Stuck in the middle of the row, nauseous, her right eye blurry for most of the flight, pain in her throat and head, she could do nothing more than smile in return and offer a small answer that calmed her by connecting her to the land and the ocean. Anytime the woman moved—to drink her wine, fan herself, or change the amount of cool air blasting on her, twisting the nozzle until her bracelets clanged together—an aroma wafted toward Vanessa. There was nothing celestial about the woman's perfume; its earthy pungency crept into Vanessa's sinus passages, prickled the inside, and intensified her pains and nausea. She swallowed hard in order to focus on the pit of her stomach, which throbbed and bubbled. The sunlight and the beeping of the Fasten Seatbelt sign as they approached the runway helped, acting as guideposts.

The man on Vanessa's right reminded her of Dan, especially when he had stowed away his jacket, flopped next to her, and fastened his seat belt, all the while absorbed with his phone until the last possible minute. She couldn't help but look at him. He had several gray hairs by his ears that stood out when the airplane crossed into more light and the cabin brightened. He had bushy eyebrows, and when he read his *Wall Street Journal*, the fold of his left cheek twitched toward his ear and then relaxed before his eyes shifted to another chart or article. During the flight, he checked his watch often; its large face flickered in the light like jagged metallic clouds; the wide band wrapped around his wrist in a steady downpour of silver. The more he checked his watch, garishly rolling his wrist so that his shirt's sleeve shortened, the more Vanessa believed he was presenting himself the way mammals do. He would roll his wrist, check his watch, and then shifting in his seat, dust off his black slacks while his loafers delicately balanced on the edge of the aisle. She may have spent too much time staring at him until she realized that she had crossed the Rockies and into Pacific Time.

After the plane landed, Vanessa's whole body ached, and her head throbbed while she stood in line at the car rental. Although her eyesight had improved, it remained blurry. *If the DMV could see me now*, she mused. Self-service kiosks and lines of people standing at the brightly lit touchscreens packed the room. Many of the people punching the keys threw their hands in the air and, spinning around, begged for help from the one employee on the floor weaving in and out of a maze of customers clogging the middle of the room; the number of people renting cars on a Tuesday afternoon shocked her. Bending and squinting at the sign, assuming that she was correctly where she needed to be, she nearly fell into the fabric belt defining the line. A wheel from a rolling bag clipped her. A young man mumbled a general apology to everyone. Vanessa gingerly navigated around him. She told herself not to check her phone until she arrived at the bed and breakfast. She closed her eyes long enough to want only the car that would take her closer to the ocean.

An hour and a half later, a voice behind the counter greeted her without bothering to look at her. "If you're driving along Highway One," the young woman said to her, typing away furiously, "you'll want to feel the ocean air, the excitement of the road. How can I get you that today?"

After stuffing the confirmation email that she had handed to the employee back into her backpack, Vanessa shook her head and crossed her arms.

"No? OK." The young employee's typing slowed to a few strokes. "The computer has found you in the system." She tottered to the rear counter on high black heels and in a tight green skirt. She waited for her turn and ripped the papers from the printer while her colleagues bounced around her, yelling out numbers and pulling managers from behind the back counter to help with customers' questions and concerns.

What a mess, Vanessa sighed. Purchasing the airline tickets had been less demanding.

On her way back to the counter, receipt in hand, the young employee grabbed a bright, colorful brochure and laid it between the contract and Vanessa. "It doesn't cost much for an upgrade, especially on a day like this. Just imagine..." She did not look at Vanessa while placing her finger on the image of a couple in their sixties laughing as they put her shopping bags and his golf clubs in the back seat of a maroon convertible. The man wore a red Hawaiian-print shirt; a white tennis sweater wrapped around the lady's baby-blue polo; both of them wore khaki shorts. After writing a dollar amount on the brochure, the employee circled it with a pink highlighter balanced in her fingers. "The upgrade is only this much more. A great deal, if you ask me. It's such a nice day out. A convertible or an SUV would be great." As the computer hummed, she clicked her mouse and took Vanessa's credit card. "Do you know about our Rewards Program? Once you're a member, we can automatically use the card that's on file. It speeds up the process, and you'd have lots of award points with your travels."

Vanessa stared at the woman's smooth, oval face and the thin red headband keeping hair away from her large eyes. The line behind Vanessa had packed itself tighter than when she first came in—more people waiting, more people crawling over each other to move forward and turning at each corner of the maze. Repeating or correcting information for the young employee, listening to all the sales tactics, and watching her type, Vanessa chuckled. Part of her thought about trying to use Dan's account, his lawyer be damned, in order to rack up enormous service fees and upgrades, rent a GPS, and throw in a ski rack—just because. But she closed her eyes and focused on what lay below the recent past and what was waiting for her once she left the line with keys in hand.

She skimmed over the contract and pretended to confirm personal information, breezing past names, dates, and addresses—all of these bits of information oscillating in and out of her as something unimportant and causing her to think of where she had come from and where she was headed to and that she now moved in a different kind of time than the world typically provided. She reviewed the dates again; she could change them whenever she was ready.

The young employee scanned the screen, "OK, Mrs. Ochoa, your vehicle is in row A, slot twenty-one."

Hearing her assumed marital status, Vanessa wanted to correct the employee, but the small pain building inside her head distracted her. The employee smiled before walking away from the desk. A few other customers in the nearby lines glanced at Vanessa as she laughed out loud at a sign on the counter that she hadn't noticed before. The rental company sold used cars, and Vanessa imagined buying one for Tim, who would recycle its gears, circuits, knobs, and fabric—all of it dangling in his studio—into a new creature. He could shape the foam from the seats into wings. Such a change flickered through her.

✹

At the bottom of the hill, she assumed that the car would have no problem getting up the steep ascent, but as the road's winding length and its severe angle seemed never-ending, she laughed—one of the upgrades from the car-rental employee may have been prescient. An SUV and its bullish V-8 engine would have no problem conquering the road. Fallen branches, large rocks, and the setting sun's glare and shadows through the thick redwoods created obstacles that required the compact car to go very slowly, which made Vanessa feel that she and it could slide back down the hill.

But up she went, reaching the peak, turning left onto a grassy plain overlooking cliffs, daffodils, and the ocean. A golden dog jogged over to greet her but kept a distance until the car stopped. Cocking its head and panting, the dog sat outside her door. As soon as Vanessa got out, the dog trotted over, tail wagging, and dropped a ball from its mouth. Dirty water dripped from its belly while bits of leaves and dirt clung to its damp, matted hair.

"Throw it," a young voice yelled behind her.

Taking off her sunglasses, Vanessa turned around and squinted at a small boy in shorts and a long flannel shirt. Mud caked his shorts, knees, and the bottom of his shirt. His eyes and smile broadened as he picked up the ball and handed it to Vanessa. The sunlight nearly blinding her, Vanessa lifted her arm back but then threw the ball underarm; the pain in her neck and shoulder restricted her mobility. The ball rolled toward the field behind the farmhouse where the boy and the dog careened after it. The dog beat the boy to it and then jumped into the pond that was near them. Vanessa covered her mouth as she laughed, which brought on a hard, guttural cough and a sharp pain tingling down her head and neck. After sunspots dissolved from her eyes, she regained her balance and slumped on the driver-side door.

"Hello there. Welcome, welcome," said a gentle female voice near her.

Composing herself, Vanessa turned toward the house. A stout woman with short hair, frosted natural white, closed the red front door and walked down the steps. "Hi. I'm..." Vanessa mumbled, losing her thought while the numbness in her tongue subsided and the golf-ball-sized glow inside her head evaporated, leaving her stranded. "Vanessa," she recovered, believing that she had mouthed her name before hearing it; the sound echoed in her mind.

"I thought it was you." The woman smiled, standing on the border of the garden brightened with flowers. "You're the last one to make it. Full house."

"I hope I didn't mess you up."

"Oh no." The owner tightened her denim jacket and slung her purse onto one forearm. "Welcome, dear. Ruth." Her soft hands warmly embraced Vanessa's. "I was just putting out a note and your key for you. I have to run into town for an errand. Dates. Ran out of them this afternoon. Arthur needs a break anyway."

"The boy? The dog?"

"No, the dog is Sage. The boy is here with his mom and dad. Arthur Itis." Ruth's grin wrinkled her face in the late afternoon sun as she held up her swollen knuckles.

Vanessa chuckled with her.

"I'll be back shortly. Make yourself at home. My husband is in and out today. You may see him puttering about the yard out there or in the barn. If you need anything, just grab him. He's Bert, not the dog...or

Arthur." Giggling, she handed a large brass key to Vanessa. "You have the Captain's Room. Upstairs, down the little hall, first door at the end."

"Thank you."

"You're so welcome. Oh, and around the corner here by the kitchen, we still have tea and snacks set out." She pointed over her shoulder at the bay window on the first floor. "Some beer and wine too. Help yourself. I'll tell Bert to hold off on ending happy hour, now that you're here. See you soon." Ruth waddled off to the truck by the barn, got in, and rumbled down the same road winding above the ocean that had brought Vanessa up to the bed and breakfast.

Vanessa stacked her arms on the car's roof and buried her face into the space between them; her head pounded more intensely. She tightly closed her eyes and pleaded for the pain to go away.

"Are you OK?" the boy asked, holding the ball in one hand and petting the dog with the other.

Her eyes red, her mouth wet, her skin pale, Vanessa turned toward them. She saw smudges that would normally be faces, eyes, and mouths. The dog was quite golden and shimmied like sunlight through a river. The colors of the young boy's flannel shirt blurred like paints mixed on a palette. His dark curls capped his soft face, and his short skinny arms and legs twitched in the cool air. Part of him stood concerned; another part of him, with ball in hand, was ready to uncoil into play.

"Are you OK?" he asked again, his voice distant like coming from inside a metal tube.

Gulping in more air, Vanessa's breathing slowed, which helped her refocus on the sights and sounds around her, sharpening them once more. "I'm fine. Thank you." She wiped her eyes and sweaty forehead. She steadied herself against the front bumper, and slinging the backpack onto her shoulder, cautiously tiptoed into the house, hoping that she wouldn't run into any of the other guests.

The bedroom's heavy door closed behind her; its dark stain matched the wood floor. "Hey, I'm home," she said out loud, panting from the climb up the stairs. The air was heavy. The soft blue plaster walls muffled the outside sounds. "Anyone..." she stopped saying after realizing that she was alone and not where she thought she was.

Dropping her backpack near the built-in bookshelves, she ran her hands over the fireplace's crimson red brick, dodging seashells, a ship's clock, and compasses. Colored-pencil drawings of nature lined some of the shelves—plants, ocean life, butterflies. Two prints above the fireplace caught her eyes. One was an old map of Monterey Bay, a faint vanilla color with red-brown foxing spilling out from under the edges and the brass frame. The ocean off to the left had no color; the space meant to be the water was nothing more than the plain paper on which it came. A thick green line meandered from the top left, horizontal until about halfway in, and then it dove down most of the map, creating a small margin on the right and spiking at the bottom—an abstract land shaped by an abstract sea.

Vanessa could see something resembling numbers in the plain water, most of them clustered near the coast, fewer and fewer further from land, like puffs of black smoke. *There*, she thought, *or there...just like that.* Blinking her eyes and keeping her hand on the fireplace's shelf for balance, she slid down to the other print—an etching of a large sea serpent with multiple fins that diminished in size toward the end of its long, barbed tail. Waves frothed and slapped against its bulky body. The leviathan had stopped its pursuit as doves and light spilling through dark clouds guided a boat to safety.

The muscles in her legs locked up, and she flopped into the chair by the fireplace; her sweaty, swollen body squeaked against the leather. She breathed more from her mouth as she sent one hand into her pocket and fished out her phone. *Haven't heard from you all day. You OK?* Tim had texted around mid-morning. Less than two hours later: *Where are you? I'm worried.* "I know," she said aloud. *Vanessa, please, please get a hold of me* was the last one before his missed calls and voicemails multiplied. Crying, she turned off the phone after listening to half of the first one from him.

Vanessa took in a deep breath and then, exhaling, pushed herself out of the chair and slogged toward the nearby bed. She struggled throwing her hips onto the high mattress, but once reaching it, she sank deeply and softly into its cloudy white sheets and blue comforter. The pillows propping her head relieved her pain briefly and allowed her to look around the room at more of the nautical decor forged in paper, pewter, or copper, all shining in the setting sun. "I know," she muttered. "But I don't want to yet."

Over the bed and centered between two oars, a mariner's astrolabe dangled by its outer ring notched with degrees; the alidade in the inner frame pivoted like a golden teeter-totter when Vanessa touched it. She pressed her cheek against the cold wall and closed her blurry right eye. The alidade swung until the small holes on each end aligned and the sunset, pouring into the window directly across from her, marked her with an orange dot.

"No, it's not like that. I'll explain later…the next time I see you. Thank you. Me too," she whispered, patting the duvet. "I'm tired. Nor Cal. No, around there. I told you. We talked about this." Sinking back into the bed, she was hungry but didn't want to eat because that would require trudging back downstairs and getting behind the wheel of the car.

"Shouldn't drive," she said out loud, covering the top quarter of her face with her forearm. Exhaustion immediately overwhelmed her, but she feared not waking up more than going to sleep. She nodded at the window. Her mouth and tongue jammed; saliva collected at the base of her throat. Her eyes squeezed shut. Having slid from behind her skull, the pain in her head sank on the right side of her face, pressing on the back of her eyeball. Her body shook, her hands quivered like wings, and she was aware of what was coming, like a train plodding down the tracks, its pale blue light becoming wider and brighter, voltage tingling throughout her body.

As Vanessa slipped into the seizure, the pale blue light bursting fully in her head, her body electric, the boy and the dog appeared in the room. The boy took her hand and led her down a trail from the front of the house, across the garden, over the slopes and humps of the land, and toward the ocean. Looking behind her, the gray house of the bed and breakfast nestled in the grass. The dog licked the boy's hand, the boy let go of Vanessa's, and she drifted out over the field of daffodils, wandering like a cloud broken free, out over the small coastal towns hidden between the airport and tomorrow morning's destination, over the hills and sheer cliffs, the lumps and ridges of the green mountains and coastal scrub falling toward the endless blue sea.

It was exactly as she thought it would be. Nearly choking herself, she took a large breath in, held it, closed her eyes, and released it. Far out in front of her, she could see the ocean rippling under the sun that was lower than when she was in the room. Oranges and pinks, metallic wrinkles in the water, golden flashes like keyholes and knobs, bright gates blinking underwater, the ocean and its consistent promise of surface and light loosening all that an eye sees, holds, and eventually releases. As the sunlight bled out, she stopped moving forward, a weight returned to her, and going any further was too soon. She would be there tomorrow, closer, no longer reaching for it through fields and fields of echoes and the invisible endurance of intuition, like a body turning inward toward itself and then opening outward, aligning with image and word and with the feeling of having been there before and of needing to come back where the place and the time would remind her of colors that have passed away but will come around again, unlocking everything as needed.

Vanessa woke in the middle of the night in a pool of sweat, shivering from the cold, drooling from her mouth, and snot running down her nose. At first, she didn't know where she was until she turned her head and saw the clock's hands at two-thirty in the morning. She tried calling for help, but, her jaw contracting, she couldn't speak, and her heavy body could not move. She laid in the darkness. The clock softly spun, its rhythm ticking in cotton. Shadows shrunk the room and the many things inside its walls. She was closer, her heart and blood hotter, pulsating like a sun continuing on its course. Another night was spinning into day as evening and its stars slid toward the other side and the oncoming light prepared what she would see.

✹

In the morning, Vanessa woke again, with a mild headache, but able to speak and move. The room was cold but warmly lit by the rising sun. She could smell breakfast, which she took as a good sign. She rolled out of bed and stiffly walked toward the bathroom's basin, where, bending over it, splashing water on her puffy face, and dabbing the back of her neck with a washcloth, she was thankful that she had reserved a room with a private bathroom. Sitting on the edge of the claw-foot tub, she sobbed, believing that by now, Tim had contacted her father. *California*, she could hear Tim say. *She said somewhere north...coastal...around San Francisco. Hurry, please, don't let her be alone. Please. We can go. I have to go with you.* Vanessa cocked her head at this voice. Had she said something to Tim? Had she told him too much at some point? Had her simple desire to be here become something else and slipped out when she wasn't watching or paying attention? She couldn't remember.

At breakfast, she was forced to be someone else for a little longer—a Vanessa who had existed when she was with Dan and when pieces of this Vanessa reconnected with Tim months ago. Swallowing hard, she scooted her chair to the table where other strangers sat waiting for tea, coffee, and the food sizzling in the kitchen. "Good morning," she said to no one in particular as she unfolded the linen napkin on her lap and relished the cinnamon, orange, and sugar that had dissolved in her coffee. *Café de olla*, she thought, acknowledging a cosmic irony placed warmly in her hands.

Ruth's large hips knocked open the kitchen's saloon doors, and the warmth that she had exuded yesterday when Vanessa met her, this stranger pulling her in, spread as soon as she walked into the dining area. "We have steel-cut oatmeal with cinnamon, butter, dates, and a splash of syrup," she said, setting down bowls. When she returned with more dishes from another trip to the kitchen, she whispered to Vanessa, "I told you Arthur and I would finish chopping those dates. I guess you could say we had our own date."

Vanessa smiled at Ruth, who giggled in return, and then looked at the bowl steaming in front of her; butter melted like a river of gold carving channels into the oats. The house and the things inside smelled like a garden filled with light and buoyancy. Vanessa glanced into the nearby study where, surrounded by shelves, her abuelita sat in a chair, her plump body wrapped in her rainbow blanket around her waist and legs, waiting quietly and always listening, as her mother had described. Her father appeared from behind a corner and, after opening a book, offered it to a pair of hands, the body hidden by a wall of light, holding a rosary with a small shell attached alongside the crucifix, where a butterfly landed after fluttering through the window.

"Bert has cooked you eggs with slices of salmon, dill, and a little cream cheese and sweet potatoes on the side," Ruth continued, her glasses gleaming in the morning sun. "Anyone need anything?" Looking at the table full of guests and their plates of food, Ruth smiled and wiped her hands on her apron.

"More room in my stomach," answered a man across from Vanessa.

The long oak table laughed in agreement. Vanessa leaned over her breakfast and inhaled deeply.

"Good. OK, enjoy," Ruth said before spinning into the kitchen and ducking under a low-hanging rack of pots. She kissed Bert on his cheek when he hobbled to the refrigerator, grabbing his cane on the way.

"It'll be a long flight back home," the man at the table continued.

"Where's home?" asked a woman sitting at one end.

"Roanoke, Virginia."

"Are you serious?" exclaimed the woman.

"Born and bred. Twelfth generation. You?"

"Yes. That was my first guess, but I didn't want to say anything." The woman blushed and laughed; she then smiled and rocked the baby on her knee. "But I know that accent when I hear one." The woman, who Vanessa guessed must have been in her forties, raised her baby up and pressed her to her shoulder with one arm while loading her fork with food in the other. "We're in Phoenix now, but I was born and raised around Bristol," she chuckled. "Left there when I was eighteen for New York City. First thing I had to do when I got to college was drop that accent."

"Now that puts a real damper on my day," the mustached man said, teasing her as he topped off his coffee. "It'll come back. Or just pass it on to the next generation." He winked at her and twirled his fingers at the baby.

"I've always wanted to see that part of the country," Vanessa peeped, smiling at the strangers surrounding her, her eyes blurrier from the night. "I've heard the Atlantic Ocean is different than the Pacific. Different colors, different sounds. Even the seafood, I've heard, tastes a little different. But I'll take the Pacific."

"Me too," the mother said. "Where are you from?"

"Tulsa. Before that, Denver." Vanessa coughed and cleared her throat. She rolled her shoulders and closed her eyes. The two cities fused in her head. Neither city seemed much different to her; they had been nothing more than cities with skyscrapers and traffic, culture, and history. One city stretched westerly until the mountains drew it in, pulling the grassland across rocks and evergreens in thin-air altitude; the other city sloped down toward the southern middle of the country where so many things could be seen in all directions from a single vantage point, past the thick woodlands, hills that build into eastern mountains, a river and streams, and patches of prairie. But the two cities had also been where she had come from and had to return to before getting anywhere else. "It was home...up until recently. Both," she said.

"Are you out here for vacation?" the mustached man asked.

"I'm out here to be out here," Vanessa answered, smiling and sipping her coffee.

"Colorado's a nice state," said a light-brown-haired man, reaching for the bowl of sugar and accidentally tipping the orange juice glass of the man next to him. "Sorry," he whispered, kissing this other man, who smiled and pushed up his glasses as his napkin soaked up the small spill. "We love traveling out there. Hiking. Good beer. The mountains. Ever been to Chautauqua?"

"No, but I've heard about it. Not too far away from where I lived."

The light-brown-haired man nodded. "They have this barn, and they showed a movie when we were there. It was a silent movie, and they had this live, little four-piece outfit playing along. Cello, violin, bass, piano. It brought this real nice feeling to the place. And it was summer at night with the mountains and the outdoors. So beautiful and peaceful."

"What was the movie?" asked the man from Virginia, wiping his mouth.

"*Sunrise*." He clicked his fingers. "Murnau. FW Murnau. It's an old black-and-white movie."

The man in glasses next to him hummed in agreement. "Really beautiful tale." Bread cracked in his hands as he spread butter and jam.

"Hey there," the mother cooed after the young boy ran into the room and hugged her. "Did you have fun playing with Sage?"

The little boy nodded.

"Is Daddy coming to breakfast?" the mother asked, sharing her plate.

The little boy nodded again and looked at Vanessa. She caught herself looking at him but didn't worry how long—and didn't stop herself from looking. The boy brought a silence and a balance that was also Vanessa's for a moment but that she would have to surrender and find somewhere else on her own once she left the table and drove further into the day.

"What's the movie about?" another guest at the table asked.

"It's about love and mistakes and a tearful reunion," the man wearing glasses said, lifting a glass of water. "And it all happens within a day. All by sunrise."

16

And then he repeated her name, not for clarification, not out of confirmation, but with pleasure and curiosity electrifying his face and his voice. Her name brought a smile to his face—and a larger smile when he repeated her name; an invitation opening more. She realized that she stared at him, his words and his face somehow familiar, already part of her life but hidden until needing to be revealed at that moment, although she had never heard or seen him before, and thought, *No, no, no, you're a white boy, güero. There's no way you'll ever be into me, and I can't be into you.* But he stood there, juggling the paper bags, which she had filled with pastries and cartons of chocolate milk, coffee cup in his other hand that he refilled before leaving. He stood there, smiling and nodding at her, a young man like no one she's been around except maybe for her friend Eric, who's sensitive, shy, and teased all the time by the rest of her friends, especially by Tanya and Jacob, who slugged his arm at lunch or after school hanging out by the fountain in the student plaza; who, after goading Eric, motioned to Vanessa to go behind the pool, away from the parking lot and their friends. But this white boy standing in front of her, repeating her name, telling her that she's cute and that he likes talking with her as he looked ready to leave but couldn't yet pull himself away, looking at her in a much different way than how Jacob has looked at her— Jacob who has always started at her chest and ended at her backside or started at her backside and ended at her chest; who could only snarl, watch, or grunt because those were the only things he knew and wanted to know; who always spun inside what he had brought with him or inside what someone had encased him. But this young man didn't do that; he said something that lingered with her and brightened around her until she had to brace herself from following it too soon. As he said her name, he looked at her wearing a t-shirt and apron, neither of which revealed her curves but also did not hide much. This young man is not like Jacob, Eric, or the fathers, older brothers, and tios and padrinos she has heard about— hiding their vulnerability and fragile secrets. *Machismo*, she thought, feeling something delicate shift between her and this young man.

"My name is Tim," he said, after stumbling into the bakery, smiling at her, and telling her that she's cute. But he also paid attention to what she said—not only her looks—as though this was the beginning where he could share something fragile and secret with her. Maybe something lightened around him as it lightened for her when he first said "Hi." And that light widened as they stood there for a few silent moments after he repeated her name and juggled the snacks and the coffee that he claimed to love. She tried shaking him from her mind, telling herself that he was just being polite, maybe fake-polite, not truly smiling at her or interested in her, the bakery, and its symbols of time and place and the cycles of life and death painted on the walls. Yet as much as she held him at bay, something also pulled her—a chasing after—the minute they saw each other. He asked for her name and stuck out his paint-stained hand. She had never seen him before in her life; he was on the wrong side of town. What else was there to do but smile back at him and pursue this light that widened the more it unfolded around her and the longer he stood there talking to her?

"Are you open?" he had asked, standing in the summer heat with his gangly body, disheveled hair, and red face. His voice cracked; sincerity filled his question and tone.

After the door chimed, Vanessa stopped rolling dough in the kitchen. Wiping her hands on an apron with flour scattered on it, she walked behind the counter. "Yes," she replied, blushing. A gold barrette with plastic jewels pulled her long hair back.

"I saw the Grand Opening sign out front and, um, just didn't know if you really were." He smiled at her.

"We are. Almost a month now."

"That's so awesome. Congrats." He nodded, kept his eyes focused on her eyes until he glanced down at her ring with the splinter of wood inside it.

She said, "May I help you with something?"

"We'd like to get some snacks. I mean, me...um, we," he stuttered, pointing to a van and a truck pulling a trailer with grills, lumber, and teenagers. "We're really hungry, and this place just looked perfect. Plus, it's near where we're working. And I was right...super-cool place."

"Thank you."

"So, what do you suggest?"

"We have all these great buñuelos."

"What are those?"

"Taco Bell calls them crispas," she giggled. "Crunchy cinnamon-sugar."

"Good ol' Taco Bell." Tim's face beamed. "I bet yours are better. Yes, please. All of them."

"All of them? OK. You really are hungry." She emptied the plastic tray of all that she and her mother had made that morning. "We have chocolate milk over there in the refrigerator. I hear it's good for building muscles," she added, laughing as he flexed his scrawny arms. "Just tell me what you want, and I'll scoop them out for you."

"That'd be great. How about some of those? Thank you." He pointed to several glazed cookies, breads, and cakes. "Smells like home in here. Is this your place? I mean, do you own it?"

"My parents own it." After shaking open several large paper bags, she placed every snack that he had selected.

"We've been helping a church over here all day. This is our break."

"What are you doing?"

"We're helping build an addition on to this church. Vida Nueva."

She corrected his mispronunciation; laughing with her, he apologized. She repeated the name until he said it the way that she said it.

"It's a really good place. Good families and new friends there," he said. "And I'm really fortunate to help another church this summer because that's what Christians do, because it's out of love, even if the denominations aren't the same." He paused to look at her. "Love builds. Love is the most important doctrine."

At first she wondered if what he said, which was so direct and pure, was scripted the way sometimes Calderon's responses seemed scripted—an indirect answer used to control rather than a clear answer allowing for the grace of discovery. But Tim's face and smile hid nothing, as though his mere presence had been brought to her, as though he had to be there in the store before anything else in her life could follow that moment. She believed him, believed what he said in his direct and pure way, and nodded but held close to her anything more about Vida Nueva. But when he said the word *doctrine*, her heart unfolded and widened more; a word that she would mention in her journal and after reading it in a book; a word none of her friends would use. She remembered Calderon and how he was no longer scary or intimidating. He had asked for forgiveness one Sunday morning in front of a packed congregation, but he did not specify. "I cleaned my heart. I cleaned my service to you and to our Lord. I cleaned the past for a better future. I cleaned the money," he said—cleaned it all, investing it in the church, its families, and community programs. Vanessa's mother told her that Calderon married a woman from a medical-supply store after meeting her when he was there. Flora heard all about this from the neighborhood ladies who loved to stop by the store and talk while flour, icing, and sugar flew through the oven-warm air. "She's helped him with his mobility, lectures, and the families coming to him and Vida Nueva for aid," Flora said. "Honest help this time around." Her parents have called Calderon's wife "a good shepherd," but her father, at first, grimaced and rolled his eyes. "Too bad she wasn't there when we were," he often muttered when Calderon's motorized wheelchair hummed by the farmers' market, his oxygen tank hissing and popping down the path. The two men nodded when they couldn't ignore each other near the tent with the poster and its hand-written Flora's Panadería Mexicana – Authentic Sweets & Breads outlined in red and green.

For a long time, Tim and Vanessa stood in the store and in the summer light as though night would never come and no shadow could dull the small skulls painted on the walls near the counter or the large circular calendar sketched on the long, main concrete wall. Fluorescent lights accented the water-damaged wood trim; a shelf of flowers, candles, a statue of the Holy Mother, and small Mexican and American flags; and photos of mountains, Aztec temples, and faces of Mexican cinema and literature. "No sports," her father emphasized—cultura only, to which her mother agreed, although Roberto would sometimes sneak a peek at a baseball or college football game on the small TV in the stockroom where clouds of flour flickered in the lights and where he grumbled about cracks in the display case, exposed ductwork, and booths in need of new upholstery; but also from where he had found his private happiness of watching lovers and families share Flora's sweets with each other. "Today, the chocolate-chile cheesecake was very popular," he would say, winking and grinning at Flora and Vanessa. "Lots of big smiles, several kisses, and joyful faces. Todos tan felices. Everyone so happy."

And as Tim picked out sweets and noticed the coffee pots by the counter, Vanessa wondered where he went to school because he was clearly on the wrong side of town. School had flown by so quickly for her that she barely noticed that it was summer again, which meant working full-time at the bakery, babysitting on weekends, swimming at the community pool with her friends when she could, and hanging out with Jacob at night after he barely made an effort at the grocery store where he avoided stocking the dairy section, stole potato chips and cheese sticks, and hated everyone and every minute of bagging and helping customers to their cars. "He looked at the floor before we opened, and he said, 'Do it again. That's a piss-poor job, Mr. Jiménez.' I mean, who does that old fat bald dude think he is? I got a güero for a manager, that's who. He ain't even the main dude. He's a shift manager. Old fat bald shift manager. You know how much bank he makes? Not that much." Jacob told Vanessa that he can't be seen as a chavala, a wussy, and she laughed but then felt guilty, and then it was suddenly summer as Tim greeted her and introduced himself with a smile and eyed the coffee, and she wanted to see him again although he had yet to say goodbye. "Strong, no sugar," he said to her, his head flopping down from laughing and blushing, his acne prominent in the sunlight. "Leaded. Just like my grandma used to say." She could tell that he was stalling and didn't drink coffee because his teeth were too white for a coffee drinker but not for a family with dental coverage and money for braces and polishing. And yet she believed that she knew something about him, but she didn't know what that something was, how to find it, or if it would find her. His presence invited her, but she didn't know where.

Was his grandma dead, like hers? Did his grandma die at forty, like hers? "Just like her mother and her mother before her," Flora had said, folding laundry outside their trailer in the lot behind Vida Nueva as Vanessa stretched her legs across the grass poking through busted-up concrete and read the tattered book that her father bought at the flea market. Was Tim able to go to his grandma's funeral because it was in the same country, maybe in the same town? Her mother has told her all about Abuelita. After Tim said, "Just like my grandma used to say," the Mexican desert and its nights swirled around Vanessa. Because of her dreams and descriptions from her mother and her abuelita, passed down like water falling over rocks, she had been to both places, stood in their grooves and on their peaks carved from the cycles of the sun and moon, cold and hot, vibrant and arid, while in her dreams, the land glowed amber, and the sun set behind the mountains and erased all the grooves and peaks until a matte black engulfed them and fell onto the waxy white desert flowers opening under the stars. In that sunset, her grandma rocked in a chair and told stories about rainbow bridges, talking turtles, and the little movie theater in the nearby city that showed all the great classics and everlasting stories. Through Flora's memories, Abuelita talked about the Aztecs and the time before the Spaniards as though she had been there or seen it in front of her—one world falling into another world; how the land connected everyone at all time; and how this was passed down to her mother and that someday, when the time was right, Vanessa would pass it all onto her descendants. But now that she possessed a driver's license, Vanessa rolled her eyes more often at these stories. Other images surrounded her—school and long summer months; watching shows with her friends on their televisions better than her family's second-hand TV; conquering her fear of drowning. Her mother reminded her, "Books are always better. That's where real magic happens." And as Tim stuck out his hand to shake hers, she thought, *At least the boxes at home are all unpacked. At least we have officially moved in.* She adjusted to sleeping on the couch in the living room.

The food at her school has paled in comparison to her mom's food, but she has loved the French fries, and she has been deliberately nice to the lunch ladies because they could, in a sense, be her mother, not biological but maternal, and because her mom could be working back there if things hadn't unfolded the way that they had. She used to stare at the lunch ladies far too long when she ordered food; one of them did a double take when Vanessa walked in front of the hot-food counter's orange lights and greasy scraps. When she first met her, Vanessa would only nod to Adelina, but now she has smiled at her while Vanessa's friends laughed, piling behind her, pushing the edge of their lunch trays into her back, nearly dragging their Jell-O or ketchup through the ends of her long hair, and teasing her for her "new best friend."

She wondered if Tim's school divided itself like hers during lunch and after school—the blacks over there; the whites over there; the

Hispanics by the fountain in the student plaza; the couples going back behind the pool to make out. One Thursday night, after Jacob parked his car in front of her family's apartment, slid her seat back, and turned up the stereo, she wanted to call a girl who was not known for going behind the pool but who had recently dropped out of school because she was pregnant. Putting his arm around Vanessa, Jacob wrinkled his nose, kissed her neck up and down, and slid his hands from her chest to her waist. She whispered, "I like that other stuff, but no, that's too far." After that night, she told him to park on the other end of the street, down by the rummage store and pregnancy center, far away from the apartment but not under a street light because his cherry red car would be seen by everyone in the neighborhood, because everyone knew Jacob and his car, especially her father, who, since Vanessa started dating Jacob, peered more from the apartment window. And so Jacob parked down from the apartment and what would become the bakery, with its For Lease sign in the front window at the time, and in the quiet darkness, he held her but only the surface of her, asking her if she liked what he held, to which she nodded and let him continue because she didn't know what else to do or say, reclined back in the passenger seat with a song buzzing from the speakers. He continued holding her body while other parts of her slipped away, not to escape but because they had to. She could have done better than eighty-two percent on her math test; she had time to double-check her work; her teacher reminded her to slow down and circled where she might have tripped over her thoughts. But she didn't care for math. She loved English class more. "Intuition can lead to new things," Mr. Overbeck once said. And after reading Steinbeck, her thoughts and dreams have drifted toward Northern California with its mountains and valleys stretched by shadows, rows of fruits and vegetables, and the Pacific crashing on the coast before lifting, reaching inland as cool mist, and transforming into clouds, rain, or snow that may or may not reach the part of the country where she lives before it circles back to the depths of its start. She looked up the ocean in the encyclopedia—*peaceful*. Steinbeck's field hands and workers were immigrants who wanted a new and better life, which is what her father has reminded her when she spent her money on a new CD or t-shirt rather than saving it for college and cultura. One of her friend's cousins lived near Salinas, and her father went all out for her quinceañera, as much as the family could afford. The dresses were like the pink frosting that Vanessa's mother has made for special-order cakes. A fountain bubbled frosty pink juice that everyone drank with commemorative glasses. Colored, spinning lights; streamers; a DJ; and the local farm boys, dressed up as the chambeláns de honor, transformed the community center. For the first dance, Stacy Martinez danced a waltz with her father. When Vanessa chose a sweet sixteen for herself, rather than a quinceañera, her friends ridiculed her, especially Tanya, who wouldn't shut up about it for days. But choosing that celebration had been one of the best decisions she made because her parents trusted her to make it. *How far I've come* she thought at age sixteen and felt old for thinking it, as though she was looking back on a life that's halfway done. "Too young," her mom has said about the women on her side dying early. "Es una maldición. It's a curse."

Looking at the mismatched cooking utensils, the flickering light in the display case, and the various supplies lying around an otherwise pristine store, she understood why Tim would ask if the store was open. When she and her parents first lived in the dingy multi-unit house in a shanty town defined by razor wire and rusted sheet metal, they shared the space with other families brought by the same Coyote whose brother helped with settlement in El Norte, avoiding La Migra, and knew Calderon. Those first several years her parents worked general labor—her mother cleaning and cooking for hotels and restaurants; her father toiling at landscaping, farming, construction, coming home every night sore and dirty and smelling of things burned and overturned. Her mother tucked her into bed at night, kissed her, and said a prayer with her. "Even though we may become separated," Flora said, "know that I love you and will always be with you." Her father, standing behind her mother, kissed her goodnight too, saying, "Go to sleep. We've survived another day." Living in fear those first years—knocks on the door in the middle of the night; cars slowing down, drifting by; never enough money—her parents told her, "No, no, you can't have a brother or sister. We could lose all of you." Calderon said that the church would always be there for them, that God would see everything through. Her father broke down in tears after he dedicated his family's life to Vida Nueva and Calderon while Flora held Vanessa's hand under the tent behind the church and said how brave Roberto was to be "tan frágil"—so fragile in front of strangers, asking for help and control for things that he could not control. But, with summer beginning, Tim, smiling in front of her, sparked a light on a distant path that has compelled her to chase it.

Months ago, in cold, bare winter, her father, picked her up in his truck and said, "I have a surprise for you." She hoped it was a gift certificate for clothes or, at the very least, a CD. They drove the long way home, past a new big-box hardware store visible from the road. Roberto stopped in front of the apartment; the For Lease sign in the store below it, which Vanessa had noticed on walks to the bus stop, had vanished. "How do cupcakes sound? Or maybe some cochas or elotitos?" he asked, humming to himself. She was confused but curious and stared at the storefront with its brown butcher paper in the window, sawdust accumulating on the sidewalk, and tools and paint cans that had appeared since she had been at school, where she didn't want to be, although her friends had decorated her locker with stickers and streamers and where Jacob told her that he couldn't wait to see her that night because he had found a perfect place to be alone where he could give his birthday gift to her. At sixteen, had she added more curves to her body? Was she now a woman? Would her decision for a sweet sixteen continue fulfilling her? Would a quinceañera have made her more or less of a woman? Long minutes in front of the bathroom mirror before breakfast looped inside her. A car would be her preferred gift, but more curves may be what she received for her sixteenth. She stared at the store window, with its broken light bulb over the front door, and laughed with her father who tossed his large eyes toward the store. "Go on, Essa, they're all in there waiting for you. Everyone you know and love." Sliding out of the truck, tightening her coat and scarf against the February wind, Vanessa assumed that a surprise party waited behind the doors and that her friends were in on it. She opened the door. The chime above it rang like a muted bird, but only paint buckets, drop cloths, and extension cords snaking into the kitchen greeted her. No friends, no car keys, no CD, no gift certificate— nothing but tools, debris, and her expectations. Dressed in a white apron, her mother walked around the corner from the back room. Flour covered Flora's hands and face with chocolate smudged here and there. She adjusted her new glasses and, brushing back her bob haircut, wiped her forehead; seeing her daughter, she smiled and motioned with her soft eyes. Flora hugged and kissed Vanessa and pulled out a plastic tray of conchas crisped in the oven and frosted with sweet icing, like their shell-shapes belonged in an electric sea. Vanessa ate just one; its melting satisfied her. And then her father smiled and paid attention to her the way Tim standing in front of her, juggling the snack bags and not yet leaving, turned his attention to her. *Maybe I am getting a car. Maybe they have new jobs.* "It's ours, all ours," her parents told her in unison. Her mom will run the bakery; her dad will renovate it. Her parents then told her to close her eyes. A match was struck; the smell of a small flame and sugar filled the air. "Open your eyes," they said. A two-tiered cake, slathered in yellow and white frosting, sat before her. "Happy Sweet Sixteen!" Her father turned on a portable stereo. When the first notes from "Sobre las Olas" spiraled out like waves, her father bowed, his paunch and skinny arms jutting out a bit more as he did; his shoulders narrowed and collapsed around his chest. He extended his rough hand, which Vanessa held after bowing back to him. Surrounded by dust and dim light, the cool air inside the store, and shadows moving on the butcher paper in the winter evening, they danced. Her mother swayed and hummed along before cutting in to dance with Vanessa and then only with Roberto. And although the waltz stopped playing and her parents stopped dancing, the music and its lyrics about the ocean echoed in front of Vanessa, blurring the start and the end. Her parents asked her to close her eyes again. Her father pressed something heavy, cold, and metal in her palm. "Open your eyes," he said. Frozen in the middle of silver, the ring glistened with its small piece from a tree that had fallen on the other side of the shore before he and Flora crossed the river sixteen years ago, almost to the day. The water had chilled them. Covered by the night and the sounds of the river, Roberto was soaked after he reached Coyote and Flora yet protected the splinter that something told him to grasp before crossing, and later spent some of Calderon's money on the bakery, the tools to fix it up, and the ring with its sliver from another time and place. And this path that her parents had tread blazed like fireflies close to the ground around Vanessa and her parents who wanted nothing more than for her to grow wherever she stood and to continue no matter how many times her destination swerved or became obstructed. Later that night, as soon as Jacob's hands moved down her legs, she let it happen and couldn't understand why she was with Jacob. "I'm not ready," she whispered as her ring shimmered, its splinter hovering in dark blue and starlight. "OK," he said, kissing her forehead and driving her home where the curtains in the apartment over the bakery opened and closed as the bass from Jacob's stereo rattled his car. And she looked at string-bean Tim standing in front of her, smiling, his clothes dangling off him, and she thought about Jacob who spent his money on clothes in order to look tougher; his parents have not liked this toughness; and his brother told him to tuck in his shirt because somebody with a gun waited to point it at Jacob because of his clothes, his loud-mouthed guy friends, and his daily-increasing smirk. Vanessa has expressed the same concerns, but Jacob has not wanted to hear it from her; he has said there's nothing wrong with how he dresses or his crew, who aren't, he had reminded her, chavalas and who don't and won't ever work as shift managers making small bank. But girls are a different story, he quickly told her, because platform shoes, short shorts, and miniskirts can be trampy, but it's different at parties because he likes it when they wear those clothes.

But this young man in front of her, this young man who said, "Hi, my name is Tim," felt different, looked different, not because of his skin color or because of his wrinkled shorts and paint-splattered t-shirt, but in ways that wait below the surface—qualities that someone would fall after; these invisible but necessary qualities underneath the skin. "Hi, I'm Tim"—this young man consuming and refilling coffee and asking for more sweets, had this impact as soon as the door chimed and this goofy, gangly teenage boy stood there, smiled at her, and talked as if he and Vanessa had known each other for years, as though somehow years had passed and he fell back into her life. He asked if they were open because the Grand Opening sign hanging on the front door was not enough for him to know; something urged him to walk in and ask, had to ask her, to ask her name, to say hi to her, and stay as long as he could.

"We're on our way back to this church," Tim said, having stopped at Home Depot to get supplies, including charcoal and lighter fluid—the same Home Depot that's nearby and not much older than the bakery; the same Home Depot that her father has secretly frequented because he did not want Ramón, owner of the local hardware store one block down from the bakery, to know that he has bought better tools and browsed more things than what's at Ramón's store. That guilt scuttled inside Roberto, like he cheated on Ramón, loving all that Home Depot offered because Ramón's little hardware store cannot hold as many things or offer better prices. But every time he has needed something small for the bakery, Roberto promised himself to visit Ramón first. He said in front of Flora, "Just the banner for now. A few nails for it. OK? Hmm, well, maybe some power tools if I have to build something. More shelves maybe." And so he has driven to Ramón's store every Saturday after the farmers' market and bought things for the bakery that the bakery doesn't need, things scattered around Vanessa and Tim with the summer light falling in. Pointing out the pile of boxes of nails by the bags of flour and sugar, Vanessa has teased her father. "It's for the renovation," he replied, to which they both laugh because the store has been open almost a month, and the Grand Opening sign that Roberto bought from Ramón flapped in the spring storms until the summer heat and humidity peeled its letters.

287

Roberto has already spent most of his free time gutting the old parts of the bakery and installing new cabinets, flooring, appliances, and fixtures and obtaining permission from Mrs. Acosta to upgrade the upstairs apartment—building a little shelf for the TV and storage for Vanessa's books and school awards that she hides from her friends. When she wanted privacy in the living room, he built an accordion divider.

Her mother has loved the idea of waking up in the morning, fixing breakfast, and simply walking down the stairs and out the apartment building's front door, turning right with a handful of steps, and walking into the bakery—her bakery—through the same door where Tim stood, smiled at Vanessa, and said, "Love is more important than doctrine," which reminded her what her mother has always said about Coyote bringing them here—they left the old land out of love for what would become their daughter and her future. When they were led to Vida Nueva, her mother was hesitant but accepted being there because God transcended denomination and could be found anywhere, anytime.

"Vida Nueva," Vanessa corrected Tim, smiling.

"Yeah, that's it!" He snapped his fingers. "Do you know it?"

"I do," she answered before ringing the amount on the register.

Tim hesitated long enough to keep her fingers in his hand as she counted the change and placed the last coin in his palm. After a deep inhale, he said, "Thanks for the snacks. They look great. Did you make them?"

Peering into the bag, she nodded to a concha. "Just that one."

"I'll make sure no one else gets it." He glanced around. "I like talking with you. I think you're really nice and cute."

"Thanks," she replied, blushing. "Me too."

"We're having this grill-out over there, if you want to come. There'll be hot dogs and hamburgers, and we'll just laugh, talk, have a good time. Bring your friends. Everyone's welcome."

"Oh...you have fun without me. I have to clean up tonight."

He nodded and, blowing the steam from his coffee, not yet drinking it, walked to the wall with skulls painted bright blue, pink, and green; flowers painted in the eye sockets; heavily outlined teeth; hearts on the foreheads; and bursts of colors around the chins and cheekbones. Pausing at each one, he said, "Did you paint these?"

"I helped my mom."

"I like them. They remind me of Disney's *Skeleton Dance*. Ever seen it?"

She shook her head no.

"It's so awesome. You'll have to see it. Do you like that kind of stuff? Old Disney cartoons?"

"I love all those old movies," she answered, looking away when he looked at her. She caught a sweet roll before it landed on the floor.

"New movies are good because of the technology, especially the special effects," he continued. "But black-and-white movies are the best."

"Yeah, they are."

"But I like the old-school special effects, too. All that makeup and lighting. It really doesn't take much to transform somebody. Sometimes just a word...like a spell or a prayer...or a symbol."

"Sounds like you know your stuff."

His blushing head nodded. "Are these the same animals over there?" He pointed to the small walnut-sized animals evenly spaced between the skulls.

"Yes. My mom's taking her time with them."

Tim walked closer. "Rabbit. A bird…snake…lizard… I don't know this." He wrinkled his nose.

"Jaguar," she laughed, standing on her tiptoes.

"What about this one? They look like two boomerangs crossing each other."

"Earthquake."

"They all mean something, don't they?"

"They do."

He lifted the snack bags and balanced his coffee cup. "I'll have to come back in here and draw them. Would your mom mind?"

"No, I don't think she would at all. Maybe you could help her."

"That would be awesome."

When he said that he would have to return and draw this world that had started but was incomplete, she imagined the many other worlds that he must open when he drew lines across a paper and filled them with colors that she would want to see; she imagined this because she wanted to see him again—the wanting opening like wings inside a day. She said, "OK with me."

"And *that*…" He walked to the long main wall opposite the counter. "This will be super awesome when it's done." He stared at faint charcoal lines and the center ring painted in gold, blues, reds, and earth tones. Animals orbited the main ring; the next layers of rings expanding from the center had yet to be finished. In the middle of the center ring, a face held two hearts. "What is it?"

"The Aztec Wheel of Time."

After his eyes roamed the store's walls, his shoulders shrugged. "I really like these things. I don't know why."

"Maybe you were there a long time ago."

"Like reincarnation?" he chuckled.

"More like a cycle coming back around."

"Maybe it's timing, like providence or...serendipity."

Her eyes brightened. "Everything is already there and planned for."

"Yeah, exactly. Everything's timely. You just have to get there before getting anywhere else. You have to get there in time." His paint-splattered finger pointed at her. "*You* have to do it."

"Right? You have to find it. You have to dig around for it."

"Yeah. It's about what's inside you, not what's going on the outside. It's already within us, and you got to build off that."

"I don't think that you can understand everything right away, but my mom and Abuelita always said, 'Your mouth speaks where your heart wants to go.' And my old pastor used to talk about how fire destroys one path in order to show another."

"I like that. They're right. Abuelita?"

"My granny."

"Grannies are good. To our grandmas." He toasted her with his coffee. "Do you go to church?"

"Not anymore."

"You should come to this one I go to. It's really good. Real Life. Pretty easy to remember."

"Maybe. I'll see."

And then the newness that Vanessa's mom had talked about happened—the newness of each day, one day giving over to another, those days tied together, necessary to each other, like corners rounding in a maze where someone inside must pass through them all before continuing on. The newness happened as soon as Tim opened his mouth and repeated "Vanessa" back to her after she had said it to him. He said it back to her, and the world she was in, the world she occupied, moved away, fluttered off into the new day on the other side, not merging, but giving itself over until the day could continue with her standing there with him. Long before she was sixteen, her father had bought a tattered *Anne of Green Gables* from the flea market with some extra cash, and she read about the road that Anne was on starting to bend toward an unknown destination—the bend itself and anything beyond it was a fascination worth pursuing. But she didn't know what Tim knew about her—if he knew she was "all-American" or if her parents were illegals or some other status. But he stood there and talked with her, and it was exactly what she had asked for, this unexpected late birthday gift inside the store near the industrial part of town; this little bakery becoming popular because word had spread about Flora's Panadería Mexicana and she had spent so much time at the farmers' markets and the state fair; this name spreading without any advertisement other than a banner out front that said Grand Opening and pulled anyone near it inside.

"I'll tell everyone I know about this place," Tim said. "Especially my mom, who will tell all her friends. She loves all this stuff. Cakes, cupcakes, all that. And the *coffee*."

"The coffee?" Vanessa giggled.

And then Vanessa's mom came around the corner, from the apartment and through the bakery's front door, the door singing its muted birdsong; she held an armful of supplies. When Tim saw her, he held open the door, greeted her with "Hello, ma'am," nodded, and smiled, these little things that Jacob never did; Jacob always snarling, staring off into space at the back of the room waiting for Vanessa to hang up her apron, wash her hands, and say goodbye to her parents who glared at Jacob as they left and his arm wrapped around her waist before his hand slid down.

"Thank you," Flora said to Tim, doing a double take, looking at the light on her daughter's face, and knowing the same thing that her daughter knew.

Tim rocked on his toes; his scrawny legs wobbled. "Well, goodbye. It's really nice to meet you. Oh, um, I'd like to hear about your drawings, especially the Wheel of Time. I really like that stuff. I'd really like to talk to you about all that. I'd like to know more."

Nodding, Flora said, "You need to come back, then. We can talk about all that. I have so much to tell."

"Bye, Vanessa. I hope to see you again soon." Tim fished a piece of paper from his shorts and slid it onto the glass case near the register. He filled his coffee cup one more time and, before leaving, turned at Vanessa and smiled.

When she said goodbye, half of Vanessa's heart followed Tim; the other half stayed put. She wondered if she would see him again and hoped that he would come back to the store and draw, ask her mom many questions about the symbols on the walls and the tales they told across from a wheel that measured time by starting again after one full turn. But she could only clutch at his simple presence, now ghostly, reverberating where he had stood and spoke to her about love, doctrine, and cultura.

"Do you know him?" her mother asked.

"No."

"He sure seemed to like you. What's this?"

"It's this thing," Vanessa answered, looking down at the neon-green flyer. "His youth group is helping Vida Nueva."

"With what?"

"He said they're building a day care and a prayer room for Calderon and the church. He said they'll barbeque when they're done and just spend time together with everyone there. He invited us."

"That's good." Her mother stared out the front window as the van and truck rumbled off. Looking at the flyer, Flora said, "You should go, Essa."

"Mom..."

"You should. You already know someone who will be there waiting for you."

17

By the time she reached the coast, Vanessa's coughing and nausea, layer by layer, had returned, tightened, and pounded her head and stomach. The rental car had shrunk since she had last driven; it was now a space for a body that existed hours ago. Her coughing brought on tears, which blurred her vision. Pulling over, she did not turn on the hazards. Neither the two cars nor the truck passing by stopped to ask if she was in trouble or needed a hand. Alongside the highway, and with the windows rolled down, she sat. The air chilled but also refreshed her. Her headache swelled, but she could breathe again; the car had stifled everything, pressed it all down on her, like when she was stuffed on the plane between the woman wearing too much perfume and the man who reminded her of an old life on her way here. Clouds drifted inland, and the Pacific crashed into cliffs and onto fields of wildflowers. She laughed out loud, and her laughs increased the more she thought about how the airport security scanners had not detected anything—not even under her skull.

She drove into the lot at the nature reserve a few miles down the road, parking in one of the middle slots, anonymous and with nothing to hide. A thick row of trees, gold-green grass, and cattails separated her from the ocean. Only the sounds of the engine clicking off and dripping as it cooled and seagulls calling out remained. Her hands shook—but not because of a spell coming on. Since arriving at the ocean's edge, the cause, be it her health or her nerves, no longer mattered. Vanessa shifted in her seat when her pelvis tingled and dampened her underwear. *Sweat...please be sweat*, she thought, shaking her head at the possibility that her body had lost control of something so basic. Before she turned on her phone, she glanced in the rearview mirror. Her lips were blue and puffy, the skin under her eyes bruised and pinkly raw. The sheen in her brown eyes had lessened; her pupils had contracted. *Did I gain another twenty pounds?* She pushed up her slumping cheeks and examined the wrinkles that had spread from her face to her throat in so few days. *So much for stopping the medications.*

Her phone glowed like a small book as she clicked the audio files that Tim had given her for her birthday. As the voices spoke, Vanessa swayed between the images in their stories, the places and people they described, and the world in front of her bending and shaking with wind and water. Wiping and then closing her eyes, she sat quietly for a few minutes before typing a number into the phone. The call shrank the distance between the past, the present, and the future. She spoke for a long time—clearly and with no hesitation. Clouds moved over the sun. She nodded. The grass and the trees around her emptied all the light that they had stored. After that call ended, she rested her throbbing forehead in her hands. She dialed another number. A little more composed this time, she licked her lips as the minutes ticked on. Before she hung up, she mouthed words with no sounds inside them as the voice on the other end reverberated. Sliding the phone into her backpack, she breathed deeply and stared in front of her: the ocean waited behind the curtain of tall grass, trees, and fog. Vanessa wobbled out of the car and walked to the trail overlooking the beach. What she had written to Dan and what she had told Tim, and what her father understood, were the same thing—to look neither forward nor backward, which was linear, but to look into the present as it spiraled down and fanned out. She did not think about any of these things. She was closer to, but not yet in, the water.

The main trail brought her deeper into the woods, brush, and wildflowers and past an old barn, its rusted metal and rotted wood sticking out like scarecrow arms. Trees arched over her; seals barked in the distance; the breeze dipped and lifted gulls. And ahead of her, on the other side of a small wood bridge, the ocean churned in late-afternoon light.

The bridge crossed a creek, wound through marshes, and dropped her off onto a terrace separating cliffs, flowers, and scrub from the coast. Her pulse raced, and she assumed that she could simply walk down to the beach, but when she looked that way, seals—some barking, some sleeping—littered the beach. The seals scrambling across the gritty sand sloughed off their coats. Vanessa caught a glimpse of one raising its head from the pack. Large flaps of skin dangled from its face, revealing a silky-smooth hide underneath. Its springtime body peeled like wallpaper in the hazy air.

Shaking and sweating more, Vanessa thought that she could at least slip past the seals because the trail continued onto the beach and disappeared into the sand. But as she stepped forward, the section of beach below her had been roped off; a tour group watched the seals from behind the rope. Her hope of being alone in the drizzle and beneath the low, thin clouds beckoned her to another point along the coast where another opportunity would open. Lowering her body as much as her aches allowed, she backpedaled into the woods and searched for another trail to the beach.

When the tour group below her moved around a rocky corner, she stopped and looked at where she had been. For several minutes, her knees swelling, her throat tightening, she waited in the shrubs and tall grass. She placed her hands across her stomach after she vomited. With the group gone and no one else around, she stepped back into the open space and found a trail hugging the cliffs' base, curling like a narrow string of gold, bypassing the seals and leading onto the dunes and through the purple patches of lupine.

Down Vanessa went, stumbling, looking around to make sure that she remained alone and unobserved. She caught her breath and opened her jaw to release pressure inside her forehead and cheeks. Closer to the edge of the ocean, she slowly walked across a ground that descended sharply after centuries of waves had exposed corals and shells and slabs of rocks the color of creamy oranges. Her feet slipped a few times because of the slick algae, the uneven surface, and her dwindling balance—and she was hungry. From her jacket pocket she pulled a muffin from breakfast, unwrapped the napkin, and broke off pieces. Only the blueberries had flavor; she tasted them immediately. Tightness spread from her ankles and lower back and crept into her legs and shoulders before she reached the end of the trail. Vanessa dropped to her backside and scooted the rest of the way.

She pulled up her jacket's hood as the coastal wind chilled her in a space more open than the trail and terrace behind her. The trail had dissolved into patches of crunchy vegetation and soft, sandy beach that didn't extend along the water as far as she had expected. It was no summertime beach: no sunbathing, no volleyball, no campfires, no strolling along the surf and sand for miles and miles. Seals, sea grass, and sea daisies occupied most of the beach's long stretches. The trees with their small spring buds surrendered to black reefs and the ocean's translucent grays and blues. Chunks of rock and knuckles of hard soil jutted from the waves and blended the land's ending and the sea's beginning. Vanessa removed her shoes, buried her feet ankle-deep into the sand, and listened to the wind and the ocean. She stuck her fingers in her ears and listened to her pulse pound after she trudged across the sand. She opened her eyes and wobbled. Off to the right, more pronounced cliffs and dunes consumed parts of the beach; on her left, through the haze and drizzle, a light burst from the island off the coast. Vanessa waited until it burst again and moved toward it.

One of the dunes held hundreds of shells stacked on top of each other. From a distance, they reminded Vanessa of the smoke-and-silver butterflies that she had chased as a child in the gardens and grass near Vida Nueva. Shuffling closer, she reached for the shells as she had reached for the butterflies when she was younger; the two moments—the past and the present in front of her—merged into one. She stretched her arms, and as soon as she believed that she had grabbed something, she retracted her hands into her pocket. But she held nothing: no butterfly fluttered in her palm; the shell remained in its place. Grimacing and digging into the sand and dirt, she forced the shell free until her fingers bled. She looked at her hands, at the white and red smashed on her fingers, and in the middle of her palm where wings dissolved into embers and ashes. "Where did you go?" she asked.

Balancing on wet jagged edges, hugging the sides of cliffs, dodging the powerful waves scoring the coast and lacing the rocks, Vanessa stumbled along her path. Each rock stepped out to sea from the low, wind-jostled point. Her isolation and pain had increased, her vision blurred again, and the air had cooled her neck and head. But she convinced her body to stay awake for a little longer as the shock of water and surrounding landscape demanded her full attention.

She found a sunken black rock, as smooth and dark as the inside of a boat, into which she could climb. The rock's tip, curved like a bow, pointed toward the island and its rhythmic light. The gulls above her warbled more intensely while the wind tossed them around the gray sky. Vanessa looked over her shoulder and could not see anything familiar. Rocks, cliffs, and ocean spray obscured the beaches and the seals, the trails, the terrace with its wildflowers and trees, and the parking lot and highway where she had started. Drizzle smoothed the sun into a yellow ball hovering over the water. Her destination glowed ghostly along the rippling horizon and inside low-hanging clouds, but she couldn't reach it across the plane of water. The lighthouse flashed from the humpbacked island while the sun intensified the fading Victorian features and colors of the keeper's home. Dark pods squiggled near the island's shore and stopped to climb over other dark jelly-like pods snapping, yelping, and barking their heads in the air. Older abandoned structures on the island twisted to the ground among debris where gusts and rain passed through scattered light and broken forms. In front of her, the unfinished calendar on the old bakery's wall burned through the haze; its faint lines and washed-out colors orbited inside each concentric circle until they retreated deeper into the island and its light like hands pulling back through smoke after having set everything in place.

Here she was now at ocean's edge, fully awake and wide-eyed in the wind and spray; here she was at a point that had started like a zero drawn in dirt and was almost complete. Watching the rapid waves, she stood against the setting sun and time splashing on the rocks. Vanessa thought of Tim and Dan and her father and mother. She closed her eyes and imagined the storm cloud engulfing her brain, pushing toward the front, spreading toward the back, multiplying, distorting her balance and vision—but also reanimating her memories: Her parents cross the river in the middle of the night; her mother is up to her stomach in the cold water; wearing his cowboy hat, her father stands in the middle, the lower half of his jeans dark from the river; Roberto looks behind him many times while wading back to take Flora's hand; he holds a plastic bag filled with baby supplies, a Bible, and some mementos before slinging it across his free shoulder; his other shoulder braces a rolled-up blanket and a plastic jug of drinking water; Coyote is just ahead, leading them all through the dark; Flora, lagging but not left behind, has to stop more than the men because the baby kicks; she emerges in the moonlight from the driftwood and the water splitting into a V-shape behind her as one of her hands reaches for Roberto and her other hand supports her belly. Their voices crackle like in Tim's recordings: "My name is Roberto Luis Ochoa...I am Essa's father...My name is Flora Maria Ochoa...I am Vanessa's mother." *They were not afraid*, Vanessa thought.

She folded her clothes on the boat-shaped rock—pants first, then shirt, socks, jacket. Her skin and hair damp, she shivered in her bra and underwear while pointing her shoes toward the island. Hearing a scuttling above her, she quickly turned and stared at the cliff's edge. A figure. Had Tim had come? Had he had found where she went? No one else was with him. She shouldn't have called him. More drizzle collected on her eyelashes, and she squinted against her poor vision. "Tim?" she asked loudly in the wind. She clenched her eyes shut. "Papá?" She shouldn't have called him either. Silence washed over her as she stared at the gray spreading in front of her; her heavy breathing was the only sound. "¿Quién está ahí? Who's there?" she shouted. The figure did not answer. She yelled her question again, louder until her throat scratched. The figure did not answer. Her cry echoed; the wind carried it off. The figure disappeared and left behind more gray sky.

Vanessa wiped her eyes and removed her bra and underwear, placing them under her jacket. She set the keys and the shell, which she had taken from the mound, on top and pointed it toward the island, like a message to be unlocked later. The shell, she believed, fluttered its wings before becoming petrified again. Her bloodied fingers curled in the cold, ocean-charged wind. The ring that her parents had given her with the splinter inside remained on her hand.

Shaking more, breathing quicker, oscillating between feeling alone and not alone, she pushed herself from the rock's edge. She struggled to stay upright and conscious and limped toward the loud rumbling waves. She could have backed away; she could have stepped from the rock's edge and put on her clothes; she could have pulled up her jacket's hood and wiped her damp face with its sleeve; she could have saved putting on her socks and shoes for last; she could have faced the edge that dropped into the water one last time before turning around and heading back from where she had come. She would have been warm and dry. But back—behind the curtain of mist, trees, and mountains—was where she could not act; it was where someone else would act for her, where only in passing she knew herself. But here, facing the ocean, the island, and the effects of landscape and memory, was where she had to act and respond to the very thing that she could not ignore.

The water between the boat-shaped rock and the island stretched like a long plaza with many doors that could open and close. Ocean swells wrapped around both ends of the island and created strong currents and a narrow, violent channel. Vanessa rocked her weight toward the water before jumping in as the light inside her head expanded its translucent ring.

She struggled to swim from the rocky point. Amassing atop each other, the waves increased their height and ice-cold grip, pushed her back, and then pulled her under. But her body found the brief lull between each one; she kicked harder, propelling herself toward the island looming before her. With each wave, her shape shifted—starfish, arrow, wings—but she also defied the waves, thrusting into them as they pummeled her, daring them to prove that here was no delusion and that back there, from where she had come, was nothing more than preparation. Here was a reminder of fluid edges and a destination shaped by time, place, and flesh.

Vanessa tired quickly, and shivering, she floated in the water. Her muscles and jaw locked up. She turned around to see how far she had come—not even halfway between the rock and the island echoing in light, movements, and sounds. She was off-center; the waves had pulled her out further to open sea. The limits of her body, aggressively shortened in the last few months, circled her. Exhaustion knotted her arms and legs. Memories cycled in and out of her head. Spitting water, she breathed rapidly.

A wave pulled her under and then another one, stronger than the first. A third wave came, smaller, but the undertow was greater, like a giant knife had opened a deeper hole. Wave after wave, one sequence complete, another not far behind, continued to assault her body, slamming her, dragging her further under the surface. But deeper into the serpentine water she paddled, struggling to stay above the feathered tips of the waves, aware that her body had burned off all that it had brought and, after being set in motion, was ready to coast forward into the unknown that was on the verge of becoming known. She refused to yield.

A light waited ahead of her, almost within reach. Vanessa could see it. She wanted it and drifted toward it, the cells in her brain popping, throwing on their full circuitry. And then, giving over, she floated, having felt that she had made it, had reached some point that revealed its location only to her, filled with peace and aware of what was happening around her, like a stranger knocking on several doors until one opened. The light expanded, as did the door through which she floated. She remained tranquil, fading, falling apart, floating through it, certain that it would go on into tomorrow.

Acknowledgements

This book evolved out of three separate stories into a publication encouraged and supported at the various stages by my wife, family, friends, and teachers; Jerry Brennan at Tortoise Books for establishing a path into the larger world for this story; Lauren Gioe, also at Tortoise Books, and her editing, input, patience, and professionalism after accepting and then managing the project; and readers who have taken and will take a chance on my work. Thank you.

About the Author

William Auten is the author of *Pepper's Ghost* (Black Rose Writing), a 2017 Eric Hoffer Award finalist for contemporary fiction. His work has appeared widely online and in print. www.williamauten.com

About Tortoise Books

Slow and steady wins in the end—even in publishing. Tortoise Books is dedicated to finding and promoting quality authors who haven't yet found a niche in the marketplace—writers producing memorable work that will stand the test of time.

Lightning Source UK Ltd.
Milton Keynes UK
UKHW011836200520
363522UK00001B/101